THE NOVELS BY ANONYMOUS
HAVE A READERSHIP SIX MILLION
STRONG AND GROWING.

The reason is quite simple: honesty. Each novel by Anonymous gives you, in free and frank language, a true look at the candid desires which drive men and women to share all levels of intimate pleasure. Rich, passionate, unrestrained, each Anonymous novel explores new territory in the endless world of erotic sensuality.

WHO IS ANONYMOUS?

The writer who signs these novels Anonymous is a well-known author whose many books have sold several million copies and have been translated into virtually every language in the world. Some of these novels have been made into films, have been dramatized on television, or have graced the Broadway stage.

This respected author has chosen the ancient and honorable appellation of Anonymous for several reasons, one of which is to know the greatest freedom that the creative worker can know—the freedom from self, the freedom to seek and penetrate those mysteries of the human soul and of the human body that are of such profound and intimate importance to all of us.

Bantam Books by Anonymous
Ask your bookseller for the books you have missed

HER
HIM
I
ME
THEM
TWO
US
WOMAN
YOU

Them

Anonymous

BANTAM BOOKS
TORONTO · NEW YORK · LONDON · SYDNEY

THEM

A Bantam Book / August 1978
2nd printing .... December 1980
3rd printing .... May 1981
4th printing .... July 1981
5th printing .... August 1982
6th printing .... September 1983

ISBN 0-553-22982-6

Published simultaneously in the United States and Canada

Bantam Books are published by Bantam Books, Inc. Its trademark, consisting of the words "Bantam Books" and the portrayal of a rooster, is Registered in U.S. Patent and Trademark
Office and in other countries. Marca Registrada. Bantam
Books, Inc., 666 Fifth Avenue, New York, New York 10103.

PRINTED IN THE UNITED STATES OF AMERICA

H   15 14 13 12 11 10 9 8 7 6

For Those Who Love . . .

Author's Preface

Anonymous did not want to write this book.
In the Author's Preface to *Me,* I said:

> *So Anonymous will now disappear, re-*
> *turning into that deep part of myself from*
> *which he, or she, emerged to write these*
> *books . . . for now, near readers in your mil-*
> *lions, that's all there is; five novels, each*
> *complete within itself and yet each forming*
> *a part of a linked whole for those perceptive*
> *enough, open enough, to divine the linkages*
> *. . . And so, fondly, and sadly, Anonymous*
> *bids you farewell.*

I was wrong. Anonymous had *not* written his/
her last book; there was at least one more; this book,
Them, written again in *the earthy language of love . . .*
the best and truest tongue in the world.

Why? Simply because *Them* insisted on being
written—even at the expense of making a liar out of
Anonymous to millions of readers.

I began the work with great reluctance. "You
can't possibly measure up to what has gone before,"
I told *Them* in my mind. "Anonymous has written

vii

five most excellent novels in which he/she has communicated the art and fact and meaning of love, and the words of love. Those books have enjoyed an enormous and continuing success. On the strength of that accomplishment, Anonymous announced his/her retirement in the conviction that he/she had completed that task outlined in the preface to *Her*, the first novel in the series:

> It has been my ardent desire to new-mint these words, this language, by writing them in the context in which they are most often spoken . . . to arouse my reader, not by the scenes and events of the book but by his own particular remembrance. I want him to recollect in tranquillity those great times when, clasped by a woman's arms and legs, a voice has breathed into his ear, "Fuck me. Oh God, fuck me." I want the woman reader to recollect in tranquillity those times she has been compelled to utter those words. I want them both to remember how beautiful and true was the language of their passion, because, in the moment of love, they were the only words that would do. I want my reader to remember those brief moments in which he has loved and tasted every pore of a lover's body, when a lover has tasted every sensuous inch of his own. And I want the lovers to know, all over again, that at such times a man is never more a man, a woman never more a woman, and that they are joined into a meaning infinitely greater than the sum of their parts, for their coupling is an equation of love.
>
> Why do we debase these lovely words? Because we are ashamed of their true emotional meaning, we are afraid to open our souls and our bodies, as these words demand that they be opened. Love is an openness.

"So why, *Them,* do you want to mess things up?"

Them smugly kept insisting that, because Anonymous had so much more to say, which could be presented only through the vehicle of *Them,* it would surely be the best of the lot.

I must admit the truth: *Them* has been a most amiable and cooperative novel. Day after day, with great ease and confidence, it flowed, writing itself in an unbelievably short span of time. It was a delight to watch as it developed, with sparkling lines, and witty asides, and some excellent observations on the modern scene. And for a reason inexplicable to Anonymous, *Them* persisted in considering itself in a subtle but unmistakable relationship with *Alice in Wonderland.* Don't ask *me* why . . . ask *Them.*

So here, dear reader, is the novel *Them,* sixth in the series at its own insistence—self-advertised as being even better than *Her, Him, Us, You,* and *Me;* and, as such, recommending itself to all those millions who have enjoyed the previous books.

This time, Anonymous makes no promises, no assumptions, about what will, or will not, happen next in his/her career. There may, or may not, be a seventh novel to add to the list. Nobody's going to make Anonymous a liar twice over.

ANONYMOUS

Them

When my international flight landed at Kennedy International, hundreds of people—it *seemed* to be hundreds, anyway—were waiting in the VIP Lounge. Among them only one familiar face: Prince Albert.

I threw my arms around him with such desperate enthusiasm that he said, "Hey! Hey now!" before embracing me as fervently.

He held me away for a good look.

"Darling Alice," he said. "You're perfectly ravishing. Doesn't time move *at all* on that island of yours? I expected a *hag,* and here you are, looking not a day older."

"Dear Albert," I said. "It's been a long time, hasn't it?"

Then, incredulously, I turned to look at the waiting reporters and photographers. Another flare of flashbulbs dazzled my senses, so that I had to cling to Prince Albert's arm. So accustomed was I to quietness, solitude, that I began to feel like a hunted animal.

Prince Albert said solicitously, "Are you all right, darling?"

I tried to smile. "I'm just . . . overwhelmed." I indicated the crowd. "But how . . . ? I asked you to keep my return a private event."

Prince Albert grimaced. "My dear, never underestimate the power of a PR man. I *swore* them to secrecy, insisting that it was the first consideration of the sale." He shrugged. "When I opened the paper yes-

1

terday morning, there was the headline: ALICE! IS COM-ING HOME."

He frowned, nodded. "The management couldn't *resist* letting the world know that *Alice!* had bought their penthouse suite. Believe me, I canceled the deal, and I *hope* you never set foot in the tacky place."

He looked at me anxiously. "I hope you're not too angry."

I took his arm. I smiled. "I know you did the best you could. But . . . do I have to talk to them?"

"Darling Alice," Prince Albert said grandly. "For the rest of her life, Alice! never *must* do anything she doesn't care to do. Haven't you realized that yet?"

My head spun again. I did know it—had known it in my very soul from the moment I had got on the plane in Athens. But everything had happened so dazzlingly fast I didn't know *what* to feel. It was as unreal as the jet lag that possessed the time-sense of my body.

That morning, like most mornings, I was walking naked on my beach. Only Alice and the shore birds, and the lovely stretches of emptiness. The firm white grains of sand tickled at my bare toes, and there was the smell of that ocean which is not like the smell of any other ocean anywhere in the world. I felt so wonderfully good. I dwelled on my is-land, in my world.

Very late the previous night, I had been brought awake by the sound of the seaplane. I had smiled to myself, going peacefully back to sleep, knowing that Stavros had arrived. I knew also that, in the morning, he would wish to make love.

I will fuck him good, Alice told Alice as she walked the morning beach. Make him happy that he traveled four thou-sand miles to spend a day with me. Be-

cause Stavros gave me the island, the ocean, all the empty spaces of my life.

I will go in to him, I thought. He will be naked, for he always sleeps naked. I will take that heavy Thing of his, so sleepy, into two warm hands. Then I will put my mouth gently on that great blunt head and I will taste It, so salty and alive in my mouth, and there will be also the salt on my lips from walking beside the ocean.

It will stir then, coming awake into a stiffening, and Stavros, still half asleep, will make the groan of pleasure. Soon, passionate and aware, his hands will reach to thrust my head down fully upon that blunt instrument.

"Alice!" he will say in that gutteral voice, "come to me, Alice!"

I will rise up naked, straddling the barrel of his body, and he will gaze upward with love and lust at the long angles of my flanks, see the nipples of my breasts also erect. Then, slowly, slowly, with such tantalizing slowness, I will impale myself and when I make the first movement Stavros will sigh deeply. We will fuck then, not without passion but also not without tenderness; and again Stavros and Alice will have come together after a long separation. And in fucking, all over again, I will bless Stavros Stephanos with all my being for the empty spaces of time and of place that he has made mine.

I stopped walking, the tiny grains of white sand delicate and real between my toes. A light morning breeze kissed at my naked body. I could feel the breeze against my nipples. I looked down. They were rosy, erect, so sensitive they made a quiver of *warmth in the very center of my physical being.*

Instead of going on the additional mile, I stopped, feeling my breath catch short, and turned back toward the house, so blindingly white in the Mediterranean sunlight. I did not hurry, though a hurry was within me. I did not wish to come to him with a spot of perspiration on my sun-golden body.

Up the steps then skirting the swimming pool, threading through the great ceramic pots that graced the area. The gardener was at work, but, knowing I always came naked from the sea in the early mornings, he kept his face to the wall.

Stavros had his own suite of rooms, the bedroom opening onto the poolside. Sliding the glass door, I groped through the heavy curtains shielding the room into a darkness for sleeping.

I could not see, after the glare of the sun, but I knew by heart the way to Stavros' enormous bed. Touching the tip of my tongue to my upper lip, I tasted there the salt of the sea. Soon also there would be added the salty taste of male sex. I breathed lightly, deeply.

I could see him now. His belly was a great barrel, not fat but strong. Hair, black-and-white, grizzled, grew thickly on his chest, on his arms and even, I knew, on the knuckles of his hands and toes.

The instrument of his sex did not shrink, like most men's while at rest, but remained strong and blunt. The head, purplish red, flared like the hood of a cobra. The penis, so thick yet astonishingly short, rested upon the heavy bag of balls.

The scenario within me changed.

Without a preliminary laying-on of the hands, I would nibble It with my lips, the warm wetness of mouth absorbing It with a teasing slowness. How It would love that teasing! . . . how eagerly It would awaken in my mouth.

Bending one knee, I eased my weight the bed. Alice! would come as a succubus in the night, to suck away his sperm.

The scenario altered again. My mouth would fasten upon It like a leech until he came. Then, when I took It into me, It would be half-limp, so lethargic in rising that the lovemaking would be sweet and long.

I bowed my head over the great thighs, my blond hair trailing its feathery touch across the sleeping flesh. I could smell him now, the slumbering man-smell of one of the powerful men of the world. He was nothing if not a man; but no one believed I loved Stravros above every other man who had ever touched my body.

I moistened my lips, wanting them warm and wet, and stooped closer, closer. It lay limply nested upon the great sack of sperm. The blunt head showed naked of foreskin, flanged and mighty even in rest. I will nibble It up. I thought voluptuously, I will lift the weight of It with the strength of my tongue.

I edged the tip of my tongue beneath the head. The under muscles feeling the strain, I had to curl my tongue to bring It inside my mouth. Slowly I slid my tautened lips over the head, savoring the anticipation of Its quickening in my mouth.

Then—I screamed.

It—that great cock of the great man, Stavros Stephanos, my lover— was cold and lifeless. Stavros Stephanos was dead.

"I really don't have to talk to them?" I asked Prince Albert timorously.

"Not if you don't want to," he said. "We'll simply walk right on past."

I gripped my hand into his elbow. "Then let's go," I said bravely.

At the movement, they realized our intention. Yelling, they surged forward in a group. Their voices were like the sounds of raucous parrots.

"Alice! Alice!"

"Smile, Alice!"

"Look this way, Alice! And smile!"

"Did Stephanos *really* leave you twenty-two million dollars in his will?"

"Alice! Are you *really* going to reside in New York?"

A self-important man with a microphone, trailed by a man with a television camera on his shoulder, thrust himself before us.

"This is *television*, Alice!" he said as though announcing the presence of God. He spoke rapidly into the microphone. "This is Carlos Romero reporting from the VIP Lounge at Kennedy International, where Alice! has just set foot on American soil for the first time in fifteen years. Alice! will tell us in her own words, I'm sure, how she feels at this great moment in her life."

The microphone. was almost touching my mouth. Something irresistible about a microphone; one feels compelled to speak.

Prince Albert rescued me. Thrusting away the microphone, he said tersely, "Beat it, Carlos. No interviews."

"But Alice! has *got* to say *something*." Carlos said, his voice a groan. "This is *television*."

"Alice! doesn't 'got' to say anything." Albert's voice was like stone. "Today, tomorrow . . . anytime."

Even as he spoke, he kept me moving. They came after us like a pack of dogs, yapping and milling. Then we were on the sidewalk, and Prince Albert was opening the limousine door. I ducked inside as one would retreat into a cave.

Albert entered behind me, hastily slamming the door. The glass mirrored on the outside; we could see out, but they could not see in.

I was safe. Yet I trembled inside. "God. I didn't realize it would be like this."

"I'm truly sorry, dear Alice. I could *kill* that PR man." Albert jerked his head vigorously. "He got fired, all right, I saw to that. And they won't have Alice! gracing their building after all." He shrugged it off. "I've found a *marvelous* place, right on Park Avenue. You'll love it. I twisted Peter Penner's arm out of the *socket* until he agreed to decorate it *completely* in four days' time. You remember Peter, don't you?"

"When I knew him, Peter was dressing windows for Macy's."

"My dear, he's *merely* the hottest interior decorator in town. He's booked up for the next two years, but I persuaded him. He is an absolute genius." He made a mouth. "But, personally, such a *whore*."

I laughed. "Albert, Albert. You haven't changed a bit."

He squared around. "And you, Alice . . . fifteen years on a Greek island has been only good. You're more beautiful than ever."

I experienced that familiar complicated reaction when anyone spoke openly of my looks. Something in me simultaneously cherished and rejected the compliment. Somehow I had never been able to believe that I was reputedly one of the five most beautiful women in the world. The idea made me uneasy. I knew the imperfect soul dwelling within that body the whole world found so irresistibly attractive.

I had never believed anybody but Daddy. . . .

The feeling stopped there, as it always stopped. By main force of will, I shoved the thought of Daddy out of my mind.

"Albert, fifteen years is fifteen years."

"Yes," he said almost sadly. "It is, isn't it?"

I looked at my friend. Still as handsome and slim as ever, his olive skin smooth as a baby's. He had always been so *pretty*. He was handsome still; but his eyes had grown old.

"Dear Albert," I said, putting my hand on his.

Albert smiled a sad smile. "Gay people age faster than anybody, Alice. Didn't you know that?" He made a small laugh. "I haven't been in love for *ages*. Only love can keep one young."

Albert had once told me that in the little Mississippi town where he had been reared his schoolmates had dubbed him "Prince Albert." It was, he told me, the brand name of a popular pipe tobacco. In defiance, when he had fled to New York to find his way of life, he had adopted the name legally.

> *"Just to remember," he said fiercely, drunkenly, tearfully. "Because, Alice, the night of the senior prom, they made me suck off the entire football team, one after the other. I had been dying all year for the quarterback, but when they made me do it . . ."*
>
> *I held him tightly while he wept, and and I wept, also. I had been a girl too beautiful for a small town, as he had been a boy too beautiful.*
>
> *"They can be so cruel to those who don't belong," I told him. "I had to be different, too, because Daddy didn't ever want me to go out with boys." I shuddered. "Why I wanted to date I don't know. They all . . . they all just wanted to brag that they'd fucked Alice Toffler, the most beautiful girl in town. Whatever happened or didn't happen, they bragged."*
>
> *Prince Albert stopped crying. He was listening now. To my secret, as I had listened to his.*

I was scared to fuck, I told Albert, because it would kill Daddy if he found out. But, when I wouldn't, they wouldn't date me anymore. And, anyway, they always told everybody they had fucked me, so every date thought he was the only one who hadn't had Alice.

Finally, one night, I was asked to go to the movies by Robert Denham, the most popular boy in school. Afterward, we drove out to neck, like everybody else did.

He cut off the car engine, he looked at me, and he said, "Are you gonna screw?"

The same old question. Demanding the same old answer. And tomorrow he would tell the boys in detail how good I screwed.

I looked at my hands. "I can't," I said.

"You've screwed everybody else," he said bluntly. "Why not me?"

It was no use. But I said, "They're liars."

He laughed. "Sure," he said scornfully. And then, "What's wrong with me?"

I don't know why. But, hearing Robert Denham speak those words in that tone of voice made me feel sorry for him. I really did want to like him.

"I'll . . . I'll get you off," I said. "If you'll show me how."

"All right," he said grudgingly. "Better than nothing, I guess."

I suppose Robert thought that once I had put my hands on his Thing, I couldn't help going all the way. That was the myth among the boys. Once she touches the old cock, she's a goner.

I unzipped his pants and took It out. I hadn't ever seen a male Thing before. Standing up so rigidly strong, I was frightened at the thought of having It inside me.

Somehow, without being told, I knew what to do. I began to slide my hand slowly up and down. He sank into the seat, arching his back, and his Thing got bigger and bigger. It was smooth and hot in my hand, and I could feel the quivering. I liked having my hand there, eliciting such response.

I don't know why I did what I did next. I hadn't heard of anybody doing it. But, leaning to watch, sensing that something strange and marvelous was on the verge of happening, suddenly I bent my head to take It into my mouth.

A hot sweetness immediately spurted. I could feel It pumping the stuff, I could taste it, but I didn't gag because it was wonderful that I could be so good to him.

Robert loved it. He told me gratefully it was better than screwing, because no girl had ever done that.

I sighed with repletion because he was gentle with me now, holding me, talking sweetly into my ear. Everything would be all right now. I could have a boyfriend like other girls, and I wouldn't have to do anything but use my mouth.

Robert took me home, kissed me lovingly, and made a date for the Saturday night sock hop. And next morning, when Daddy left for the office, he saw spray-painted on the sidewalk: ALICE THE COCKSUCKER OF CLANCY STREET.

The limousine going over a bridge now; the city spread itself before us. I looked at the skyline, feeling excitement and fear at once. There's nothing in the world like coming into New York. No matter how many times before you may have arrived, it is always full of threat and promise.

I wondered, then, what threats, what promises,

Alice was now seeking. Why, after fifteen years, had I found it necessary to come back to the United States at all, much less to this city where I had first lost and found myself?

That was it, of course. I had believed in sanctuary; but sanctuary had not been. And, in the years of self-sought solitude, the world had moved on, leaving Alice behind.

Now Alice, bereft of sanctuary, bereft even of the island-Alice she had created out of herself, had to catch up. Where better than New York, the city where I might hope to recover the innocent Alice I had abandoned so long ago?

Prince Albert, sitting quietly, was watching my self-absorption. He smiled when I turned to him. Gently he took my hand. With the other hand, he pointed toward the city.

"There's your wonderland, Alice," he said quietly. "It's all yours."

The apartment was perfect. Prince Albert stood beaming as I inspected the handiwork of his friend Peter. The residential hotel was a new building on Park Avenue, very modern, full of glass. One side of the apartment revealed the panorama of New York City below.

"Peter and I spent a great deal of your money very hastily," Albert said. "After all, it had to be ready in four days."

"It's worth every dollar," I said, sighing with the achieved subtle perfection.

The colors were the colors of the Mediterranean, white and gold. The walls seemed to emanate a sea-light. There were also the rich tones of old wood, for Peter had furnished entirely with antiques. The Persian rugs were deep and rich.

"You *must* see your bedroom," Prince Albert said excitedly.

In the doorway, I gasped. The bed was virtually a duplicate of Stavros' bed in the island house, large and very old, with massive carvings in the headboard. A coincidence, for Peter could not have known.

I moved across the room to touch it.

"Stavros died in just such a bed," I said tremulously. I looked at Albert. "He lived and loved in it, too. With me."

Prince Albert regarded me. "I've been *dying* to know why you decided to come back," he said. "Not that it's any of my business."

I smiled. "Everything about Alice is your business, Albert. You know that. But I don't want to talk about it. It's too . . . painful."

Turning away in a futile effort to hide my feelings, I walked into the living room to stand before the expanse of glass that gave me the great city.

"The place of refuge for Alice is gone," I said softly. "I must return into the world, find myself all over again."

Albert spoke quietly. "With the millions you dispose of now, Alice, you can insulate yourself in New York as successfully as on your Greek island."

I turned quickly. "There is no sanctuary in mere money. Besides, I mustn't do that. I have to be open now. Wide open. To everything."

"Why?"

A simple, hard question. I thought about that hard question before I answered.

Then I said, "I don't *know* why. It simply must be, that's all."

He gestured toward the city. "What do you expect to find out there?"

"Me," I said soberly. "The true Alice."

My voice throbbed in my throat. "There must be a true Alice. I've never found her, though at times I believed that I had. Not at home in Iowa. Not during those years in New York when I became Alice! instead of Alice Toffler."

I paused. I spoke the final truth of my soul. "Not even on my island. Perhaps, Albert, least of all there."

I felt sadness, and fear . . . and an exultation, a

readiness, a promise. Suddenly I spread my arms wide. "I'm going to make love to the entire city," I cried. "The city will make love to me."

Prince Albert chuckled ribaldly. "Sounds like a lot of fucking going on!"

I laughed with him. "Some fucking, sure. But love, too. Love."

I fell into silence. The words were startling, unexpected; I had not realized such feelings had been growing in me.

I added more quietly, "Because Alice has never been loved. Alice has never known how to love."

I gazed again upon the city. Intensely I said, "I must know the city all over again. As I must know myself."

The good time? A beginning time. But, I knew deep down, a frightening time. Because now, for better or worse, I was out of sanctuary.

I turned to my friend. "Albert. Stay with me tonight? I can't be . . . left alone just yet."

He touched my arm with his hand. "Yes," he said. "Of course I will stay."

The Daddy Dream came to me again. It had not been alive in me for such a long time. But suddenly there it was, as real as if it had never been dreamed before.

Daddy stood naked at the foot of my bed. As in life, he was lean and hard, with flat stomach muscles and sinewy legs. So I had to believe also that the Thing between his legs, enormously round and enormously long, was also real; though, as was only decent in a Midwestern household, I had never gazed upon my father's nakedness.

In the dream he was naked, and It hung nearly to his knees. I was six years old, the age when I had first known Daddy, and I crouched afraid upon the bed.

Daddy had been away in the war when I was born. In the first six years of my life I had not seen him. Daddy was in the Pacific, I was told, though I didn't know where or what the Pacific was, and because he was fighting a fierce war he could not come home until it was over.

Then Alice was six years old and there was Daddy, lean and fierce in a colonel's uniform, his face like a blade, his eyes like the eyes of an eagle.

Picking me up high in his arms, he held my thighs strongly against his chest, and I could feel the beating of his heart.

But now, in this bedroom that I had come to tonight from the Mediterranean, his dream-voice was like thunder.

"Alice! Did you suck that boy's cock?"

It thundered and trembled at once, so great was the rage, so great the love. The words beat at me with the rage of love, and so I could not lie.

"Yes, Daddy. I sucked his cock."

"Why?" the Daddy-voice thundered. "Why, in God's name, WHY?"

I trembled. "Because he wanted me to," I whimpered. "He really wanted me to, Daddy."

"DO YOU HAVE TO DO EVERY-THING SOME BOY WANTS YOU TO DO?"

I trembled more violently. "Yes," I cried. "YES!"

Then I couldn't breathe, because that great Thing between Daddy's legs was stirring into life. I stared, fascinated, as It jerked repeatedly, rearing Its head to gaze one-eyed at me.

Daddy stood with legs braced, letting

his Thing do what it wanted to do. Second by second It engorged itself, turning redder, glistening now, until It pointed like an accusing finger. Then It was higher yet, more rigid, thumping against the base of his belly. It struck fear into me, and I wanted Daddy to take me into his arms, hold me safely high against his muscled chest so that I could feel his heart beat strong and true.

The voice rolled again with thunder, but so far away it seemed to come from a distant mountain.

"Then you are The Cocksucker of Clancy Street. Admit it. Say it. SAY IT!"

I put my both hands over my face. I could only whisper the words. "Yes. I am The Cocksucker of Clancy Street."

"SAY IT OUT LOUD. AND LOOK AT ME WHEN YOU SPEAK."

I took away my hands. I did not look at him. I looked at the great Thing thumping against his hard belly.

"Alice is The Cocksucker of Clancy Street."

The voice was close again, thundering. "Then, by God, suck this cock."

Frozen. I stared at his Thing. Then, for the first time, I looked up into Daddy's face.

He gazed at me over his great Thing, and the planes of his cheeks were hard, silvery. His eyes were fierce. His eyes were fiercely loving, and he was my Daddy.

"Do you want me to?" I whispered.

The voice did not thunder when he answered, "Yes. More than anything else in the world."

I smiled. I hitched myself forward to the edge of the bed. I touched Daddy's Thing most tenderly with my small hands. And then I put my mouth on It, sucking hard, feeling it cramming my mouth full. At the same time, I raised my eyes to see the pleasure in his face.

He stood tall, reaching toward infinity. Daddy filled the world, from the sinewy legs I grasped like twin tree trunks, to the eagle eyes. I wished I could swallow the Thing all the way down, engulf It, feel It throbbing against the walls of my throat.

He pushed me away. And the voice was not thunder.

"Alice. Did you fuck that boy?"

"No, Daddy," I said. "I didn't fuck him."

He put his hands on my shoulders. "The truth, now. The truth."

"I'm telling the truth, Daddy. I've never fucked any boy."

He leaned closer. He smiled tenderly, lustfully, as he said, "That's what I wanted to hear."

"I'm glad, Daddy," I said.

He pushed me suddenly backward on the bed. With irresistible hands, he spread my legs.

"But one of these nights you will fuck one of those boys," he said harshly. "So you must fuck me now. First."

In the dream, Alice is always six years old. In the dream, Alice lay quiescent, her nightgown lifted to show her secret, Daddy's hands holding her legs apart so it could not be hidden, and Daddy's great Thing throbbed against the small entrance.

Alice stared at the Thing, knowing that she could not hinder Its entrance into her body.

"But, Daddy," she whimpered. "It's so big. It'll kill me."

"You will take Daddy's cock," Daddy said. *"Because Daddy wants you to."*

With his hand holding the staff, he pressed the enormous head against the lips. It probed there as with a life of its own, sending through Alice's flesh a thrill of terror. It pushed, and pushed again, and Alice screamed, because It was IN, every inch enormously embedded into her tender flesh.

Alice whimpered again. But she did not struggle, because she knew she could not fight Daddy. Alice had to do what Daddy wanted her to do. Then, slowly, Daddy began to fuck the six-year-old Alice. So strong and lean, with each quickening stroke he pulled all the way out, he plunged all the way in and, in spite of all, it felt good, so that Alice wriggled her body trying to get closer, trying to take it all.

So, in the dream, Daddy and Alice fucked, and Alice felt so good. She was doing what Daddy wanted most of all; and if she ever did fuck a boy, Daddy's Thing had been first, making everything as it should be.

As they continued to fuck, Alice was no longer six years old; she grew under the prodding lust of Daddy's Thing, to ten years old, and twelve, and finally sixteen; so that when he came Alice came also, trembling, with one continuous orgasm. It was so overwhelming that she knew without a doubt this was the Great-and-Only Fuck of Alice's life.

I startled awake. I was cold inside. I was also sweating, and the silk sheets tangled me like a shroud. Panic-stricken, I wrestled with the sheets as vividly as I had wrestled with the Daddy Dream.

Free at last, I lay panting in the darkness. Why had the Daddy Dream returned *now?* Since I had gone to the island, I had thought it was conquered forever. But all this time it had been lurking, waiting to be dreamed again.

Lonely in this darkness of myself. Daddy, Clancy Street, were far away. Equally distant was the sanctuary of the island. I am usually good within the solitude of myself. Now, the Daddy Dream newly alive, as though it had never been dreamed before, I was so lonely I could feel the aching in my heart.

Getting out of bed, I padded across the room to part the curtains. The city lay sleeping below in all its millions of sleepings. I shivered. Why had I come back to New York, of all places—where, at the core of success, had lain an ultimate failure?

In the hope of sleeping again, I returned to the bed. But, with the jet lag, I was out of joint with the time.

The only recourse available to me in this great city was Prince Albert, asleep in the guest bedroom. I went to tap on his door.

He was instantly awake. "Alice. Are you all right?"

I entered. In the darkness, I took his hand. He would feel, I knew, the clammy sweating of my palm.

"I had a bad dream," I said. My voice sounded like the little child I had been in the Daddy Dream.

He gripped my hand. His tone was calm, reassuring. "It's gone now, Alice. When you go back to sleep, it won't be there anymore."

I shivered. "I'm slept out. The jet lag, I guess. Will you . . . come talk to me?"

He swung his legs over the edge of the bed. "Of course."

I returned to my bedroom. When he came, he switched on the bedside light.

"Let's not sit in the dark."

He was wearing dark blue silk pajamas, a dark blue robe to match. Before going to bed he had run home to fetch his "overnight kit."

Prince Albert, sitting beside me, put an arm around my waist. "What was your dream?"

I shuddered. "It's too horrible to talk about."

"All right, then," he said in his soft, still Southern voice. "Don't talk about it."

How could I describe, even to Albert, the tangled webs of the Daddy Dream? It held, I knew—even though my waking mind would not, could not, face it—the major themes of my life. That was why it recurred during the crises.

Tremulously I smiled. "Will you brush my hair?"

Without a word, he brought a silver-backed brush from the dressing table. Sitting half behind me, one hand under the fall of hair, he made the first gentle stroke.

The brushing of my hair had been a ritual between us even before he had gone to school to learn the art of hairdressing. Indeed, it was his hands, so deft yet so firm, so loving in the attention they gave to the task, that had inspired his career. I had suggested it, at a time when he had been floundering unhappily through a series of meaningless jobs, from selling neckties on Times Square to demonstrating appliances at Macy's. Now one of the great hairdressers, it was a media event when he invented a new hairdo for his sparkling clientele.

His voice was a low murmur. "Your hair, dear Alice, is *still* the loveliest I have ever touched. A bit sun-bleached, of course, but it does go with your shade of blond. And so *silky, so fine.*"

He made a small laugh. "You ought to see *some* of the haystacks I have to deal with. *Horrible* hair. And of course they always expect *miracles.*"

He kept on brushing. Steadily. Gently. Hypnotically.

Dreamily I said, "Albert, don't you wish it was still the old days in New York? We were so young then, so unfulfilled, yearning for all the good things, love and money and life. And . . . *happy.*"

Prince Albert chuckled. "Darling, those were the *bad* old days. Your memories are betraying you. We were young, but we were running scared. Have you forgotten trudging about to agency after agency, day after day, with your pathetic little portfolio? And me . . . demonstrating a fancy new *toaster* in *Macy's,* for Christ's sake. One year, when old Saint Nick turned up drunk as a skunk, they pressed me into playing Santa Claus. Can you *imagine* a gay Santa?"

He laughed. A light and happy sound. "No, Alice-my-dear, *these* are the good days. You have twenty-two million dollars, and I am so great in my profession it's an *event* when I actually touch a client's head."

"But . . . I hate to say it, Albert, after you've worked so hard, but I wonder if coming home isn't a mistake."

"No," he said firmly. "I feel it's right for you."

"But how can I live in the city if it's going to be like today?" I faced around, making him pause in the brushing. "I wanted to . . . Albert, I must tell you. For fifteen years Stavros has been the only man. He wanted it like that, insisted upon it. It was a part of the bargain."

I was breathing hard again. "And . . . before Stavros . . . when I went to bed with a man, it was because *he* wanted to. Somehow, it always seemed to work out that way. But now . . ."

I stopped because I did not know how to say it.

Albert was watching my face. He was very serious. "What are you trying to tell me, Alice?"

I made an impatient movement. "I don't know. That's it . . . I don't know *anything* about *anything* anymore. I thought the island would be *me* for the rest of my life. Now I have to catch up."

His voice was thoughtful. "Singles' bars, then? Consciousness-raising sessions? Feelie groups?" He paused to laugh. "That's what you might call *grope* therapy. Biorhythms, est, Kundalini yoga and orgies, all that modern scene?"

"I don't know what you're talking about," I said. "What are singles' bars?"

He regarded me. "My God, it *is* innocent-Alice, isn't it?"

He laughed, began brushing my hair again.

I was insistent. "What *is* a singles' bar? Tell me."

He smiled. "I really wouldn't know, my dear. I understand it's *rather* a meat market."

"Meat market?"

"Single men and single women go there, make their choice of who they want to fuck. Then they go fuck." He laughed. "Gays have had their meat markets for years, you know. The idea of a singles' bar was really *borrowed* from the gay culture."

"Will you take me to one?" I asked.

He shuddered. "Darling, it's really not my *milieu*. Besides, you're *supposed* to go alone."

I slumped inside myself. "I won't be able to go about alone. You saw what it was like today. The photographers are probably camped outside this building right now, in the middle of the night."

Prince Albert's face showed a serious expression. "If you really wish it, I think you can establish your privacy. Greta Garbo has lived in New York for *years* —nobody bothers her because she truly wants to be left alone. Now, Jackie Onassis . . ." He laughed. "Jackie hates it and loves it at the same time. She doesn't *want* all that publicity—but if it suddenly went away, she would be *bereft*. The press understands that, subliminally at least, so they keep after her."

He paused. "If you truly wish it, it can be done. To begin with, you'll have to hire a publicity agent to keep your name out of the papers."

I laughed. "Sounds rather silly."

He laughed with me. "Yes, isn't it? I know just the man for you. He has good credibility. When he tells the press you don't want to be interviewed, you don't want to be photographed, they'll believe him. Eventually."

"But . . . those pictures today. If I show up in a gay bar, I mean a—what did you call it, singles' bar? —everyone will recognize me."

"Without the reinforcement of continuing publicity, by day after tomorrow everybody will have forgotten. New York is so *ephemeral* nowadays, my dear. As Andy Warhol once said, 'Before long, *everybody* will be a celebrity for fifteen minutes.' "

I raised my eyes to Albert's face. "I've always been somebody else's Alice," I said. "Now I'm looking for the true Alice. Do you . . . think I can find her?"

He nodded. Seriously. "Yes. Because you have the courage of innocence."

Suddenly I felt it all over again. A great lift of happiness rose in my heart. My body tingled. Still dwelling in me, I realized, was the warm eroticism of the Daddy Dream.

I lay back on the bed, opening my legs. I could feel the throbbing deep inside.

"Oh God, I need a man," I said passionately. "A man I've never seen before. It's been so *long*, Albert. Fifteen years."

Prince Albert regarded me ironically. "Well, darling, don't look at *me*. Or are you going to try to turn a silk purse into a rawhide *man?*"

> Those many years ago, Albert had used that same wry phrase. They had been words of despair.
>
> Both of us, then, had been so desperately young. Though I had been in New York only a few weeks, I was finding an occasional modeling assignment, mostly underwear stuff.
>
> I came home to the tiny West Side apartment that day, mad at the entire world. We had been shooting on a grinding schedule to finish a new catalogue. The client, silently observing, had been in the studio all day. It was always more difficult when the client was watching.
>
> Finished at last, bone tired, I was dressing behind a screen when Len, the photographer, came over. I was in underwear—my underwear, at least—but as far as Len was

concerned I might have been wearing a Mother Hubbard.

"Alice, the client has picked you to treat for dinner," he said. "All right?"

I looked over the screen. The client stood waiting beside the door, too fat, in an an overcoat too long. Carefully not watching us, he studied the wall panel of photographs displaying Len's work.

I tried to imagine being under that mound of blubbery flesh. He would pant and huffle, getting it off. I was not as innocent as the day I had started carrying my "pathetic portfolio" about New York.

"Len, I'm tired and I'm hungry," I said. "When I go to bed tonight, it'll be by myself. Believe me."

Len regarded me. "You're hungry. So enjoy a nice meal. Choose the most expensive item on the menu." He waited. Then he said, "The man has given us a beautiful commission. There's more to come. If you want the job."

"Do I have to fuck to work?" I said harshly.

Len shrugged. "Suit yourself, baby. I told him I'd ask. Don't put me in the middle."

I smiled. I laid my hand on his arm. "You're a good friend, Len. But . . . I just can't. Not tonight."

Crossing the studio, Len shook his head at the client. He disappeared into the office.

The client still waited, however, when I came out. His hands were in his overcoat pockets.

"Hello, girlie," he said. "What's your name?"

He was looking me up and down. His skin was dark, with a grayish, unhealthy pal-

lor. The whites of his protruding eyes were muddy yellow.

"Alice," I said shortly.

"Alice what?" he said. "I want to remember the name of a girl like you. Your name ought to be remembered all over the garment district."

"That's it," I said. "Alice. It ought to be easy to remember."

I went on past him.

So that's that, I thought wearily as I gained the street. Never have to worry about working for him again. Or any of his friends.

Seeing an empty taxi, I thought, What the hell, it's raining, isn't it? and lifted an arm. The taxi driver eyed me in the rearview mirror. A young man, probably Puerto Rican from the Catholic medals hanging from the mirror. His hand was on the meter, ready to flip the flag.

"Hey, kid. Want to ride with the flag up?"

An undertone in his voice told me his meaning.

"Mister, I'm tired and I'm hungry and I feel very dirty," I said. "Just let me pay the fare, all right?"

"Too bad," he said unabashedly. "Beautiful girl like you, ought to ride free all over this town."

I sank into the seat. There was anger in my soul. Since I was twelve years old, male eyes had been watching me, in their depths an aching hunger that, they seemed to insist, I was born into the world to satisfy.

Why does it have to be so, I thought, feeling as disgusted with Alice as with the dirty world. Why isn't it enough to be photogenic, and eager to please? It was a job, *wasn't it, like any other job? And I could do it well.*

The very first assignment of my professional career had remained a bitter rankle in my mind.

I had arrived breathless for the fashion show being staged for out-of-town buyers. The girls all in one dressing room, the place was a disturbed beehive, the designer fussing about, screaming, beating his hands against his forehead, enjoying a nervous breakdown out of the sheer excitement of the event. For the first time, I was a part of it.

The owner beckoned me to one side. He was smoking a vile cigar.

"You're the new girl, ain't you?"

"Yes," I said, quivering with anxiety. Had he changed his mind?

He looked me up and down. "Well, baby, I'll lay it on the line. Fuckee, workee. No fuckee, no workee."

"What?" I said.

His eyes narrowed. "Not me, understand. I got a good wife, kids at home, I don't mess around. But I got this big buyer in from Seattle, know what I mean? Always counts on a fresh piece of ass." He shrugged, spread his hands. "If he's satisfied, he buys. Big. If he ain't satisfied, he blows his budget somewhere else."

"But I can't . . . I don't . . ."

Indifferently he turned away. "Suit yourself."

I was suddenly terrified. I might not ever get another job in New York if I lost this first one. "Wait," I said, clutching at his arm. "Wait. I'll . . . I'll be nice."

He smiled. He puffed cigar smoke.

"That's my sensible girl. Believe me, you'll go a long way in this business."

Each time I went down the runway, I watched faces in the crowd, wondering which of these men would use my body tonight. Their eyes clung to me like leeches as I paraded and turned, paraded and turned. But I could not recognize the eyes which would see me naked.

A cold knot gripped my stomach, I tapped on the door of the hotel room. It opened immediately.

"Hello," I said in a shaky voice.

"Well hello there," he said as if surprised. "Come on in."

Not bad looking, I thought, not too old. A sturdy man, short, not over five-seven. There was a glass of whiskey in his hand.

"Want a drink first?"

"I don't drink," I said.

He looked at me, looked away, gulping at his drink. Suddenly I realized he was as nervous as I was.

Feeling better for some reason, I sat down on the bed. "I believe I will have a drink."

We drank. We took off our clothes. We fucked. I felt nothing.

When he came out of the bathroom in his underwear, he regarded me. I was still on the bed, my face turned into the pillow.

"You're a beautiful girl," he said. "But you fuck lousy."

I rolled over to look at him. "I'm sorry," I said guiltily. "I tried. I just . . . I never did it before. I'm sorry."

His eyes quickened. "That so? You mean, I got your cherry?"

Speechlessly, I nodded.

*He sat down on the side of the bed.
"So that was the trouble! I figured you just
didn't want to put out." He placed a friendly
hand on my shoulder. "It was all right,
wasn't it? I didn't hurt you or anything?"*

*The sympathy touched my feeling of
desolation, I scrounged closer. His arm sliding around my shoulders, he held me, telling me how nice it was to meet such a nice
girl, if he had just known he would have
handled it better.*

*Within minutes, of course, a renewed
lust began to penetrate the sympathy, and
he wanted to fuck again. Knowing now that
he was my first man, he whispered, it was
up to him to leave me with a beautiful memory.*

*He fucked me again. This time, still
slick and unfeeling inside, I pretended it was
better. Because he wanted so very much for
it to be better.*

*The taxi stopped. The driver looked
anxiously over his shoulder. "Are you all
right?"*

*I was crying, and he knew it. I straight-
ened my shoulders. "Just tired, that's all.
And ... dirty."*

*Resolutely I opened the door, got out.
"How much do I owe you?"*

*"Listen, forget about the fare, all
right?" He paused. "Want me to park it,
come on up? You look like a girl needs a
friend."*

*I looked at him. Something newly hard,
newly cynical, in my soul said, Yeah. Sympathy.*

*"I always pay my own way," I said
coldly.*

*He shrugged. "If that's how you feel
about it."*

Why, I thought, do they always shrug?
To show they don't care about the sex, even
though they've been panting for it?

When I went up to the stoop, I saw
Prince Albert sitting forlorn, huddled into
the hallway out of the rain.

"What's the matter with you?"

His eyes were haggard. "Kicked out of
my place. I've got no place to sleep."

I smiled. "Of course you have, Albert.
You can sleep with me."

Feeling better, I laughed. "I mean,
not sleep with me."

Albert, standing up, laughed also, saying almost gaily, "I knew I could count on
Alice."

"Dear Albert," I said fondly, putting
my arm through his. Together we trudged up
to the top floor.

I took off my coat. I wasn't so tired
anymore, and I didn't feel dirty. Albert was
the best friend I had ever had. Every girl,
I thought fondly, needs someone like Prince
Albert. He was the only man I had ever
known who didn't lust to get into my pants.
He loved me simply for the sake of myself.
As I loved him.

The apartment was tiny, one room and
a kitchenette. Albert would literally have to
sleep with me; there was only the studio
couch. Unless he curled up on the floor,
which would be silly.

Albert was prospecting in the gas refrigerator. He still had on his battered pea
jacket. "All you've got is soup." He smiled.
"Just have to make out on chicken soup, I
suppose."

"I've got money," I said. "I've been
working. We'll have a feast, if you don't

mind making a trip to the grocery store in
the rain."

Albert returned laden with the ingredients for beef stew, salad, and milk and eggs
and bacon for breakfast. An extravagant
buying spree. And, most extravagant of all,
a bottle of wine. While he was gone I had
taken a bath and I was now comfortable in
the quilted robe that had been Daddy's fif-
teenth-birthday present. With experience of
the cold rain outside, the apartment felt snug
and safe.

"I do a marvelous beef stew," Albert
proclaimed as he unloaded the grocery sack.
"With herbs and everything." He looked
anxious. "You do have herbs, don't you?"

"Afraid not," I confessed. "I'm not
much of a cook."

"Worcestershire sauce, anything."

"I think there's a bottle of Worcestershire. If it hasn't dried up."

I curled up on the couch, watching him
work. Albert had opened the wine. It was
harshly sweet in my mouth.

"I thought you liked this landlord, Albert," I said. "You told me he was very
nice."

He made a grimace. "When I didn't
have the money for the rent, Mr. Hyde was
suddenly on the scene."

Picking up his glass, he gulped from it.
"I haven't worked for a month, you know.
I've simply pounded the pavement, but—"

"But why didn't you tell me?" I cried.
"I could have lent you enough money to
tide you over."

He looked abashed. "Well, I kept thinking something would turn up."

"He literally threw you out? How
mean."

The stew on, he came to sit beside me.
"Worse than that. A lot worse."

Because he had shuddered, I put my
hand on his shoulder. "What happened?"

"I got home late, dead tired from
tramping all over town. The rent was already overdue about three days, so he came
up the stairs right behind me. He'd been
watching for me, obviously."

We drank from our glasses.

"He came right on into the apartment. 'I
need your rent money,' he said. I faced him
squarely. 'I haven't got it,' I told him. 'You'll
just have to wait.'

"He kept on looking at me. 'Ain't you
working?'

" 'No. But I'll find something tomorrow for sure. One place today told me to
come back, they . . .'

"He came close. 'Pretty boy like you
ought to do all right hustling,' he said.
'Young stuff, too, not used up like most of
these hustlers in the Village.' "

Albert looked into my face. "I knew
what he meant, all right. And don't believe
for a minute I hadn't already thought about
it. But . . ." He shivered. "I just don't do
that. With me, there's got to be love, some
promise of love. Even if you're only kidding yourself, and you know it."

He finished his wine, poured again.
"Not bad stuff," he said. "Pretty cheap, but
not all that bad."

"You mean he wanted you to . . . to
do him?"

Albert shook his head. "Not that simple.
'Boy, let me tell you something,' he said.
'I'm gonna get you out of your trouble. I
know these guys, see, they go ape over a

good-looking boy like you. I'll see to it you won't ever have to work at a job again.'

" 'I don't hustle,' I told him.

" 'Wouldn't be what you'd call hustling,' he said. 'You wouldn't have to cruise the bars, looking for the chicken hawks. No sir. You'd be cozied up right in your own apartment, making money like there's no tomorrow. So, how's about it?'

" 'No,' I told him.

" 'Hell, you're queer, ain't you?' he said. 'You got to be queer, pretty boy like you. So what difference does it make?'

" 'Just all the difference in the world,' I told him."

Prince Albert's voice was shaking. Beginning to cry, he put his face into his hands. "Then he said, 'Hustle or get out.' So . . . I got out."

My arms were holding him tightly. He leaned his head against my breast.

"God, I wish I was straight," he said brokenly. "Everybody just beats on a person all the time. Nobody's got any respect, they don't even think you're a human being."

I rocked him in my arms. "It's all right, Albert, everything will be all right. One of these days you'll be on top, and so will I. They'll know we're people then, not just somebody to be used."

It was all coming out; the anger I had felt today, the frustration, the hunger. Coming out in both of us, so that we huddled together, holding each other.

Prince Albert, forcing composure, got up to check on the stew. He came back, poured the last of the wine. We drank again.

"Haven't you ever thought *about* being

straight?" I asked curiously. "Maybe you're more normal than you think."

Prince Albert shook his head. "Darling, I never had a chance. I was raped, my dear, before I was thirteen. And I loved it."

"But . . ." I said. "But if . . . Have you ever kissed a girl?"

He made a mouth. "I can't imagine it. Oh, like I kiss you, sure. But, with passion?" The shudder was exaggerated.

I watched him. "You really would like to be like other men, wouldn't you?"

He was morose again. "It'd be a different world. I'd be a different person." He sighed. "I never have liked myself very much, you know. Even if I do have a normal *amount of vanity.*"

"Listen," I said. "Why don't . . ."

He stood up abruptly. "You know what I'm going to do? There was some money left over from the shopping, so how about another bottle of wine?" He giggled. "We'll just get drunk tonight, darling. Drunk as skunks."

He was at the door. "Now, you keep an eye on the stew. Ought to be about ready by the time I get back."

I lay back on the studio couch, wondering why he had departed so suddenly. I felt a bit tiddly from the unaccustomed wine, but warm, safe, not thinking at all about my bad day.

Idly I put my hand on myself, then, Daddy striding sternly into my mind, I snatched it away. I pushed Daddy away and the hand crept again to the secret place.

When Prince Albert returned I had to get up to open the door. He had brought two bottles of wine, not one. He waved them triumphantly.

"Two for the price of one," he crowed. "One for our elegant repast, another for afterward."

We waited a bit longer on the stew, drinking at the second bottle, talking quietly about nothing at all. In abeyance from ourselves, with the time, we floated dreamily.

We were quite drunk by the time we ate, so the stew, whatever its real character, was delicious. I did have a vague feeling it was undercooked; the potatoes were still hard.

Conscientiously, enforced guest that he was, Prince Albert wouldn't let me help with the cleaning up. Finished, he brought the third bottle of wine, placing it carefully on the floor beside the couch.

"Are we both going to sleep in this tiny bed?"

I giggled. "The only bed I've got. Unless you want to sleep on the bare floor."

He looked embarrassed. "I don't . . . have any jammies. My last pair wore themselves to tatters, and I haven't had the money to buy new ones."

"You can sleep naked, for all of me," I said. "Unless you'd like one of my nightgowns."

"My dear, I'm not a drag queen," Prince Albert said loftily. We collapsed in laughter.

Sobering, he said, "I'll get undressed after the lights are out. That way, I won't embarrass you. Or me, either."

"Albert," I said, suddenly serious. "Why don't you fuck me?"

He was very still. "Alice!" he said.

I sat up. "Well, you said you'd like to be straight. Maybe, if you tried it, you'd like

*it so much it would take the place of . . .
the other."*

He wanted to make light of the matter. "My *dear! Are you trying to turn a silk
purse into a rawhide* man?"

I refused the laughter. "*After all, Albert, we're good friends, we do love each
other. It wouldn't be like we were strangers.
You'd just be making love to Alice.*"

His voice was a mumble. "*Don't keep
talking about it, for God's sake.*"

I hesitated. But after all, I thought, it's
a better reason than that other time. It is,
at least, for love. A special kind of love.

I reached for his hand. Boldly I placed
it between my legs.

"Put your finger there," I said. "There."

I pressed his hand against me. "See how
nice and warm? See how she likes to feel
your finger rubbing?"

Albert was trembling. Gripping his reluctant hand, I forced his finger deeper into
the groove, up and down, up and down.
But when I stopped, he did not continue
the motion.

Standing abruptly, I said, "Get naked."

My voice was commanding. Numbly,
he moved to obey. I watched, as severe as
a schoolteacher, until he was naked. Then
I dropped to my knees to take his limp
Thing into both hands.

"See how beautiful It is," I crooned,
my warm breath blowing against his flesh.
"Any woman would love to have a beautiful
Thing like that in her."

It was nice, I thought warmly. Not at
all like those gross Things I had sucked in
high school. The long shaft was slim, delicate; the foreskin, the pink head, smoothly
bright. Only a light fluff of curly hair, and

the ball sack was small, rounded, snugged up tightly.

He endured it for a minute, two minutes. Then, lurching sideways, he snatched up the bottle of wine. Tilting it, his throat pulsed with the swallowing.

He handed the bottle to me, and I drank. Holding the last swallow, I put my mouth on him, bathing his Thing in the wine. Albert shivered. In spite of himself, he was beginning to get an erection.

"Oh, God," he gasped. "Oh God, Alice."

I leaned back to look up. "You see?" I said. "It's good, Albert. So good."

Turning, I laid myself down on the studio couch. The quilted robe divided, leaving me naked to him as I opened my legs.

"Get in me," I said. "Hurry."

Prince Albert was into it now; he wanted to fuck like a man. He came eagerly upon me. But when I scissored my legs around his slender hips, drawing him down, he abruptly lost his good hard-on and his penis was limp against my crotch.

"I can't, Alice," he said helplessly. "I want to, and I can't." He began to cry.

I stroked his flanks with both hands. "Don't worry about it," I told him. "I'll do it for both of us."

I put my hand between his belly and and mine, fingertips touching his Thing. I inserted the flaccid head between the lips, rubbing it gently against the clitoris. He flinched away, but, with the other hand pressing hard on his rump, I held him close. I was moist now, open; I waited for him to respond to my arousal.

Prince Albert's face, pressed against my cheek so he wouldn't have to see me as a woman, was wet with tears. He trembled in tiny spasms. Knowing his mingled fear and desire, I perversely felt a greater lust to have his reluctant Thing inside me. Wet now, aching to be filled, I began to move, grinding against his unresponsive limpness with mounting desperation.

My womanly frustration produced an inspiration. I put my index finger on his anus. Pressing hard, I felt it flower warmly. When the finger slipped inside, Albert groaned.

His Thing came suddenly to life. He didn't go hard-erect but he was inside, at least. I held him in, half-limp though It was, and as I continued to massage his anus the warm flow of his come began an orgasm slow and deep like a woman's climax.

Seeking my own release, I began to thrust frantically, yearning for a ruthless hard-on stroking into my seeking flesh. But he was finished, ebbing away like an outgoing tide until It slipped too easily out of my grasp.

Prince Albert raised his upper body to look down into my eyes. His mouth, soft and inviting like a girl's mouth, was trembling. A rictus of pain fled across his face. He wrenched his body away and fled to the bathroom.

Sitting up, I huddled into myself, listening to the sound of his retching. Beneath the misery I felt for Albert still dwelled the unfulfilled desire for some sort of completion. I hated him, in that moment, for arousing me, then not performing the part of a man. Though it had been my own idea.

He came shamefaced from the bathroom. "It was the wine," he said, not looking at me.

"No," I said sadly. "Because I am a woman."

Bravely he came to cradle my head in his arms. My cheek was against his naked belly.

"But I came, didn't I? I came inside you."

My arm was around his waist. I patted him on the fanny. "Come on, let's get to bed," I said. "I'm tired and I'm sleepy, and I've had too much wine."

Through all our following years, we never spoke of that night.

I liked Mark Judson from the first moment. A tall, lean, knobby man, his face showed high cheekbones, like an Indian, and a sad mouth. Stooping his shoulders, like most men who feel themselves conspicuously tall, he walked with an awkward, bent-kneed stride.

He did not look prosperous. His trench coat was ratty-looking and, beneath it, he wore a shapeless tweed suit. An ex-newspaperman, Prince Albert had told me, now scuffling around town doing publicity for a handful of second-rank theatrical talent. With most of the old gossip columns no longer in existence, it wasn't exactly the easiest way to make a living in Little Old New York.

While he shook hands, he looked at me with eyes that had seen much, very clearly, and had not liked what they had seen. Yet in them was the quickening every man exhibited when gazing upon Alice! for the first time. I won't let it turn me off the man, I told myself. I need him, if I'm to do what I must do.

"I told Mark you were anxious to explore the modern scene," Prince Albert said. "You won't find a better guide; Mark has been exploring New York ever since he came up from Virginia to work on the *Times*."

Mark was still holding my hand. Taking it away, I sat down again at the breakfast table. "I'm sure you can. But . . . can you arrange it so I can go about as a private person?"

Albert, busying himself, poured fresh coffee. "Mark's got a plan," he said.

I looked to Mark.

His voice was a low rumbling in his chest. His accent showed not a trace of Virginia; one would have thought him a New Yorker born and bred.

"Lady, you got to give me a week before you stir out of this apartment," he said. "Photographers are waiting outside right now."

I looked at Albert reproachfully. "I thought they didn't know about *this* place."

He shrugged to show his helplessness. "They've got ways of finding out what they want to know. We were probably tailed all the way in from the airport yesterday, though I *told* the chauffeur to use up Queens before he headed for Manhattan."

Mark was waiting patiently. "If you'll agree to stay under wraps for a week, I think I can get things fixed. I'll talk to the people I know, explain how you're doing a Garbo, you'll be around from now on—*if* you can live privately."

He smiled for the first time. An unexpectedly sweet smile, glowing out of that worn face.

"I'll tell them, the surest way to run you out of town is to hound your steps everywhere you go."

I kept my eyes on him. "Will I be able to go to singles' bars, places like that?"

A flicker in his eyes. Surprise? Interest?

"Discreetly. You might consider a wig to cover that spectacular hair." He smiled again. "Good God, if you walked into Maxwell's Plum looking like that, everybody would fall off their stools."

Prince Albert regarded me anxiously. "Alice, I don't know *anybody* who could do the job better." He turned to look at Mark. "Of course, my dear, you'll have to get him some new *clothes*. That ex-news-paperman bit, with the tweed suit and the battered trench coat, is too *too* for doing reverse flack for Alice!"

I expected Mark to be offended by the arch criticism. He only smiled tolerantly. "I'm certainly not going to dress like you, pretty boy."

"Oh, you manly *thing*," Prince Albert said mockingly. "I could do you a dozen *times,* with you sitting there like a wooden *Indian.*"

They both laughed. I relaxed, seeing that, though of different sexual persuasion, they were truly friends.

But still . . . I looked at Albert. "Go away," I told him. "I must talk to Mr. Judson."

Prince Albert elaborately elevated his wrist to look at the time. "I really must get to the shop today," he said. *"Grace* is coming in, and she always expects to experience the expensive touch of Prince Albert's own personal hands."

He came around the table to kiss me on the cheek. I held his hand pressed against my other cheek. "Stay with me again tonight?"

"I am not Alice's guide to this wonderland they call New York. I've done my job getting you settled in. You're on your own now."

"But . . ."

He shook his head firmly. "I have my own *crowd,* you know. Certainly you don't want to be a part of *that* scene."

"But your clientele . . ."

"Darling, I learned long ago not to mix socially with the clientele. It simply doesn't *work.* Accept their invitations, soon they begin to feel like they *own* you. Prince Albert is *aloof.* Prince Albert is *mysterious.* It's the only way to develop enough personal clout to tell them what they need to know about themselves."

He shook hands with Mark. "Look after Alice, man. Or I'll kick you right in those lovely balls."

Mark had stood up. He gazed down on the diminutive Prince Albert. "You can't even reach that high, fellow."

Prince Albert chuckled. "Just *try* me."

"But, Albert, won't I see you . . .?"

He waved a limp hand. "I'll come often enough to do your hair, my dear, and hear the *details* of your sex life."

Mark Judson gazed fondly after him. "That's a ballsy little guy."

I laughed. "That's the best description of Prince Albert I've ever heard."

Mark Judson was still looking toward the door. "He's the only hardcore fag I've ever been around who didn't make me just a bit uncomfortable. But he knows how to be a friend. You know?"

"Yes," I said soberly. "I know."

Mark Judson turned. He said directly, "What did you want to tell me so privately? That you don't think I'm the right man for the job?" He paused. "If that's the bottom line, lay it on me and I'll be gone."

I looked at my hands, placed flat on the table. I raised my gaze to look into his eyes.

"I don't know yet," I said. "Do you want the job?"

He moved his big shoulders. "I can use the money."

Both of us were being tentative in the absence of Albert as a go-between.

Mark Judson looked at me inquisitively. "Do you really want to experience everything that's going on in this New York City of the nineteen seventies? Let me warn you. It's pretty grubby, sometimes violent. A lot of greedy people out there. Hungry for the gratification of their appetites—food, shelter, for sex and love and friendship. Everybody, it seems nowadays, carries a monkey on his back. It's been drummed into them that they can let it all hang out. Everybody's into primal screaming and acting-out. Utter permissiveness. If they feel like banging somebody on the head, they got a right. They often *feel* like banging somebody on the head."

He took a deep breath.

"I'm a night-walker. Know what I mean? I don't go home unless I have to. Because I want to see it all, too."

His mouth was tight.

"But you can't do *your* night-walking with me at your side for protection. Go to a singles' bar with an escort, you've closed out the deal. Understand? You've got to hang it all the way out, too. And, a woman looking like you look . . ." He shook his head.

"So you disapprove," I said steadily.

His mouth twisted.

"You're just about the most beautiful woman I've ever had in the sight of my eyes," he said. For the first time, I heard the Southern eloquence he had put away long ago. "You've got the kind of money most people can't even dream about. You can live anywhere, do everything you want to do in high style, with whomever you choose to share it." He moved his hands. "So why this?"

My voice held steady. "Because I lost myself, a long time ago, for a lot of different reasons. The true Alice is out there somewhere among all the people. I've got to find her again."

"It looks like, to my simple mind, that fifteen years on your own private island should have been sufficient for finding yourself."

I felt a tremor inside. "I thought I had. I was deceiving myself."

He looked directly at me. "With the money your friend left you, you can buy your own island, you know. If you're looking for sex, import your own studs. Twenty-two million dollars can buy a lot of love. It'd be a hell of a lot better than looking for it on *this* island."

The words were as ruthless against my soul as he had meant them to be. Because I knew he had spoken the truth.

"Sure," I said. "I can do that. If it were the thing to do. But it isn't. *This* is what I must do. I feel it strongly."

He smiled faintly. "Well, just know what you're getting into. That's all I'm trying to say."

I said sharply, "Of course I don't know what I'm getting into. That's the name of the game, isn't it?"

"I suppose so," he said grudgingly. Disapproval showed in his tone. "I guess it's settled you won't let your mind be changed. So . . . what about me?"

I regarded him. "Do you want the job?"

"I don't know," he said slowly. He looked surprised at himself. Quickly he added, "I can use the money. Believe me."

"All right, then. Employment interview. Are you married?"

"Yes. If you can call it that."

"What do you mean, *call it that?*"

He looked away. "Like I said. I'm a night-walker. I go home only to sleep."

"Why?"

The single word was so blunt, so direct, he could only answer.

"My wife is not the woman I married. I suppose that's why."

"What do you mean?" I said again.

He looked at his hands. "Well, Marsha's into Women's Lib. You know?"

"What do you mean by Women's Lib?"

His expression was wry. "Good God, you *have* been away, haven't you? Betty Friedan's *Feminine Mystique.* Gloria Steinem. ERA."

"ERA?" I said.

"That's the big battle now, an amendment to the Constitution guaranteeing women equal rights with men. There's also the abortion issue, with the Right-to-lifers and the Catholic Church fighting it tooth and nail."

He sighed. "I can't explain to you in fifteen minutes the entire women's movement that has grown up while you've been away."

"Then just tell me about your wife."

A long-suffering look. "Marsha? A nice Catholic

girl when we got married. Younger than me . . . too much younger. We had three kids in four years because she didn't even believe in birth control, you know?"

He was not looking at me. "Then she happened, by chance, to go to a meeting over there in Brooklyn where we live. Friedan was there, and Steinem, and Phyllis Schafly on the other side, because it was, you know, a big debate." He made a pained expression. "She came home to tell me I had to have a vasectomy before she'd make love with me again. And a week later she was driving a cement truck. Because, she claimed, she'd grown up wanting to be a truck driver and now she had as much right to do what she wanted as I did."

He laughed. It was wry, bitter.

"So she drives her truck, and the kids are at home alone after school unless I happen to be there sleeping. She won't even wash the dishes. I tell her I still have to take out the garbage, but that doesn't cut any ice. She's given up cooking, too. We eat out of the corner delicatessen."

"Did you have the vasectomy?"

He looked at me. "No."

There didn't seem to be anywhere to go with that.

"Listen," I said. "Something else. I saw the gleam in your eye when Albert introduced us."

I had tautened myself to bring out those words. But it had to be clearly understood. Had to be.

His voice rumbled. "Lady, you've got to be used to it by now."

"Don't call me *lady*. Call me Alice."

"All right. Alice."

I forced myself to speak as ruthlessly as he had done before. "I just want you to understand one thing. This job doesn't carry the side benefit of an occasional piece of pussy."

I had startled him, all right. His eyes flared before he looked away.

I kept my voice from trembling. "The deal won't work unless our association is thoroughly professional. Just because I might be sleeping with a man—or men —don't think there'll come a time when it's your turn."

"A wry quirk. I see where you're coming from. You'll go to bed with any man who happens to strike your fancy. With the sole exception of one Mark Judson. Right?"

"Right," I said coldly.

His eyes were cool. "What if you happen to want to fuck Mark Judson?"

He was playing games now. Sexual games. Exactly what I had tried to avoid, right here at the beginning, by an open discussion.

I stood up. "It's not likely," I told him furiously.

He stood up also, saying ruefully, "I really blew it then, didn't I?" He sighed in resignation. "Well, in spite of what Prince Albert said, I didn't think you'd go for me. So I can't call myself disappointed, can I?"

Moving away from the table, he picked up his shabby trench coat and draped it over his shoulders without putting his arms into the sleeves.

I surprised myself.

"You've got the job," I heard myself saying. "If you want it."

He looked at me for a while. I thought he meant to turn it down.

Then he said, "Do you mean it?"

I nodded quickly, before the residual anger could change my mind. "If we understand each other."

He stood quite still. Another threshold. Then he said, "What about the money?"

"Albert told me I ought to pay you a thousand dollars a week."

It wasn't a smile this time. A greedy grin. "My God, Alice! I've never earned that size of money in my life."

I liked the frankness of his delight.

"You've got it," I said. "As long as you can

keep me out of the papers and off the television screen."

"Lady," he said earnestly. "I mean . . . Alice, I'm gonna be the best anti-publicity man you ever saw."

He looked down at himself, smiling. "If you'll advance half of the first week's salary, I'll even buy a new suit."

"That one looks fine to me. Regardless of what Prince Albert had to say."

He leaned forward to regard his trousers dubiously. "I bought this Harris tweed on the occasion of going to work for the *Times*," he said. "Which makes it an ancient suit indeed."

I laughed. "All right. Buy yourself a new suit. But not a Pierre Cardin, like Albert was wearing. I'd suggest another Harris tweed."

He looked thoughtful. "Spring coming on, wrong time to invest in Harris tweed. I'll just go looking." He laughed. "But, I promise you, not Bloomingdale's. More along the lines of Brooks Brothers, right?"

"All right," I said, laughing. "I'll tell my bank's trust department to put you on salary, and let you have the first week in advance."

He was regarding me. "Maybe you ought to go shopping with me," he said. "I want to be sure you're satisfied before I spend my good money."

I turned abruptly away. "You told me I had to stay incommunicado for a week, remember?"

"Yeah," he said ruefully. "I did, didn't I?" He smiled again. "So. I'd better get about your business."

I went to him, holding out my hand. "I must thank Prince Albert for bringing you to me."

"Yeah," he said. "Me, too."

And he was gone.

The week I spent in that elegant, empty apartment, before I sallied forth for the first adventure, was a strange time indeed.

I was not entirely alone; Prince Albert came daily for an hour to do my hair and share a glass of white wine and much gossip about people I didn't know.

Mark Judson reported daily, also, on his progress at getting across his point that I truly meant the Garbo act.

"I describe you as a frightened bird, fluttering and ready for takeoff. Any pressure for an interview will send you winging, never to return," he told me jubilantly. "I'm convincing them, I think, that they can't win; even *trying* to get something will lose the game."

On the first return visit, he was wearing the new suit. Inspecting it, I said, "Men's clothes haven't changed while I've been away."

He smiled at my naïveté. "They've changed a great deal. It's just that, this year, the unflared cuff and the narrower lapel is coming back. Not to mention shorter collars and the neat collar clip."

With the conservative chalk-stripe suit he wore a striped shirt with a white collar, a safety-pin stay of gold at the neck, and small round cuff links. He looked very good, though as ever he stooped his tallness.

Basically, however, I was as solitary as on the Mediterranean island. The phone never rang, unless Mark or Albert called; the switchboard operators had their instructions no calls were to be put through without the code word.

For some strange reason, I had chosen "Peacock" as the code word.

So much alone, yet so internally restless, I found myself dwelling on the past—both the good and the bad. And perhaps it was right for me to review the events that had brought Alice to this critical juncture of her life.

There was a waiting in me . . . in my mind, in my soul, in my body. For, somehow, all my feelings, all my needs—all my desires—were in my memories.

Daddy. Always first and forever was Daddy. For years, now, I had not allowed him to dwell in my mind. Though inevitably, like a persistent ghost, he appeared whenever I least wanted him.

I had always been a daddy's girl; because, I suppose, I did not know him until I was six years old.

As a lawyer, he had told me a thousand times, he could have enjoyed a comfortable war behind a desk somewhere. But I am a man, he told me proudly, and a man goes to war when it is the real war of his time as a man. He had taken his commission with the paratroopers—even in middle age he was lean and hard, ready—and he had returned a colonel with ribbons on his chest and the look of eagles in his eyes.

And, when he held me safe and strong in his lean, muscular arms, against my thighs I could feel the strong true beat of his heart.

Even at that age, I was acutely aware of Mother's jealousy. Smugly Daddy's girl, every night I sat on Daddy's lap, in his leather chair before the television, until it was time to go to bed. Often we weren't even watching television, but talking, laughing, playing the games we shared only with each other.

There were also the moments when he warned me seriously about the perils of being a beautiful girl-child. Never must I talk to strangers, or accept a ride in a car I didn't know. Telling me these frightening things, both strong hands would grip my thighs, holding hard to keep me forever safe. He was frightened, too, by the perils made tempting by Alice's beauty; fearful that even Daddy was not strong enough, watchful enough, to ward off the myriad dangers.

I knew he was afraid, because I could feel the palms of his hands sweating against my legs.

In later years, at twelve and thirteen, he began to talk about boys. They all wanted the same thing, he impressed upon me. If I should give them what they wanted, I would lose their respect forever. Any decent girl saved herself for the man she would marry. Yet, somehow, the man Alice would marry always remained a dim, remote figure. No man could take the place of Daddy.

From the kitchen, cleaning up after dinner, Mother would clash the plates, muttering to herself just loud enough for us to hear. But, when Daddy went into the kitchen to investigate, she denied vigorously that anything could be wrong.

As I grew toward teen age, Mother's performance became steadily worse. Now starting before dinner, she grumbled steadily under her breath as she cooked. She half-smoked too many cigarettes, putting them out by wetting them under the faucet and then dropping the sodden butts into the sink.

Though for a long time I didn't know it—and, even longer, refusing to recognize it—Mother was drinking. Not an all-day, everyday drinking, with the empty vodka bottles accumulating in the garbage cans, but sporadically signaled by the cigarette butts clumped wetly into the dirty sink and the meals not fit to eat. And the under-the-breath bitterness.

Until that ending night, when she said it all out loud, and brought my childhood to a ruinous, shattering end.

*I also, I realized too much later, was
jealous of Mother. When I was very young,
no matter how I cozened Daddy into just
one more game, one more story, one more
rapturous hugging and wrestling, sooner or
later the time would come when Daddy
rose, holding me against his chest, my arms
tight around his neck, to carry me to bed.*

*Another small time, then, while he un-
dressed me, put on my nightie, and rubbed
my legs until I was drowsy. His story-telling
voice came deeper and deeper, from farther
and farther away, until I had slid safely
into sleep.*

*But never a sleep so deep that I did
not know when Daddy left me to go to
Mother, in their bedroom; where, sleeping
beside him, she could touch him anytime
she wanted to.*

*It was a great victory for Daddy-jeal-
ous Alice when Daddy moved into a separate
bedroom. Not as good as if Alice had shared
it with him. But better than Mother being the
one to share.*

All right, I told myself in that New York apartment, you've got to remember the bad parts, too:
Those times you won't let yourself think about, much
less remember in complete emotional detail. For
there, where the Daddy Dream had its genesis, Alice
had begun to lose herself.

Cold inside, shaking, I stood at the window to
look out over the city. As naked of flesh as of soul,
the apartment was always at exactly the right temperature, so there was really no reason not to dwell body-
naked in this sanctuary, as I had so often been naked
on my island beach.

My mind must be, I told myself, as naked as my
flesh. I must touch myself in the sore places of memory.

A strange time, that week in the apartment. Even more strangely, a beautiful time, though often so frightening that in the midst of remembering I would feel the cold sweat trickling clammy down my ribs.

Alice is strange. I know how strange, how complicated. Too deep at times, and often too shallow. Thoughtful, yet so thoughtless, careful and heedless, trusting too much to instinct and yet, somewhere deep down, distrustful even of herself. Lusts and appetites, too, acknowledged and unacknowledged; and longings to be loved. Most of all, perhaps, the longing *to* love.

For, I knew now in my penthouse sanctuary, I had never understood the men. Yearned for Them, yes; lusted after Them, tried to love Them. Hated Them. But, to Alice, the male of the species has remained always and forever a mysteriously opaque being.

They are always *Them*.

An alien race, perhaps, come unto us, the women of the earth. Hadn't I read in the Bible, during all that reading on the island, that *There were giants in the earth in those days . . . when the sons of God came in unto the daughters of men . . . ?*

To Alice, men had always been giants in the earth. *Them.*

Alice, like all women, had sought for shelter, for love—and to experience the stroke of passion cutting hot and true into her receiving depths. *That the sons of God saw the daughters of men that they were fair; and they took them wives of all which they chose.*

Standing to gaze down upon the great city, thinking these thoughts, I trembled and was lustful. I desired that a giant might come in to me, and see that I was fair. I lusted for him to take me unto him as wife, marrying me to his great flaming sword of flesh.

For Alice, in her innocence, there *had* been giants in the earth. Daddy, first of all.

But then Daddy . . .

My trembling hands pressed against the insides

of my thighs. I told myself, I *will* think about it. I *will* remember.

> *Daddy came back into the house.*
>
> *I looked up in surprise, for he had just kissed me on the cheek, there at the breakfast table where I sat eating Cheerios, and as always, was gone early to the office.*
>
> *Daddy worked hard because, as he so often told me, it was all for me. He already had the trust funds set up so I wouldn't ever have to worry about money, and every successful year added its quota of security.*
>
> *I looked up. I froze. Never had I seen such a look on his face. He was pale, his lips a bloodless line, the eagle eyes flat and dead in their sockets.*
>
> *I couldn't recognize his voice. "Alice. Come here."*
>
> *Beginning to tremble, I stood up, saying, "Daddy! What's the matter?"*
>
> *"Come here, I said."*
>
> *His eyes were terrible against me. Going to him, I felt as if I were walking through neck-deep water.*
>
> *When I was near, he stepped aside as though fearful I would touch him. A nameless guilt smothered in my soul. No idea what I had done wrong; whatever it might be, it was surely terrible enough to kill Daddy.*
>
> *I went through the doorway, stopped to look back. His voice was as harsh as a crow. "Keep walking."*
>
> *I kept on walking. He was behind me, but not close. Keeping his distance as though I were a leper.*
>
> *Clancy Street looked the same as always; green lawns and white houses, two boys on bicycles on their way to the gram-*

mar school. Big white houses, on large green lawns, with expensive automobiles in the driveways—Cadillacs, Continentals, Imperials—for we lived in the best part of town, with the other lawyers, the doctors and bankers and the successful businessmen.

No change. Nothing to account for that stricken expression in Daddy's face.

"Look," he commanded. "Look at it!"

There at my feet, written indelibly on the concrete sidewalk with red spray paint, were the words:

ALICE THE COCKSUCKER OF CLANCY STREET

The burning spread from my face over my body, a flash of fever that felt as though it would consume my flesh. Daddy will see me burning up, I thought wildly, and he will be glad that Alice is gone, never again to shame him.

Though I knew I could not look at him, I knew Daddy was watching me. Clancy Street whirled about me in a red haze. I wanted to fall down, clutching at the earth to hold it steady. If it kept on spinning, I would be whirled into outer space, farther and farther until I had used up all the farness there was.

"Get back into the house," he said.

That same harsh, strangled sound that I couldn't recognize as Daddy's voice, because Daddy had never talked to me in that tone.

Again, somehow, I began walking. Again he came behind me, maintaining the leper-distance.

"Into your room."

I went into my room. I stood with my head down, waiting. I knew that he would

*come; this exile was not, could not, be all.
My stomach, twisting violently, was hurting.*

Daddy stood suddenly in the doorway.
He had taken off his suit jacket, pulled the
tie loose on his throat. In one hand he held
the belt that went with his wartime colonel's
uniform. Broad and brown, it waited terrible in his hand. Daddy, except in play, had
never spanked me.

I had to look at him. His face was pale;
he was sweating. A bleakness showed in his
eyes.

He began to unbutton the shirt. He
took it off, wadded it up, threw it on the
floor. I could see his rib cage, so lean and
muscular, rising and falling in a hysteria of
breathing as if he could not get enough air
into his lungs.

"Alice. Did you suck that boy's cock?"

Robert had been so polite for our first
date. Instead of blowing his horn at the curb,
he had come into the house, politely saying
"Hello" to Daddy where he sat before the
television set.

Daddy turned his head to look at Robert, grunting a reply.

Robert had said, "How are you today,
Mrs. Toffler?" and Mother said, "Just fine,
Robert. How's your mother's cold?"

"It's better," Robert said, and Mother
said, "Good, maybe she'll be able to help
with the Organization Committee tomorrow
night after all."

Then we smiled at each other, and he
opened the door for me, and I said, "Good
night, Daddy," and Robert said, "Good night,
Mrs. Toffler, Mr. Toffler," and then we had
gone out on the date and I had sucked him
off.

"Yes, Daddy, I sucked his cock," I said, because it was the truth and I did not not dare tell Daddy a lie, not with the terrible look of dying in his eyes, and the sweating paleness of his face as if he were suffering from heat exhaustion.

"Why?" he said. The single word was a knot of pain in his throat.

I trembled again. "Because he wanted me to."

"Do you have to do everything some boy wants you to do?"

I put my hands over my face. "I don't know, Daddy. I just . . . did, that's all."

"Don't call me Daddy," he said. His voice was so quiet, so fatal, I couldn't bear it. I wanted to cry out against the edict, Daddyyyyy . . . , but the plea strangled in my throat.

"Then that's not just somebody's idea of a bad joke. You are *The Cocksucker of Clancy Street.* Admit it."

I knew now how Daddy must have looked when he was killing people in the war. Because he was going to kill me if I didn't say it.

"I am *The Cocksucker of Clancy Street.*"

He did not relent. "Did you do anything else?"

"No," I cried. "That was all."

"All!" he said scornfully. "Don't lie to me now."

"I'm not lying," I whimpered. "He didn't touch me. He really didn't, Daddy."

"I told you," he said. "Don't ever call me Daddy again."

He stopped talking. He looked at me. I tried to meet his eyes, but I couldn't.

His voice had thickened. "I tried to tell

you about boys. From the time you were a little girl, I told you how they'd be if you let them. But you thought it'd be a secret, didn't you? You didn't think he'd betray the nasty thing you did to him. But he painted it on the sidewalk in front of your house to let the whole world know. And, believe me, he's already told every other boy in school. Your reputation is ruined in this town. Ruined forever."

I trembled violently under the steady impact of the words. "I'm sorry, Da—I'm sorry. I won't do it again. I promise."

His mouth tightened. "You're going to be more than sorry. You're going to remember this day the rest of your life."

It was coming now. He meant to kill me. He ought to kill me, I thought crazily, because I can't go to school again anyway, with everybody knowing I'm The Cocksucker of Clancy Street.

"Bare your ass," Daddy said.

"What?" I said, as if he had spoken in an unknown tongue.

His voice rose. "You heard me. Lie down on that bed and bare your ass."

I was wearing white shorts, a boy's shirt. White always looked so good against my golden skin—even in the wintertime I always appeared as if I had a new tan— and I knew my legs were marvelous in shorts. The boys, the men, always turned for a second look.

I fumbled to unzip the shorts, felt them drop to my ankles.

"The shirt too."

I took off the shirt. I stood now in bra and panties. White panties, a pale-blue rose covering the mount. Because I could not

bear to take off the panties in the sight of
his eyes, I turned and lay down across the
bed.

His fingers clutched at the waistband
of the white panties. I could feel his knuckles against the base of my spine.

"In the war, I whipped one of my
men," Daddy said from somewhere above.
"With this very belt. I gave him a choice
between being shot between the eyes or taking a hundred lashes. I told him it would
have to be in front of the other nine men,
the only ones still alive after his mistake.
He consented to the beating."

He stopped talking. His hand, gripping
tightly, snugged the panties into my crotch,
hurting me.

"If one man had told the tale, I would
have faced disgrace, years in Leavenworth
Penitentiary, perhaps even execution. But
not one man betrayed me. Because they
knew, like I knew, that that man had to
be made to remember, out of all the days of
his life, that one day when he turned coward."

His voice had changed again. Thin now,
hard as a blade of steel.

"Do you consent to the punishment?"

"Yes," I said muffled into the crook of
my arm.

"Do you deserve it?"

"Yes."

His hand ripped suddenly, tearing the
panties. It left me naked, exposed. I tightened my buttocks, waiting, waiting, and then
I heard the belt swish. I jerked before it
lashed across my rump, then lay quivering
under the stinging impact.

One hundred, I thought. Ninety-nine
to come. I can't bear it.

I bore it.

As steady as a metronome, the broad leather belt whacked against my quivering flesh. I did not cry out; not until the very end, when I began to believe he had gone long past the decreed one hundred lashes, meaning to stop only after he had beaten the life out of my evil flesh.

I moaned and then screamed, "Stop! Stop! Stop, oh please God stop now!"

In the next moment, the intrusion of my mother's voice, saying, "What's going on in here?" and then, gasping, "Oh my God, Darrell, what are you doing to her?"

The whipping stopped. In a voice as unforgiving as ever, Daddy said, "I'm giving her what she deserves. Just wait till you see what's painted on the sidewalk in front of the house."

"But, Darrell. She's your daughter." Mother's voice was shaking.

"Not anymore," Daddy said flatly.

I could stand the beating. I couldn't bear that.

Thinking I couldn't but doing it anyway, I rolled over painfully and sat up. Blood stained the sheets where I had been lying. I could feel the wetness, as though I had suffered a heedless period.

Then, somehow, I stood on my feet, naked and bleeding before them.

"Whip me again, Daddy," I said. "Please, Daddy. Whip me until I'm your daughter again."

It was as if Alice were not there in the sight of his eyes. Even with the nakedness. Even with the blood.

He dropped the belt to the floor. Picking up the crumpled shirt, he said, "I've got to put on a fresh shirt before I can go to the office."

"Daddy, please don't stop," I repeated hopelessly.

Daddy was looking at Mother. "Call the Dilbro Brothers. Tell them that by ten o'clock this morning I want that whole stretch of sidewalk torn up. Tell them it's an emergency, and I don't care how much it costs. But I want those words destroyed before the next person walks in front of my house."

"Yes, Darrell," Mother said.

He left, then. Gone for good, I knew. Even with the hundred lashes he had not relented, had not looked at me, had not heard me.

My head whirling blackly and redly at once, I cried out wordlessly, collapsing with the cry.

For three days I was confined to my bed. At first I was out of my head with the fever of hysteria, tossing and turning, crying out for Daddy to keep punishing me until I was again his daughter.

Only Mother tended me; the doctor was not called.

When I became clear-headed, it was only to realize the agonizing pain in my body. Mother kept warm compresses on my buttocks to soak away the soreness. A hundred times, as if it mattered greatly, she assured me there would be no permanent scars. The broadness of the belt had made only great bruises in my flesh.

In that convalescence, I was close to Mother as I had never been. She quit drinking. She spent hours sitting with me without talking, simply there, a presence in *the room, loving me for my hurts though she did not own the words to tell me of her motherly love.*

We could hear the sounds of the men pouring new concrete in front of the house. But we did not talk about the now-destroyed words, about the beating itself, not even the fact that not once had Daddy set foot across the threshold into my bedroom. We were Mother and Daughter. She fed me, she bathed me gently, she sat with me and was silent.

On the fourth day, she entered without a breakfast tray to say: "Alice, you're going to have to get out of that bed sooner or later."

I got out of bed. Strange to be on my feet. I felt weak. I put on a robe and went into the bathroom.

"Hotcakes and country sausage?" Mother said from behind me. It was my favorite breakfast.

"Yes," I said.

"It'll be ready in the kitchen when you are."

"All right," I said.

Then, still from behind me: "You must remember, Alice, your father is only a man."

I turned. We looked at each other. I turned away, leaning over the sink to wash my face.

Mother said, "Hotcakes and country sausage, coming up!" and left me alone.

Once up, I stayed up. I did not leave the house.

I watched all the mindless kid shows, the mindless soap operas, then all the mindless game shows. When I heard Daddy's car, I retired to my room, sitting in the chair before the floor-length mirror Daddy had given me, with the card that read: Mirror, Mirror on the wall, Alice is the fairest of them all, With love from Daddy on her fourteenth birthday.

I studied my face until it became strange and ugly in my eyes. Then I looked at nothingness.

The door opened, closed, and I heard Daddy's footsteps. He went to the bar; the clink of ice, a sound of stirring, as he fixed the one gin martini he allowed himself before dinner.

Then silence, and I knew he was sitting before the television set. Without turning on the evening news, for the silence continued.

Mother stood in my doorway. "Alice. Dinner's ready."

"In a minute," I said clearly.

I was still wearing the nightgown and the bathrobe. Taking them off, I went to my closet and selected a print dress. Before putting it on I stood before the mirror, twisting to see my behind. The bruises were scarcely visible now, and I knew Mother had told me the truth about the scars.

I dropped the dress over my head. Then, on a strange impulse I did not pause to investigate, I went into the living room without adding the accustomed underwear. It made for a strangely naked feeling.

They were already at the table. I slid into my place, unfolded my napkin. Daddy did not look at me.

Through that interminable dinner, not a word was spoken.

Daddy rose, returned to his big leather chair. Real leather, not plastic, and it had always been for me the safest, warmest place in the whole world.

I stopped in the doorway to the dining room. I looked at him for a long moment. Then I said, "Daddy."

He did not turn his head. He did not speak. It was as if Alice did not exist.

I don't know, now or ever, where I got the courage to do what I did. But from the time I was six years old, when he had come home from the war, until this very week, I had sat nightly in his lap.

I walked across the room, turned, sat down in his lap.

Strangely different. I felt naked without panties beneath the thin cloth of my dress. Strange, and good; because I was closer to Daddy than ever before.

For the beat of a minute his legs were rigid under my weight. Seeking comfort—the soreness was still in my flesh—I squirmed a bit, yearning for his lean arms to embrace me.

One beat of time—then, violently, he shoved both hands against me, catapulting me to the floor.

Stunned, I got to my feet.

He was panting, his chest heaving with the effort. His face was red now, not pale, his eyes glaring.

"Don't ever do that again," he said. His voice was a rasp. "Do you hear me?"

I did not cry. I said, "All right, Daddy. I won't do it again," and went to my room.

I came voluntarily to breakfast the next morning, but only after Daddy had gone. Mother gave me eggs and toast. I was hungrier than on the previous day.

When I had finished, Mother said quietly, "You can't stay in the house the rest of your life, Alice."

"I'm going to school today."

As I rose to go, Mother tried to tell me again: "Remember, Alice. Your father is only a man."

"Yes, I know," I said, and went into the outside world.

The sidewalk gleamed newly white in contrast to the stretches of concrete in front of the other houses on Clancy Street. Pristine, uncorrupted of legend. The barriers, marked with the sign, PROPERTY OF DILBERT BROS. CONST. CO., were still up. Walking across the cement, my faint footprints registered permanently in the not-quite-hardened cement.

I had always liked walking to school through the early morning, the old oaks, freshly dressed now for spring, a few cars hurrying to carry the men to their offices, students clotting into laughing, chattering groups.

Except, this day, I had gone scarcely a block when George Bering pulled his noisy jalopy to the curb.

"Hey, Alice! Where you been?" he yelled over the sputtering noise of the cutout.

"Sick," I said, and kept on walking.

He cruised alongside. The jalopy had been cut down from what had once been a decent car, the engine exposed, the sedan body removed except for the windshield. It was daubed crudely red and green, with screamingly funny sayings inscribed in white paint.

"Want a ride?"

George was the captain of the football

team. He played center, so he was big and blond, with muscle and baby fat.

"All right," I said.

All the way to school I didn't have to talk; George kept chattering about spring practice starting today, and how he was really gonna play that center position this year, there was this kid, you see, only fifteen but already he weighed two hundred pounds, and Coach liked his hands.

"He ain't gonna blow me outa my job," George said happily. "Some o' the guys, they're gonna show him what a tough job it can be to play center."

In the parking lot, he glanced hesitantly in my direction. "Hey, Alice, listen. You want to hang around till practice is over, we'll go for a Coke. Okay?"

I got out of the jalopy. "Okay, George," I said.

Before classes—even in the classes—I could feel the eyes prowling at me. I didn't let myself think about it. I thought instead, They can look at me all they want, but they can't see I'm not wearing pants.

It felt strange, moving through the school corridors with that nakedness under my clothes and nobody knowing.

After class hours, waiting for George, I went to the library to catch up on the work I had missed. There was a lot of it, and I wasn't through when I heard "shave-and-a-haircut" sounded on a car horn.

I went out to the jalopy. George was sweaty and happy from the football practice. He had showered, but in his excitement had immediately started sweating again.

"Hey now, Alice, you shoulda been out there watching," he chortled. "The Blue Squad, they give my competition a lesson he

*won't forget. By the time practice was over,
he was coming out of the snap mighty damn
slow to throw his block. No guts at all."*

There was a drive-in where everybody
went after school. George drove right on by.

"Where are we going for a Coke?" I
asked quietly. "Not Todt's?"

"We'll come back for Cokes," George
said happily. "I need some fresh air, down
by the riverside, down by the riverside. . . ."

He sang the last words. Then he
glanced at me with a sidewise anxiety.

"All right? Too sweaty and tired right
now for a Coke. Drive a while first. Okay?"

"Okay," I said.

There was still no need to talk. George
had enough words about the joys and trials
of football to fill the silent spaces between
us. Only when we were on the bluff looking
out over the river did he allow my silence to
prevail.

This was where the neckers came—
where I had come, that night, with Robert.
But only at night, so we were alone on the
bluff point.

The silence was taut, because I was
waiting. Alice was waiting.

Then George said, "Hey, Alice. You
want some o' this?"

He had It out of his pants. Astonishingly small, I thought, for such a big boy.
Even though It was erect.

"Yes," I said, and leaned to put my
mouth on It.

"Hey, you do suck, don't you?" George
said happily. He squirmed up against my
face. The sweating was sexual now. I could
smell it, musty and male.

I raised my face. "Yes, George, I love

to suck," I told him. "I'd rather suck than anything in the world."

I went down again. It was tiny and hard in my mouth; I could take it all without gagging. I wondered how a boy large enough and strong enough to play center could be built so small where it counted. Rather sweet, to feel it so tiny and needful in my mouth. I played with It as long as I could. George was begging for relief when finally I gave him the last long strokes up and down the wet shaft that brought his come.

He collapsed. "Oh God, Alice, that was good," he said. "Good."

"I know," I said serenely. "I'm the best cocksucker in the world."

Somewhere inside myself, after the remembering, I found a saving laughter. Prince Albert had told me, once, about his traumatic experience, being forced to go down on, one after the other, every member of the football team at his high school in Mississippi.

The varsity football team had been been Alice's first project. I tasted the cock of every boy who wore the blue-and-gold; not all in one night, like Albert, but throughout the last weeks of my senior year.

I had my niche. Some of the girls screwed, and everybody knew who those girls were. Alice sucked, and everybody knew that, too. In the school corridors I walked proud, holding my head so high no one dared sneer at me. Because I had my standards, and I made my standards prevail.

The older boys, the seniors, persisted in considering my specialty a preliminary to the main event. But not one ever even discovered the vulnerable fact that beneath my outer garments I was always naked.

At the core of each performance lay a curious gratification. In the beginning, I only took It out through the fly. But soon, seeking a greater sense of the male flesh, I made them undress from the waist down. I could put my hands on them then, holding their tight young asses, stroking their thighs, cupping the scrotum when they were ready to come, and feeling the balls draw up tight as the sperm jetted into my mouth.

Most of them I did only once; but Alice had her favorites. George, so tiny and hard, was sweetly fulfilling. A thin, tall right end possessed an enormous tool, long and fiery red, that made my jaws ache when I tried to swallow It whole.

I got more excited with him than with anyone else, so I persistently, masochistically, returned to Rolf. Yet, though my naked bottom was always wet and warm by the time I had finished him, I never experienced a desire to feel the great Thing inside me.

Nor any of the others. No. I was fulfilling Them, in a peculiarly intimate way, in their deepest desires. They might screw those other girls who consented to screw; but only Alice cherished them as potent male without asking for anything in return.

Except, I thought in the darkness of the apartment, never again did I suck that original cock of Alice's experience, the Thing belonging to Robert Denham. With a touch of sadness, I reflected that I should have had the love, the generosity, to have sucked off Robert at least once more.

Even after he had destroyed my life.

I was sixteen when Daddy whipped me with his Sam Browne belt. It wasn't until graduation week that the rest of it took place.

During the balance of that year, the three of us lived within a web of silence in the house on Clancy Street. Daddy came and went from work as he had always done, drank his single gin martini straight up, ate dinner, and went to sit in his leather chair.

When the boys came to the door—I was very popular—Daddy acted as though they did not exist. He took no apparent note of their names, their faces, not even the fact there were many instead of one.

If Mother noticed, she made no comment.

Mother, by now, was deeper into her own pattern of self-destruction. Drinking more, and more openly, I realized that she was an alcoholic. Her face had become bloated, unhealthy-looking, and she was putting on weight in her shoulders and around the middle.

People can't live together in a house without a minimum of communication. We talked when it was necessary to talk, made idle conversation over the dinner or breakfast table. My grades were discussed regularly and, toward the end, whether I would major in communications, as I wished, or English, which Daddy thought was best.

Politely, with never a raised voice, we settled that I would go to the University of Iowa, where Daddy and Mother had both gone to school—I had wanted the University of Missouri because it was farther away —and I would get my Communications major and go into radio or television when I graduated.

Life continued strained but placid. Until the night it shattered around us, exposing us naked to ourselves.

I was chosen Senior Prom Queen—with the entire football team on my side it was really no competition—so I had to have a special dress for the occasion.

Mother sobered up for a week so we could plan and execute the dress. I had sketched out exactly what I wanted, and Mother knew a seamstress who could run it up properly. After intensive consultations, in which the seamstress made workable my amateur design, Mother and I went all the way to Des Moines to buy the material.

Now, after countless fittings, the dress hung ready and perfect in my closet.

Daddy had not seen the senior prom gown.

Tomorrow night I would wear it before the world. So tonight I tried it on for the last time, standing a rapt hour before the full-length mirror and believing for the first time in my life that I was truly beautiful.

And, again, I don't know why I did what I did.

Perhaps it was because, for the first time since we had started on the gown, Mother was drinking again. Going into the kitchen for a drink of water before the try-on, I had spotted three soggy cigarette butts in the sink. I looked at Mother in sudden shock. She was sitting hunched on the kitchen stool, an apron streaked with flour across her broad middle, stirring spoon in one hand. Oblivious to me, she stared straight ahead, her lips moving not quite silently.

She's really drunk, I thought in dismay. *Dinner won't be fit to eat.*

Or perhaps it was because, standing before the mirror, I knew Alice as truly beautiful. I swayed dreamily back and forth, thinking of the moment when Alice would be led out by the class president to take the traditional first turn about the floor, the handsome pair of us flowing into the waltz step; and all the time, a secret known only to me, Alice would be naked under the lovely gown. It would be, I knew, the greatest experience; even better than when, at evening's end, still wearing the prom queen gown, I would give our class president the greatest blow job Alice had ever performed.

Then, I thought in sudden sadness, it will be over, and I will go away to college. Away from everyone who knows that Alice Toffler is The Cocksucker of Clancy Street; away from Mother's drinking, from Daddy's silent distance.

Yes. I felt sadness enough for us all. Soon, now, Daddy wouldn't have to pretend that I was not alive in the house; I really wouldn't be there. He would still, however, have to walk twice a day across that stretch of sidewalk, still so much whiter and newer, which bore, indelibly though invisibly, that fateful legend which had destroyed our father-and-daughter love.

In the end, however, it was everything, not just one thing, that made me do it.

Turning from the mirror, I walked into the living room. Spreading the full skirt in a tiny pirouette, I said in a timid voice, "Daddy. Do you like my senior prom gown?"

For a space of time that stretched so long I thought he would never respond, he sat still. Then—he turned his head. He looked at me.

The gown had a gold top, with a diagonal of sparkling white satin from the left shoulder across the breast and down to the waist. The other shoulder was bare, the cup of gold cloth revealing the first faint rise of breast. The plain white chiffon skirt fell full to my feet, hiding my secret nakedness. Twin panels of free-falling gold satin draped my body in front and behind, bringing the eye down the length of body to the golden slippers peeping from underneath.

Daddy looked for a long time. His face was working, fighting against a pain so visible it struck at my heart.

He gripped the leather arms of the chair with clawlike hands. The tendons stood out on his lean arms.

"Come here."

His voice choked. But I would have heard those two words if Daddy had uttered them from the ends of the earth.

I went to Daddy. The right arm circled hard around my waist. I could feel the strength, the agony of feeling. It drew me down into his lap. Then the other arm came around, embracing me fiercely.

"Oh, God, baby, you're beautiful enough to break my heart," he said brokenly.

"Daddy!" I said.

Putting both arms around his neck, I clung to him. My face pressed tightly against his chest, I could smell the Daddy-smell I had lost for so long. I squirmed in his lap, trying to get closer. All the way close. He trembled with the nearness. I was weeping softly because it was so good to weep within the sanctuary of Daddy.

"I suppose you've made it up at last."

Mother's voice, so harsh and raw it snapped our heads around simultaneously.

The sight shocked me. Mother was so angry her eyes bulged, her face was violently red.

"It must be nice," she said, her voice mocking the words. "Sweethearts again, aren't we? Daddy and his little girl."

"Helen," Daddy said.

She straightened. A painful movement, as though she had been hunched over her bitterness for so long she didn't know how to stand straight anymore.

"Alice, get up off your father's lap," she said sternly. "You're ruining that gown I worked so hard on."

"No," I said. I was clinging to Daddy by main strength against her assault. "I won't."

She stared at us, her face changing, becoming so hateful I tried to close my eyes against it.

Then, in a voice soaring startlingly out of control, she spoke the words that had dwelled so long in her jealous heart.

"Instead of just coaxing Alice to sit on your cock, Darrell, why don't you take her into your private bedroom and fuck her in that beautiful gown? That's what you've always wanted to do, isn't it? Fuck your precious Alice."

We sat frozen.

Mother began to look sick as she realized what she had said. She sagged, her mouth working as if she tasted vomit. Then, precipitately, she fled out of our sight.

I couldn't look at Daddy; I knew how terrible his expression would be. Instead, I pressed my face into the warmth of his neck.

The words were ready in my mind.
"She's just drunk, Daddy. Drunk."

But—then I felt Daddy's Thing.

Alice knew, now, about men's Things.
Alice was experienced. Maybe, all those
thousands of times I had sat in Daddy's lap,
It had been hard under me. But Alice had
not been aware.

But now, unmistakably, I did feel It.
Daddy's Thing was pressing hard against my
bottom. Closer to my secret nakedness than
any boy had ever been, the only barrier to
penetration the cloth of his trousers, the
filmy texture of gown.

I drew away in horror. "Daddy!" I
whispered.

Self-knowledge showed in his shame-
ful eyes. Incredibly, his erection did not wilt;
the shared awareness only caused It to
thump rebelliously, like a knock at a door
commanding entrance.

A crashing cascade of awful realization
flooded through me. He had never loved me
as Daughter. Always it had been this, this
—and vividly I remembered the many times
his hands had caressed my flesh, those moments when, held high against his chest, my
naked thighs could feel the powerful beating
of his heart.

Daddy did not love me. He lusted for
Alice-his-daughter. And, I realized as vividly, Mother had always known that terrible desire which had dwelled for so long
in his heart, in his flesh.

As even now, in this terrible moment,
the insatiable Thing burgeoned beneath me,
burrowing at my flesh, conscienceless in Its
passion to possess.

Without transition, I merged into another dimension of terror. Pulsing inside, in-

*voluntarily I ground my bottom against It.
I was suddenly wet, ready for penetration.
I wanted to feel It in me, hard and thrust-
ing.*

*I had to move before something ter-
rible and irrevocable happened. Springing
out of his lap, I stood with trembling legs.
Free for the moment, I was yet afraid that
I would find myself fumbling after It with
both hands, compelled by the desire to stuff
It under the prom queen gown where I was
waiting so nakedly.*

*Daddy, suffering an agonizing pain in
the throes of exposed desire, sat looking
straight ahead.*

*"You've always been so beautiful, Al-
ice," he said. "I could never quite believe
that you were my child."*

*The apology, explanation, exculpation
—whatever it was—released me. I fled to
my room, where, still wearing the lovely
gown—ruined now, forever ruined—I threw
myself across the bed.*

*Still suffused by the desire to feel his
Thing in me, I had to touch myself. I was so
hot and wet, I instantaneously began to
come. My hand trapped between my straining legs, I thrust against it, writhing frantically until I was exhausted.*

*Late night, the house dark and still.
Mother had not come to me; Daddy had
not come. Utterly alone in the house—in
the world—I rose from the bed. I took off
the prom queen gown and threw it without a second glance into the closet. Reaching up on a shelf, I pulled down a suitcase.
I packed it with everything it would hold.
Going to my student desk, I found my new
checkbook. The account had been estab-*

lished only a week earlier with the budget for my college wardrobe, the fall-semester tuition.

Quite a lot of money, at least to my mind. There was also the savings account I had kept since I was six, always adding in but never taking out. I took the savings-account book, too.

Carrying the single suitcase, I walked through the dark living room, so empty because I was leaving nothing behind, and quietly opened the front door. I paused on the sidewalk to look down, wishing I could see in the darkness the faint trace of my shoe-prints marked into the cement. But that was all right, too. I went on.

At the bus station, I sat in a booth and drank coffee until the sun was up. Then, leisurely waiting for the bank to open, I ate a hearty breakfast. When the time came, I left my suitcase under the watchful eye of the counterman and walked to the bank. When I got back to the station, the Chicago bus had just arrived.

I took it. But Chicago was only a way station. Alice's destination was New York.

New York was exciting in those young days. The city was full of lovely, ambitious girls, walking Fifth Avenue as if they owned the world. Living three and four and five to a cramped apartment, subsisting primarily on hot dogs and orange juice, we were yet dedicated to dressing smartly in the New York image of that time.

Prince Albert not only did my hair, but taught me makeup and coached me how to walk and stand. I had an apartment to myself because, working steadily, I could afford the privacy.

But I was only anonymous Alice, not Alice! until Paul Riff came into my life.

I was excited about the call because acceptance meant a trip to Cypress Gardens. I had never been to Florida; and it was February, with spring seemingly never coming again.

A dozen of us, six to be chosen. My heart sank as I studied the competition. Though a bathing-suit catalogue, it looked like a high-fashion deal; the other girls were the hollow-cheeked, rib-starved clotheshorses so popular at that time. No Florida for Alice, I told myself dolefully.

"All right, girls, this is swimwear, so we're going to have to see some skin," the agency man announced. "Strip down, please."

We stripped to bra and panties—in New York I had resumed wearing full underwear—and shaped up into a line. It was cold in the studio loft and I shivered, holding my upper arms with each hand.

The agency man walked down the line looking at our legs, then walked around behind us, appraising our asses.

"Paul," he called. "Come here, please."

Paul detached himself from the two representatives of the client. The agency man indicated the tallest girl.

"I like this one but you're going to have to watch the crotch shots. Have you ever seen one stick out like that before?"

A dispassionate criticism. The girl stared haughtily into space. She had beautiful legs, an elegant face, body thin as a rail. Her pubic arch, however, was almost abnormal, a prominent bony thrust under the almost-transparent underpants.

Paul shrugged. "No problem. Have to shoot away from the crotch anyway."

The agency man nodded to the girl. "All right. You're number one."

The haughty look turned into a smile. Not a chance, *I repeated to myself against the inevitable disappointment.*

He walked on down the line, snapping thumb and finger at number two and number three. When he passed me by, I turned to go behind the screen and get dressed.

"Okay, fellows?" the agency man asked when he was finished. "Any second thoughts?"

They shook their heads. I hurried to get out of there, thinking they could have specified high-fashion models, and saved me the trouble of showing up.

"Wait a minute," the man named Paul said. "What about this one?"

He was pointing to me.

"No way," the director said. "I knew that the minute she walked in." He grimaced at me. "Sorry, dear. But that's the way it is."

"Look at that skin," Paul said. "She'll be the only one in the lot looks like she belongs in Florida."

The director looked doubtful. "Well, Paul, you're the photographer. But . . ."

"I want her," Paul said decisively. "We'll build the catalogue around her."

The other girls looked hatefully at me. They knew they'd only be background figures. But, wanting a Florida trip, too, this cold February, no one made a point of quitting.

I was watching Paul Riff. So this would be the one this time. I knew quite well why he had chosen me; a week at Cypress

Gardens, he wanted a grateful girl in his bed.

An ugly man. Face lumpy and acne-scarred overshadowed by a great nose. His eyes were black and piercing. Legs too short for his normal-sized body, he looked almost dwarfish. His pants bagged at the knees.

"All right, girls, nine-thirty in the morning at the National Airlines counter in the terminal," the agency man said in brisk dismissal.

Turning away from my perusal of Paul, I shrugged inwardly. What difference did it make who I fucked in Florida? Better than a client's representative, at least. I preferred —when I had a choice—the working guys.

Still in underwear, I walked across the room to say, "Thank you, Paul."

He smiled. "No favor. Liked you the minute I laid eyes on you." He laughed, nodding his head in affirmation. "And we'll have fun in Florida. I guarantee it."

Yeah, I thought as I got dressed. I'll bet you'll want to fuck all night and expect me to be fresh-looking as morning dew for the next day's shooting.

The rustic cottages at Cypress Gardens were remote from the tourists. The client's representatives and the agency man took the big cottage; there were three girls in each of two smaller ones. Everybody had a quick swim, of course, then we were invited for drinks in the big cottage. The agency man jovially made much of the fact that he had imported, at great expense, an ample supply of booze in his luggage because this was a dry county.

Quickly he got a game of strip poker

started; to "break the ice," as he cleverly put
it. When he lost the first pot, he promptly
took off his pants rather than beginning discreetly with a shoe. He seemed to be in a
hurry for the ice to break.

Noticing that Paul Riff was not in evidence at the rapidly changing party, I wandered about the big room, a glass in my
hand, humming to the music. I knew what
must come, and I always kept my part of
a bargain. The laughter becoming more boisterous, I poured a second drink and departed unobtrusively.

Paul Riff sat before another cottage,
wearing violently flowered bathing trunks and
a terry-cloth robe. Sipping a drink, he gazed
peacefully toward the sunset.

"Hello, Paul," I said. "You're missing
the party."

He shrugged. "Parties, shmarties, I can
take 'em or leave 'em." He looked gloomy.
"I hope they don't carouse too late . . . we
start shooting with the sun in the morning.
I want some very fresh morning shots of
some very fresh girls."

I looked at him. His feet barely
reached the ground. Black hair showed thick
and curly on the short, crooked legs.

"Why aren't you staying in the big cottage?" I asked curiously. "That's where the
action is."

"That's exactly why," Paul said. "I always insist on having my own quarters on
these expeditions. I'm not much of a drink-
er, anyway. I'll go over when I smell the
steaks cooking." He smiled. "Why aren't
you over there raising your share of the
hell? . . . and ruining your looks and dispo-
sition for tomorrow?"

I made a smile. I drank. I looked at him over the glass.

"I wanted to thank you again for insisting on Alice." I shivered. *"Think how cold it must be in New York tonight. It's so lovely here."*

I stopped talking. He was giving me a very straight look.

"Listen, kid," he said. *"I picked you because I liked the way you walked into that studio. You have something. You know?"*

So that's how he wants to play it, I thought. I put my hand on his arm.

"I like you too, Paul. That's why I came over from the party."

Deliberately he took my hand from his arm. "I don't fuck around," he said shortly. *"All right?"*

The words were crisp and unmistakable. What kind of game could this be?

"You didn't use your clout just to get yourself a good lay in Florida?" I said incredulously.

Paul studied me. Very directly. "Good God, kid, how old are you, anyway?"

"Nineteen."

He snorted. "You talk like you're a hundred." Deliberately he added, *"I'd feel silly, fucking a nineteen-year-old kid. So let's forget about it, huh?"*

I began to believe him. "Paul," I said warmly. *"I'm beginning to suspect you're a pretty nice guy."*

He smiled. "All I ask, kid, don't get a sunburn and mess up my plans. I'm even gonna put you on the cover."

So Florida was fun. I didn't have to fuck anybody—the other guys committed themselves for the week that first night—and Paul Riff made it Alice's catalogue.

Nor was that the end.

Riding in to the airline terminal, Paul came to sit beside me. "Kid, why don't you come to dinner Sunday night?" he said without preamble. "The wife's a great cook, and I want to talk to you. All right?"

"I'd love to meet your family, Paul." I laughed. "And I haven't had a home-cooked meal since I left home."

He gave me his ugly-faced grin. "You're gonna be surprised, take my word. My wife don't exactly cook kosher."

Paul Riff lived in the basement and first floor of an old brownstone house north of the Village. He owned the house, he told me later, renting out the top two floors.

I was startled when Paul's wife came out of the small kitchen to greet me. Broad-faced and broad-bodied, not at all pretty—and she was black.

Paul and Zella were the first interracial couple I had ever known. But quickly Zella made me comfortable . . . and the food odors from the kitchen were tantalizing. Pork chops, turnip greens, and cornbread; it was the first time I had eaten real Southern cooking. A bottle of wine graced the meal.

The three boys, nearly as dark as Zella but looking more like Paul, were quiet and well mannered. Zella took them upstairs to bed as soon as the meal was finished.

Paul, carrying the half-empty bottle, led me to a battered sofa against the living-room wall. Pouring wine, he said, "Fun?"

"Fun," I said. I stretched. "Wonderful meal. I've never eaten turnip greens cooked like that."

Paul raised his eyes toward the ceiling. We could hear Zella's footsteps as she moved about in the first-floor bedroom.

"Zella is a marvelous cook," he said. "Wonderful woman, too." He paused. "My father had a heart attack when he found out I had married a Negro. It nearly killed him."

"I guess it would be a problem," I said carefully.

He laughed wryly. "It wasn't that she's black, it's that she isn't Jewish. My father is very orthodox."

He drank, put the wineglass back on the table. "But enough about me already. I want to talk about Alice."

I felt uncomfortable. "What do you want to talk about?"

He looked into his glass. "Want to know why I picked you for the Cypress Gardens deal, Alice? Because I'm sick and tired of photographing these neurotic broads who haven't had a square meal in so long they'd throw up if they ate one. I suspect a lot of people are tired of looking at those racks of bone, too."

I shook my head. "I don't know. I find it hard to get fashion work."

"You know why? For exactly the reason I liked you on first sight. You look like a woman, for God's sake, that a man can touch without shattering into a million pieces. You looked like Florida in the winter. How do you keep that tan, anyway?"

"It's just my natural skin coloring."

"And look at you now, with the Florida sun for a week," he said. "You're absolutely tawny. I'm gonna buy you a sunlamp tomorrow. Want you to use it every day." Pause. "All over. No white areas showing."

I felt my breath catch.

"What have you got in mind, Paul?"

"It was really just an impulse, that first day," Paul said. *"But working with you all week, studying those hundreds of shots I took . . . You're something special, Alice. You've got a quality I've never run into in all my years as a working photographer."*

I was puzzled. "I don't know what you're talking about."

"I can't put a name to it. You come out of the photograph. You're . . . touchable." He took a deep breath. *"Alice. What are your plans for the future?"*

I felt my mind darken. "Model all I can, I guess. Make money. I . . . I really don't know, Paul."

"Can you act?"

"No," I said honestly. *"I was in the high school plays, all right, but I always got the pretty-girl parts, simpering and flirting. You can't call that acting."*

Paul drained his wine. "I'm a photographer pure and simple," he said slowly. *"All I've ever wanted to be."* He turned his head *"Until now. Now, Alice, I want to be your manager."*

I looked at him as directly as he was looking at me.

"Why, Paul?"

His eyes did not flicker. "Because you can become the world's great symbol of feminine beauty. If you can learn to act, you'll be a movie star . . . maybe television. But you will be famous. I will make you famous."

I faltered. "Paul, you're out of your mind. New York is full of girls better-looking than me, with more talent, more—"

"*Alice,*" Paul said quietly. "*You don't know what you are. I know. Enough of it, anyway. So listen for once in your life.*"

He nodded thoughtfully. "*We'll have to start small. If I had the money to invest, we could make it in a year. But at first I'll have to keep on working, too.*"

He looked at me quickly. "*It's strictly a business deal, understand? We'll sign a legitimate contract, twenty-five percent off the top for me.*" He paused. "*What about it, kid? Are you game?*"

I was flustered, excited . . . scared. "*Paul, you make it sound so exciting.*"

His voice turned cautious. "*You're not already signed with an agent?*"

I worked out of an agency at times, but it was only an informal arrangement.

"*Nothing I can't get out of.*"

"*All right,*" he said. "*I want you to think about it for a week. Talk to your friends, if you have someone you can trust to advise you on this sort of thing.*"

He looked at me hard this time.

"*I warn you, Alice, I'm gonna work your ass off. Acting lessons, dancing lessons, a voice coach, charm school . . . you won't be able to go to the bathroom without my permission.*"

Breathless again, I grasped his hand warmly. "*I'll do it, Paul.*"

He shook his head. "*It's important, Alice. Take a week to decide.*"

"*All right,*" I breathed. "*But . . . I've already made up my mind.*"

"*A week,*" he repeated. His hand over mine was warm and solid and real.

"*I'll tell you the first thing. You're not going to put out anymore just to get a job.*

From now on, you're exclusive. You will go to bed with a guy only if you happen to want to. Understand me?"

"I understand." Then I said, "You know, Paul, I never have. I mean, got into bed with a guy just because I wanted to."

"Can I go out now?" I asked Mark on the fifth day.

"Let's don't rush it."

I felt stubborn. And restless. "I'm getting tired of being cooped up inside these four walls." I looked directly at Mark. "I need some action."

His eyes flickered. He knew my meaning.

I pressed on. "I want to visit a singles' bar. It sounds . . . exciting."

Mark shrugged. "Singles' bars aren't any different from what bars have always been, Alice. It's just that everybody's out of their sexual closet now. They don't pretend anymore they're not looking to get laid. Women as well as men." He chuckled. "It's your basic up-against-the-meat-rack time."

"Then why all the *talk* about singles' bars, as though they're something new and special?"

"The human animal—especially the New York animal—has a peculiar habit of mind in that respect. They think, if you give something a new name, it's a new thing." He stood with hands in pockets, regarding me. "If you ask me, this Great Sexual Revolution everybody believes so unquestioningly doesn't exist. I have a sneaking suspicion nothing very much has changed over the centuries. Except there's less pretense. In my opinion, just about the same amount of —of sexual intercourse—goes on that has always prevailed. Most girls today, just like always, still manage to lose their virginity somewhere about the age of eighteen."

He laughed. "I'll tell you one thing. If all the statistics are true, somebody's sure getting *my* share."

I watched him. "Do you have a girlfriend, Mark?"

"If you can call her that," Mark said shortly.

He had used the same phrase about being married. So self-deprecating, as though anything that pertained to Mark Judson couldn't possibly measure up to the human standard.

"What's she like?"

"Nice girl. About twenty-five. Secretary in a publishing house, wants to become an editor. She'll make it, too."

"Pretty?"

"Attractive, rather. A good mind, fun to talk to."

Drily, I said, "You make it sound like she's pretty lousy in bed."

He moved his shoulders. He was wearing a new overcoat today, very smart, very conservative. A melton.

"She starts out enthusiastically enough. Active as hell." Puzzlement showed in his eyes. "But the same damn thing happens every time. She gets off pretty rapidly, then . . . just at the point where a woman gets to feeling tender toward the man that's got It in her—just at that point, she closes up shop."

"What do you mean?"

"I can feel it," he said. His voice was tinged with embarrassment. "She suddenly turns off, goes dry and tight. As though a little voice had spoken somewhere back in her head. *Watch it, girl. You can't let yourself feel anything.*"

"Must be strange."

He nodded. "Puts a fellow right off. You've been rejected just when . . . It's not only Carol. I've run into the same problem with other girls."

I was frowning. "Women often sense that, to the man, they're only a warm hole. Once he's got his, he's ready to turn over and go to sleep. It makes a woman feel like she's . . . being used."

He eyed me. "That's exactly how Carol m⸺"

me feel." He became animated. "Hey, maybe that's *it*. These girls, they're the first generation to be raised on Women's Lib. They're intent on *using*, not being used. They're afraid, if they let themselves feel anything beyond naked need, they *will* be used. So they turn off."

"Sad, isn't it?" I said. "And yet . . ."

"Yes," he interposed. "Sad for everybody."

I reverted abruptly to my original theme. "When can I have a simple drink in a bar, Mark? That's all I want to know."

"A couple of diehards are still hanging out downstairs. Let one of them get a picture, every photographer in town will have to get into the competition."

"You suggested that I might disguise myself."

He wasn't listening. "I think I'll lie a bit. Tell 'em you took off for Acapulco yesterday. The way the weather has turned winter again, they'll believe it."

I sighed. "So not yet."

He watched me. "You don't *have* to listen to me."

I laughed. "If I won't listen to you, why am I paying you such a salary?"

He looked relieved. "Exactly what I was thinking."

"Albert, bring me a wig," I said.

"You're dying to get out of here and get *laid*, aren't you?" Albert said disapprovingly.

"How would *you* like to spend a week cooped up inside four walls?"

He looked about. "Pretty fancy walls to make a prison of. Isn't Peter's work *staying* with you?" His tone showed hurt.

"I'm not faulting Peter, or anybody else," I said. "I'm only thinking ahead to when Mark Judson tells me I'm free to go and come as I please."

"Oh. I see." His interest quickened. "I was afraid you were thinking about kicking over the traces." He studied me speculatively. "A nice problem. How to make Alice! into an *un*spectacular, yet not ruin her entirely. After all, you don't want to be a *dog*."

"Maybe a red wig?" I suggested.

He shook his head. "No. I think, blond."

"That's no change."

"Blond," he repeated. "But just a *little* tacky, you know. A bit *much,* as though you didn't have any sense of yourself as a woman." He chuckled. "I've never tried to make a woman not-beautiful. I've built my career and my fortune on improving the raw material I had to work with."

"I tried, once, to change a silk purse," I said, laughing. "So it's the least you can do."

The next day, Albert brought along a selection. Seating me before the mirror, he placed a red wig on my head.

"See. It doesn't work."

I had to agree.

"Now try this one."

Not my kind of blond, but darker, with a coarser texture. Even when hairdos were more elaborate, I had always worn my hair simply, whether long or short. The wig had a flyaway curl that quite transformed my appearance into that of a chancy, impulsive creature. The quiet elegance Paul Riff had groomed into me had quite disappeared.

"Amazing," I said.

Prince Albert, with a worried frown, was still studying me.

He sighed. "Now I've got to teach you how to make yourself up *badly,*" he said. "Obscure those lovely bones, not enhance them." He threw up his hands. "You'll have to unlearn everything I taught you years ago."

With rapid applications of face cream, he bared my face of all artifice.

"Look at that," he murmured. *"Shiny* with cre_
yet still beautiful enough to knock a man to

He began to work. "Now, we'll use a bit too much eye shadow, and *ignore* the cheek planes as though we don't know we've got them. Are you following me?"

"Yes, Albert," I said dutifully.

"Of course we must keep you *young*," he said. "They're all under *thirty* out there, you know. Everybody *dies* when they reach thirty." His voice was bitter beneath the surface scorn.

"I brought some clothes. Try them on, so I can look at you."

He knew my sizes. He had bought barrel boots, the leather too bright, a skirt a bit too fussy with western motifs, a leather vest with rosettes. The leather coat was more expensive than the rest, and far more elegant.

"You've put all your earnings into the *coat*," Albert explained. "It's your only extravagance. Understand? This little adventure will require a *modicum* of acting, you know."

He stood away. "It'll have to do," he said at last. "There's nothing to be done about your body lines . . . I'm certainly not going to insist that you get *fat*." He surveyed me inch by inch. "You're no longer Alice! But any perceptive man would see you underneath. There's no disguising the true Alice."

If I knew who the true Alice is, I thought.

I studied myself head to toe in the mirror. "You've done a marvelous job, Albert." I laughed. "I do look as though I'm trying too hard, don't I?"

"Exactly the effect I was after. A couple of years over the edge into thirty, but striving to get back on the good side of time. Yes. It'll do."

I kissed him on the cheek. "What would I do without you? My very own Prince."

Pleased, Albert hugged me. But then he said what, until now, he had avoided saying.

"I really don't think you're going to find what you need out there, Alice." His tone was serious.

"And . . . it's dangerous to go looking. Girls have gotten killed, you know."

"One can't hope to live safely," I said quietly. "I tried it for fifteen years, and it didn't work." I looked at him pleadingly. "I must find another sanctuary, Albert. Don't you see that? But . . . it can only be inside me."

He nodded. Tears were shining in his eyes.

I had kept on the clothes. To get used to wearing them, I had told Albert; but there was in me a hard kernel of need.

And . . . a sense of excitement. After all, I reminded myself, the mandated week is *nearly* over. Soon Mark Judson would have to give his consent. So why not now, tonight, when there was a burning need in my loins to know a man, any man with a passionate need corresponding to my own?

A long time since I had made love without love. But now, I thought with excitement, it will be on my terms, under my conditions. At my desire.

I thought suddenly of Mark Judson's friend, the girl who turned herself off when she felt tenderness toward a man. Pushing away the thought, I went to the phone to ring the building manager.

When he came, promptly as usual, I told him, "I need a way out of the building where no one will have a chance to recognize me."

He nodded with benign tolerance. If he had registered the alteration in my appearance, he didn't reveal it. "A way back in also, I presume."

I laughed. "I will have to come home eventually, won't I?"

"I think I've got it," he said. "You'll have to wait for me to bring you a key, though."

He returned with two keys on a Tiffany key ring. "Come. I will show you."

He stopped the penthouse elevator at the second floor and led me down a corridor. The service elevator took us the rest of the way to the basement.

"After twelve, the elevator is off," he said. "So, when you come in late, you'll have to use this key to turn it on. You can transfer on any floor to the penthouse elevator." He inquired anxiously, "Will that be satisfactory for your purposes?"

"Yes," I said. "Thank you."

He opened the basement door into the catering kitchen. The workers stared curiously as we threaded through the work islands.

"Our people are discreet, naturally," the manager said. "I don't think anyone will betray you . . . though it might be worthwhile to allow me to scatter around some extra gratuities."

I recognized the waiter, John, who brought up my meals. I smiled at him as we passed.

"I'll let Security know you'll be using this route," the manager went on.

We had stepped out into an alley.

"The other key fits this outside door," he said. "It's kept locked at all times." He gestured. "The alley leads a block away before coming out on the street."

I thanked him again. He stood watching as I walked down the alley into the night life of New York. Where I would seek love without love, without commitment; where I would, hopefully, discover the true Alice I had never known. She had to be out there somewhere. To find her was the true hunger in my belly.

But there was also the hunger for a man . . . sharpened by the fact that now it was Alice seeking, not Alice who was being sought.

> *That first six months with Paul Riff had been a revelation of what real work, real dedication, meant. Paul prescribed my diet, regulated my sleeping time, arranged appointments, handled the money—I had twenty-five dollars a week of my very own —and worked my ass off. Just as he had promised.*

Paul had moved me into one of the upstairs apartments in his own house, conducive to his intensive supervision. It was the roomiest place I had had in New York, comfortably furnished with sturdy secondhand pieces Paul had picked up here and there.

Even with the hard work, it was a satisfying life. My time was filled, between modeling assignments, with a heavy schedule of lessons. I even enjoyed a family life of sorts; at least once a week I ate with the Riffs, and I was the baby sitter for their three boys on the rare occasions Paul and Zella went out.

In those six months, a man had not touched Alice. I don't know how Paul arranged it; but on assignment no one dared even a gesture in my direction to indicate that he had sex on his mind. So much better; I knew at least that I was hired because they thought I was right for the job, not because I was an easy lay. My rate-per-hour was rising, too, as my photograph appeared more prominently in higher-quality magazines and catalogues.

Paul's plan was definitely working. And I was happy. Until the day Andy Glenn made me so angry I had to cry.

Andy was the reigning star of my acting class under Raskin Wells. He was tall, with the shoulders of a fullback, the wiry legs of a cowboy. Handsome, too, in an ugly, rugged sort of way. A white scar an inch long marred his left cheek.

He dominated the class by the sheer energy of his presence. He fought with Raskin over every assignment, fought with everybody in the class. Playing a scene with Andy Glenn was like getting into a wrestling match. But he woke us up, he kept us alive, for it was obvious he would become a star.

Andy, I learned later, had been reared on Long Island. His father was a prosperous realtor. Leaving home at seventeen, he had thumbed across the country half a dozen times, working in the Kansas wheat harvest, as a logger in the Pacific Northwest, a cowboy on the King Ranch in Texas. He had been in Acapulco, working as a resort-hotel beach boy, when he had decided his true destiny was to become an actor. Hitching a ride in a plush private plane to New York, he had talked his disapproving father into financing a year's study with Raskin Wells.

All the girls in the class were in love with Andy. Except Alice; I considered myself too busy to think about love.

The "school" consisted of a great loft, a tiny stage at one end furnished with a sofa that puffed dust every time one sat on it, a few chairs and stepladders, and a few props. We were playing the balcony scene from Romeo and Juliet. *The balcony was a stepladder, so Romeo could climb the other side.*

I thought the scene was going well, until Andy stopped in the middle of a speech.

"I can't play this scene with this girl," He told Raskin bluntly. *"Get somebody else up on that ladder."*

Raskin Wells, costumed in a ratty old sweater and a pipe, was a deceptively mild-mannered man. "What's the matter this time, Andy?"

Andy scowled at me.

"Just look at her, for Christ's sake. That's a pinup *girl. She'll never be able to act her way out of a paper sack." Angrily, he shook his head. "All she'll ever be good for is to show her nakedness in* Playboy *magazine. Or walk around a movie set in a bathing suit."*

Maybe I wasn't the best actress in the group; I knew that, stiff and self-conscious, I couldn't let myself go. But Raskin Wells had praised my efforts, and he was chary with everything but criticism.

You have to make yourself open to get into a role—I had already learned that, at least—and up on the ladder I had been feeling myself as Juliet, so innocent yet so lustful for Romeo. (Raskin had told me, "Now, Alice, Juliet is not innocent, as she's so often played. She may be only fourteen, but she's a hot-blooded Italian, and she wants to be fucked. Understand? Now play it that way, see how it feels.")

I was playing it that way, and I had felt it. I was wet down there, because I had made myself see Andy-Romeo with his naked Thing bursting out of the beribboned codpiece a real Romeo would have been wearing.

In the midst of such self-engendered emotion, this brutal attack.

"Get down," Andy commanded scornfully. "I want a real Juliet."

Raskin Wells ambled up on the stage. He pointed his pipe at Andy.

"Now listen, Andy. You're not a star, yet, who can pick his supporting players." His voice was gentle, unforceful. "You might well find yourself working with a Juliet too dumb to learn her lines. Or a fifty-year-old woman struggling to project the innocent lust of a fourteen-year-old girl, when innocence vanished from her soul forty years ago."

His voice sharpened. Raskin Wells had dominance at his command, or he couldn't have been the teacher of acting that he was.

"So get up there and work, Andy Glenn. Temperament is fine in an actor, but

I've had just about enough of yours. So act this scene with Alice—and you'd damn well better be good—or quit the class. I don't much care which. I've had you—" with the pipestem he indicated his throat"*—up to here."*

Andy looked sullen. But he remained silent.

"Take it from the top," Raskin said as mildly as if nothing had happened.

We took it from the top. Andy threw himself passionately into the scene, his voice soaring with the beautiful words. Then he was up on the ladder, reaching for me. In that pause when we look at each other, seeing a great love, his eyes went cold on my face, his mouth curled.

"So you're fucking your way to stardom," he whispered. *"I should have known. But I didn't think the old goat could still get it up."*

No one had heard but me.

I simply stared. I couldn't believe he had broken the scene in such a ruthless manner. Bursting into tears, I climbed shakily down my side of the ladder and fled across the narrow stage.

"Alice!" Raskin shouted, rising to his feet.

I did not heed him. I had to get out of there. And I knew that I could not return.

Reaching the street, I slowed to a walk. But, inside, I was still fleeing. Oh God, I thought, I'll have to tell Paul I've quit the class.

A terrible thought.

I couldn't go home now. Home *meant* telling the truth to Paul, as I told to him the truth of all my days.

There was a coffee shop on the block

*where we hung out after class, talking about
the day's work, dreaming out loud about
the time, sure to come, when we would be
established actors working on Broadway or
in Hollywood.*

*I took the back booth, where I hud-
dled miserably. The coffee went stone cold
in front of me as I reviewed helplessly over
and over again, the brutally devastating attack.*

*With the session only half over when
I had fled, I had expected to be safe. Apparently, however, Raskin had dismissed the
class immediately, for suddenly they were in
the coffee shop, chattering excitedly.*

*In their midst, Andy Glenn stalked si-
lently aloof. I picked up the cup, drank
blindly. The coffee was bitter in my mouth.*

*They had seen me, of course. Sensitive
to my distress, the group took another table.*

Except for Andy.

"Can I sit down," he said.

I looked up. "No," I said stonily.

*He sat down. "Listen," he said, "it was
nothing personal. It's just that you're too
beautiful to be an actress."*

"Thanks a lot," I said bitterly.

*He was very earnest. "I couldn't get
into Romeo because I couldn't see Juliet on
her balcony. All I could see was Alice beautiful on a stepladder."*

There was nothing in me to say.

*"Your coffee's cold," he said. "Want
another cup?"*

*I didn't say anything. He got up, re-
filled my cup. In that place we were free to
serve ourselves.*

*Andy sat down again. "An actor's got
to be honest, or he's no actor," he said. "Got*

*to feel what he feels, then project it. So,
feeling like that about you, I had to say it."*

*I looked at him for the first time. "Who
are you to say I'll never be an actress?" I
demanded in sudden anger.*

*He moved his hands. "I'm sorry, Al-
ice, but that's the way it is. All you'll ever
be is a beautiful piece of meat. They won't
let you be anything else. Can't you see that?"*

*Hard words, thudding against me. This
time it only made me angrier.*

*"Well, who the hell is Andy Glenn
but beef on the hoof?" I said challengingly.*

*"Sure, I got the beef," he said un-
ashamedly. "It'll take me a long way, too.
But I'll act whether they want me to or not."*

*Quite self-satisfied about his integrity of
purpose.*

*I challenged him again. "How do you
know I'm not the same way?"*

*He looked at me. With interest this
time. "You work as a model, don't you?"*

*"I have to make a living," I said short-
ly. "Not like some people I know who get an
allowance from home."*

He flinched under that blow.

*"You've got to use everything you can
use," he said defensively. Then, with some
astonishment, "You mean you're entirely on
your own? Your folks aren't helping out?"*

*"They don't even know where I am," I
said bravely.*

*He stared. He said, "You've got guts,
anyway. I'll give you that."*

*I was warmed by the spontaneous
compliment. Promptly he took it away.*

*"That guy brought you around to class
that first day . . . you sleeping with him so
he'll pay your bills?"*

"Paul Riff?" I said. "Not on your life."

I reached again for the anger. "It's my money, earned by my work. Paul is my manager. That's all he is."

Andy nodded, impressed by the statement of independence.

I carried on the attack. "You can't know another person by looking at them, you know," I said scornfully. I tossed my head. "You couldn't know me in a thousand years."

He muttered, "Who needs to know somebody who calls themselves by one name, anyway?"

I was cool now. "Is Andrew Glenn your real name?"

He looked startled. "Of course."

"Well, it could have been Ignazio Pumpernickel for all I know," I said loftily.

I had him backed up to the wall. He looked over his shoulder as if thinking of fleeing to the group. They were gone.

Turning to me, he smiled, held out his hand. "Hey, Alice," he said. "Truce?"

The charm. Oh, yes, he had it then, too. Had it, and knew how to use it. Except, this time, it didn't work.

"You started the feud," I said inflexibly. "But if you think you can run me out of the class, you've got another think coming. What's the matter? Can't you stand the competition?"

He wouldn't fight anymore. "All right. I misread you. Okay?"

"That's better," I said grudgingly.

He quickened. "Listen. Let's go back up there, do the scene right. I'll show you how Juliet ought to be done. We'll work on it."

"The studio will be locked," I said indifferently.

He looked abashed. "I got a key," he

*said. "I . . . talked Raskin into letting me
have it so I could work solo. There's some
things I'm trying I can't show even Raskin
yet."*

*"I've got a fencing class at four," I said,
looking at my watch.*

*"Plenty of time," he urged. "We'll sur-
prise old Raskin with our beautiful balcony
scene the next class session. Come on."*

*The loft was empty, afternoon sunlight
slanting through dirty windows to highlight
the unevenness of the old wooden floor.
The dirt, the shabbiness, didn't matter. To
us, it was a place of enchantment, where we
would become great in the sublime art of
acting.*

Andy sat me down on the dusty sofa.

*Warily, I said, "I thought we came to
do the scene."*

"We've got to talk first."

"What are we going to talk about?"

*"Us," he said ingenuously. "Me and
you."*

*I sat straighter. "There's no 'me-and-
you,' " I said firmly. "There's not going to
be, either."*

*"No," he murmured. "But we're going
to get into each other's heads. Then we can
do the scene."*

"All right," I said. "Start talking."

*He didn't start talking. Instead he put
his hand on my breast. He performed the
move with precision, cupping his hand underneath, catching the nipple, through fabric
of bra and shirt, between thumb and fore-
finger.*

*Startled, I sat quite still. The pressure
alerted the nipple. Warmth moving slug-
gishly through my body, I leaned against
him.*

Pushing me down, he sprawled his legs across me.

"Oh God, Alice. I was so mean because I didn't want to want you this much."

His voice was low in his throat. I put my hand on the back of his head. I wanted him to kiss me. He kissed me. It lasted a long time, engendering a mixture of feelings and sensations I couldn't sort out. I didn't want to be taken like this. Yet I had to be taken like this, I had to taste in my body the thrust of his Thing.

Going cold inside, I pushed him away. "Stop it now."

He fixed me with his burning gaze, and immediately I wanted to put my palm against his face. His hand was under my skirt, seeking the mount and finding it all in one sure stroke.

"No," I said, grasping his wrist in a frantic effort to stop the touching. He resisted with unassailable male strength because he was making me so weak with kisses I couldn't get my breath. I succeeded, once, in removing the stroking hand, but then it returned, sneaking under the panties to touch me so directly I felt that I would faint.

Alice went through, in one brief afternoon, the frustrations and needs and desires and fears of adolescence. It was as though I were virgin still, for I experienced all the emotions and sensations of surrendering for the first time. Only now did I realize that, when I had sucked at home, fucked in New York, it had been in a soul-less state of non-feeling.

I was feeling, now, all the permutations of resistance and surrender. In spite of all desire, I would not give in to him. Time and *again, kissing, wrestling, panting, disheveled, we fought our way to the brink. Each time, I forced a retreat.*

At last I lay exhausted, yielding him the freedom of my body. He took off my panties, leaving me naked and vulnerable. His fingers were busy in me, his mouth on my breast. I lay trembling and open. But when he withdrew to unlimber his artillery the sight of Its arrogant stiffness evoked a final barrier of resistance. When with his hand he bent down the rosy head to press It between my legs, I could feel intensely the betrayal of my own desire to be entered. Even yet, however, resistance dwelled unbowed, and it stayed him.

The windows were dark with twilight. Lying quiescent on the dusty sofa, Andy's weight oppressing me, I thought peacefully, I've missed my fencing lesson. With indefatigable optimism, Andy was using both hands in one more futile effort to spread my legs. My legs parted. Startled by the sudden ebbing of resistance, he hesitated.

I touched the scar on his face. "Love me, Andy," I said. "Will you love me?"

I had never spoken those words to any man.

His face tightened. Suddenly fearful that I had lost him, I thrust my hips upward, seeking consummation. It slid into me so suddenly I could not encompass the sensation. Having resisted so long, It hurt and felt good at the same time. As though he couldn't believe in success, he held still. Slowly, coaxing him to action, I slid up on the shaft, down again. It didn't hurt anymore.

His face changed. Reaching to take my knees into the crook of his elbows, he arched my body into a tight bow, lifting my eager bottom into position. Slowly he pulled out, hung rampant for a moment, then rammed It home. The air was driven out of my lungs. But I didn't need to breathe; all I needed was for him to do it again and again and again, without end.

He withdrew once more, plunged, and on this second stroke he was already coming. Knowing he was in orgasm drove me wild, so that our bodies rocked together in a wedded rhythm of downward stroke and upward thrust. He came forever, it seemed, and when it was finally done he started all over again, rising quickly to a greater crescendo of frenzy.

We were too frantic, however, to keep it going for long. When at last he lay still, his exhausted instrument limp inside me, I embraced his head with both arms, feeling myself assailed with a great tenderness.

So this, *I thought deeply, is what it's all about. Why did it take Alice so long to find out?*

Andy stirred, wanting to get up. Regretfully, I released him. He sat up, wiping the sweat from his face.

"My God, Alice, I thought you'd never break down—and I didn't even get your cherry."

"Yes," I said. "Yes."

True, somehow, though not physically true. From the way he looked at me, he didn't feel it as the truth. As I did.

He laughed shortly. "I was ready to quit a dozen times."

"I'm sorry," I said. "It . . . had to be that way, I guess."

I stopped talking. No way to tell him how all the growing up Alice had missed out on had fallen upon me instantaneously in one short afternoon.

I sat up. Too warm, too sweaty, my clothes disheveled. "I've got to get out of here. Paul will be wondering where I am."

"Not yet," Andy said tenderly. "Please."

"But . . ."

He put his hand on my hip. "I haven't even seen you naked."

I stood up. I took off the shirt, the crumpled skirt.

"All right?" I said softly.

His hand trailed down my flank, tickled through the damp pubic hair. His eyes were devouring me. "Alice," he said throatily. "There's so much loving in that lovely body."

"Yes," I said.

He looked up. "All for me?"

"Yes," I said intensely. "Yes."

His arm circled my waist, drew me close. He cradled his head against my naked belly. He didn't say anything. There was no need.

At last, reluctantly, I stirred. "Got to go. It's late."

"No." He stood up. Unbelting his pants, he let them drop. He took off his shirt. He stood naked, his Thing erect.

"There's loving got to be done yet," he said.

I wriggled my crotch against his thigh. With one hand I encircled It fiercely.

"Oh God yes," I said.

Without separating we went down on the couch, our bodies melting together.

Longer this time, not so frantic. There was time to explore each other. He held back until we were coming together. Then he

*glued his mouth to mine, as our bodies were
glued, and it was so good and loving I began to cry.*

*In the circumstances of sex, Alice had
never cried before.*

Lord Harry's on Third Avenue was very nice,
I thought. All red and black, the vinyl plastic looking
almost like leather. The lighting, low-key and flatter-
ing, was excellent.

A few couples sat in the booths along one
wall—I wondered if they had come as pairs, or had
started the mating dance here. Most of the small tables
in the center were occupied by groups of men or wom-
en. A lot of back-and-forth attention, I noted, but no
one as yet committing themselves to a pairing. The
long bar was mostly stag.

Not wanting to sit alone, I took one of the two
empty bar stools. By remaining near the door, I realized, I was avoiding committing myself deeply, as yet,
to the adventure.

"What'll it be?" the barman asked, working toward me with his polishing rag.

I could do worse than him, I commented mentally in deliberate appraisal. Handsome in the Latin
manner, thin mustache on a long upper lip, liquid
eyes. But of course he would have to work until closing time.

A weird sensation, to be considering so directly
the potential of a strange male. I had always, I realized suddenly, remained quite passive, dealing only
with what fate, circumstance, accident, had brought
within my orbit. A heady feeling, to think I might
initiate sexual intercourse with some unknown male
presently within range of my gaze.

Because I hadn't responded, the bartender was
impatient. "What'll it be? Or are you just shopping?"

"I haven't made up my mind yet," I said. "What's
your name?"

"Pete Regalado," he said. "How about a nice Chablis?"

"That'll be fine," I said, relieved the choice had been taken out of my hands.

I sipped the dry wine, looking again around the room. An undercurrent of excitement in the air; speculation, the scenting of opportunity, an exposure of needful seeking that I was not accustomed to. People *were* more open, as both Prince Albert and Mark Judson had told me. A sparkle in their eyes, a brightness in their voices, as though they would surely discover tonight a fulfillment that until now had escaped them.

The next observation was a shock: they were all so young. Not a woman in the room, it seemed, over twenty-five; the men thirty at most. They exuded a youthful vitality; even, it seemed to my innocent eyes, a certain innocence.

The youth of the crowd struck at my heart. For the first time I understood emotionally the bitterness Prince Albert had occasionally revealed about his age. Involuntarily I thought, You missed it, Alice. You were young at the wrong time.

This, I couldn't help but feel, was no place for a thirty-six-year-old woman.

In my day, I remembered, females who went alone to bars tended to be older women, lonely, perhaps as much in need of a drink as of a man. There had been in them a desperate quality. But, these young, handsome, vital people—why did they need this? Had the structure of social life so deteriorated that the young people must go to a public bar, desperately institutionalized as the only possible meeting place?

A horrible thought, casting a pall over the lively scene.

But you didn't come here to philosophize, I told myself resolutely. Like everybody else, Alice, you came to get laid. On your own initiative. Of your own free choice.

So—how did one go about it?

Sitting in a corner of the bar certainly wouldn't do it. One stool away, a man's back was turned. He was talking to the chunky girl on the stool beyond. She wore, I noted, heavy turquoise bracelets on both arms. She was dressed in skintight blue jeans and a T-shirt that announced she was THE BITCH OF THE WEEK. It was obvious that she did not wear a bra; large nipples thrust with naked boldness against the flimsy cotton fabric.

Well, I told myself, a lady can always go to the ladies' room.

I finished the wine and gestured for a refill. Sliding down from the stool, I threaded my way through the tables. Speculative eyes felt at me as I passed.

In the rear corridor were three doors, one labeled MEN, another WOMEN. The third declared: UNISEX. I laughed; then, on an impulse, pushed open the UNISEX door. As I did so, somewhere a bell chimed.

Rather to my disappointment, the place was empty. I looked about curiously. There was a urinal, two compartments, two basins sharing a long mirror. And a bidet. I gazed speculatively at the bidet, wondering what woman would have the nerve to use it. But, I had to admit, it was funny.

Going to the mirror, I studied my makeup. Quite all right. But there was no way I could look as young as those people out there. Well, I thought defiantly, if I'm choosing, it might as well be a younger man. Most of my lovers had been older than I; maybe it was time to turn the tables.

When I emerged, everybody was looking. Why? I wondered. Then, remembering the chime, I looked over my shoulder. A sign on the wall: UNISEX NOW IN USE. The red light blinked out as I looked.

I smiled. A college-fraternity trick, like the nude man with an obvious figleaf on the wall of the ladies' room. When the figleaf was touched by an inquisitive hand, a red light would come on in the social room, generating ribald laughter.

When I resumed my stool, I realized that I had been followed.

"This seat taken?"

I looked at the man, ready to shake my head. But, for no particular reason, my impulse moved against him. And it was my option, wasn't it?

"Sorry," I said. "It's taken."

He stood uncertainly between embarrassment and anger. Turning with a jerk of the body, he marched away. Well, I thought to myself guiltily, I didn't *have* to let him sit down, did I?

The girl with the turquoises put a bill on the bar, slid down from her seat, and walked out the door without a backward glance. Immediately her companion turned to me. He looked me up and down, a faint smile showing.

"When was the divorce final?" he asked suddenly. "Last week? Or did it take you an entire month to get here?"

I looked at him coolly. "I've never been married."

He shook his head in disbelief. "I know where you're coming from. Never been in a singles' bar in your life. Right?"

"No, I haven't," I said. "How could you tell?"

"I hang out here, my apartment's just around the corner. We get your type all the time; older woman, been married for ages, with kids and the whole bit, maybe all she's had in all those years a quick hump at a country-club dance. So she's curious, and now that she's divorced she's gonna satisfy that curiosity if it kills her. Am I reading you right?"

Compared to the rest of the crowd, he wasn't so young himself. He displayed the stigmata of youth; the long sideburns, expensive sports jacket, a discreetly elegant ascot. Obviously he belonged to a health club, kept a pretty good tan even in the wintertime, and he held in his stomach muscles—he tended to stockiness.

"Wrong," I said. "Except it *is* my first visit to a

singles' bar. I've been . . . living abroad quite a long time."

His eyes remained speculative. "Of course, most of these older women, they don't have the class you've got."

My God, I thought in laughing despair, after all Prince Albert's hard work, my male stranger thinks it's *class* he's looking at.

"I'll bet you give good head," he said judiciously. "European women are noted for good head."

"Good head?" I said.

"Myself, I come from a long line of French ancestors," he added coyly.

A thrill of shock coursed through me. He's talking about me going down on him, I thought incredulously. When we didn't even know each other's names yet.

There seemed to be a lot of shortcuts in a singles' bar.

"I'm not European," I said. I smiled. "Originally from Iowa, if you want to know the truth."

He smiled confidently. "But you *lived* abroad. Most of these girls, they'll give head, but they don't *like* to give head. You got to love it to give *good* head. You know?"

"I've never gone into the matter on a scientific basis," I said carefully.

He nodded seriously. "Now me, I *like* to give head. But I'm choosy. Know what I mean? I go by instinct. Sometimes that's the first thing, sometimes I won't touch it. Sometimes it's *all* I do."

He considered the matter. "I don't really know *what* it is. The way a woman *smells,* maybe. Know what I mean? An olfactory instinct. When it turns me off, it turns me off. If your personal smell turns me off, don't expect to get good head from me."

I felt a strong sense of the absurd. Here was Alice, discussing seriously, with a man whose name she didn't know, the more esoteric aspects of going down on each other.

Overwhelmed by a sense of unreality, I sought a steadying banality. "What's your name?"

"Herbert Gloss," he said. "You can call me Herb. And yours?"

I thought swiftly. A false name? But suppose I might want to see him again?

A feeling of certainty seared through my mind. When had I decided?

Had that absurd conversation about "giving head" captured me after all?

I laughed inwardly, with a certain euphoria. It had been fifteen years since a new man had come into me.

"Alice Toffler," I said. It was the first time I had used my last name since the night I had left home and Daddy. To slide over the scar of memory, I said quickly, "What kind of work do you do?"

"Stockbroker."

He was watching me intently. I didn't know how I was supposed to react.

"I'm actually a very creative person," he added apologetically. "I can paint, I can write, I make things with my hands. Creativity is really where my head has always been."

He paused to beckon to the bartender. I let him order for me. I knew now, didn't I?

"After Yale, I went out to British Columbia," he said. "Bought a piece of land there, along with some good friends who were in the same bag. Handicrafts, you know, authentic stuff, based on Indian motifs. I *love* to work with wood."

I looked at his hands. They were tanned on the back. But the palms were smooth.

Herb saw my glance. "Of course, I haven't kept it up," he said. "I'm into *living* now. You know—style and substance. That's the *real* creativity, making your life into something that's *you*."

It's a new language, I thought. I'll have to learn a new language.

"But, being a stockbroker . . . how did that come about?" I inquired politely.

"Dad had this heart attack, you see," Herb said. "So I got a hurry-up call to come home. Dad and I had never been that close, but he wanted to see me before he went in for open-heart surgery."

He looked down at his glass. "We . . . talked. Quite a creative talk, actually, for the first time in our lives." He looked up. "Sort of nice, you know? Communication on all levels. So I went into the firm. Now I manage the uptown branch, over on Park, as well as handling accounts for my own individual clients."

"And Dad?" I said.

"Oh, he's fine now," Herb said. "You wouldn't know he's been to Houston for surgery. Walks four or five miles a day, plays golf, his weight is down, and he's quit smoking cigars." He smiled. "Dad will probably outlive *me*, though I keep myself in shape as one essential element in my life-style." He chuckled. "Dad even divorced Mom and married a real cool chick not much older than I am."

"So you like being a stockbroker?" I said.

He gazed at me earnestly. "People insist on thinking of it as just *money*, you know. But being a stockbroker is a very creative thing, once you understand it. You're using people's money to *build* something. A decent capital is a very solid foundation for a self-fulfilling life structure."

I thought about my twenty-two millions of dollars. I didn't even know what my trustees were planning in the way of investments. A "decent capital" was unreal to me, anyway.

"What about marriage?" I said. "I should think . . ."

"Oh, my life-style doesn't include even the *prospect* of marriage," he protested. "That's a whole different bag. You know? You have to think about things like houses, and having children, and whether to live in the city or commute. My life-style is very *personal.* The entry of another ego would require a drastic restructuring of priorities."

He shook his head firmly. "No. For the first time in my life, I know where I'm really *at.* I have the sense that I am utilizing my basic creativity in a very satisfying way."

Does everybody talk this way now? I was wondering. Or is it just Herb Gloss? Ready to spill out his deepest thoughts and feelings to a stranger in a bar. Even assuming that before the night was over he would fuck that stranger, it was unreal.

If I satisfy his *olfactory* instinct, I thought drily, he might even give me head.

The Unisex chime sounded. We both looked up. With everybody else, we waited.

It was a young man. He swaggered out of the corridor, paused as though to take applause. Down the length of the room, he was looking directly toward me.

He came to me, very young, very arrogant. His hips were slim, and there was a knife scar on his neck.

"Can I sit down?" he asked, indicating the empty seat between me and Herb.

A tough young boy; he'd be like a pile driver in one's body. I felt the thrill of attractive danger. There was temper in his mouth.

But—then I looked at his eyes. As predatory as the eyes of a hawk. I chilled inside.

I glanced at Herb. The more he talked, the more doubtful I became. He talked so much, but there was so little—what had he termed it?—*communication.* The language he used seemed to deny meaning, not embrace it.

But Herb, in comparison to this boy, was safe. Those predatory eyes had searched me out, obviously an older woman. He had gone to Unisex deliberately to attract my attention. Now, with his native arrogance, he was invading my conversation with Herb.

"Sure, sit down," I said. "Slide over this way, Herb."

Herb slid over, leaving vacant the stool on the other side. The boy sneered at my clever ploy. Turning quickly, he walked out of the bar.

Herb smiled. "You're right to stay away from that one. The word is, he likes to play rough." He shrugged. "Of course, some people are into masochism, it's the only thing that can turn them on. I've run into *that* type myself."

Maybe *I* was into masochism; something in me yearned after the boy. To take all that arrogance and energy into one's body, feel it pounding there . . .

"Besides, he'll cruise a man as quick as he will a woman," Herb said. "Basically, about as bi as they come."

I smiled. "He's gone, Herb," I said. "And I'm still here."

Herb looked at me. For a long moment. He seemed to be considering me all over again.

"You sure you're not putting me on about not just being divorced, all that?"

I shook my head. But I said, "You can believe me or not believe me, Herb. If it's that important to you."

He looked at my breasts. His eyes slid down to my lap. Finally he spoke.

"Whaddya say we get out of here?"

From the door, I looked back. No one was watching us. Everybody is so absorbed in his own lifestyle, I thought, they don't care who leaves with whom.

Those first weeks we were together, Andy and I made love like people possessed. My body, my mind, my entire soul, was suffused with sexuality. And with love —I floated inside myself in an elixir of happiness. The world was soft with beauty, all the colors bright and strong, and it was good simply to walk a street smelling all the varied smells of a great city.

Andy lived in a tiny room on the sixth floor of a building that was virtually a tenement. The single window opened on an air shaft; he had a hot plate for cooking, and the bathroom was in the hall.

It was terribly hot that summer in New York. Fucking in the afternoons, our bodies gleamed slickly with sweat, slapping against each other with wet sounds. Sweat dripped off his face stinging into my eyes. The dirty sheet under us was wringing wet with our effluvium. When, at the heights of exertion, I began to get dizzy, we laughingly bought salt tablets to restore the chemical balance in our bodies.

I was both giving and demanding, soft and passionate. I couldn't get enough of his beautiful maleness. When I stayed over instead of going home to Paul's house, even though the nights were hot I slept spooned into his backside, one hand holding his cock.

Waking in the morning, there would be in my hand the gift of a hard-on. I would kiss his back. Turning over in one move, he would put It in me and I was immediately so ready that I would orgasm at the first penetration. So often those early mornings, with his piss-hard he could go on even after I couldn't climb up to orgasm anymore. Then I would melt under him, feeling him sinking deeper and truer into me, until I began to cry.

Andy Glenn never understood why I cried so much while he was fucking me.

At first the sex was more than enough; both so young and unskilled, we had to learn together, investigating our bodies step by step in a continuous exploration.

We were lying quietly one day, sweaty and exhausted, his cheek resting on my breast, his tongue occasionally flickering against the nipple. Playfully varying the rhythm, he tantalized my erotism until the nipple stood rigid.

Turning over, he slid his tongue slowly to my belly. A pool of sweat stood in my navel; he lapped it up gleefully, flicked his tongue in the empty depression. I put my hands on his curly head, trying to hold him there, but he escaped, dragging the rough side of his tongue all the way to the thigh. Shifting over, he licked his way up the other leg.

Suddenly pausing, with both hands he parted the lips of my pussy. Kneeling over me, he gazed with intense curiosity. I felt a pang of lust. Slowly, deliberately, he put his mouth on me. Starting low, flattening his agile tongue against the slit, he lapped upward to the clitoris. Once he had found it, tiny and hard, he brought his lips into play, sucking the clitoris into his mouth.

I didn't know whether it felt good, or painful. I sat halfway up, thinking to escape the frightening new sensation. At the same time, I was begging, "Don't stop. Don't stop."

He didn't stop. Lifting my thighs, he buried his face into the blond muff. His tongue was probing deep now, so deep, and it was different from his cock, softer and warmer, so skillful in its flickings and dartings that it aroused in me a passion beyond anything I had experienced. Surging my pussy hard against his tongue, I wrapped my legs around his head to hold him forever. Trapped into me, fighting for breath, he became yet more ferocious in the eating, and I began to come.

*Different from the fucking orgasms.
Deep, slow waves, broaching from the depths
of my being and rolling through me toward
that point of contact; with each successive
wave my legs tightened, holding him pris-
oner against my pulsing cunt. He was fighting to escape now, needing to breathe, but
I wouldn't let him go until my legs had
slackened in satisfied weariness.*

*He came up red-faced and grinning. "I
think you like it."*

I grinned in return. "I like it, I like it."

*We laughed at our sparkling wit like the
young fools we were. He pulled himself up
so we could hold each other. Stroking the
curly locks of his head, I felt a tenderness
and fulfillment so great I didn't know when
I went to sleep in his arms.*

*Andy was doing me all the time now;
not only, unselfishly, because I loved it so
much, but selfishly because it warmed and
opened me, as nothing else did, for the fucking to follow.*

But I did not volunteer to reciprocate.

*One night we were resting, side by side
on the narrow bed. The sheets were damp
under us, from the come and the sweat,
but to us it was like lying in a bed of roses.
The odors of lust were strong in the room.*

*I sat up to stretch my back, relaxed to
lie down again. But his hand was at the
nape of my neck, pressing me down toward
his used-up cock. My mouth was almost
touching It before I realized what he was doing. I rebelled violently, but he only pressed
harder.*

"No!" I gasped. "No."

*He took away his grip suddenly.
"What's the matter?"*

I bent my head so the long hair would obscure my face. I stared dumbly at his waiting cock. The warmth of my mouth, the sliding motion of lips, the flicker of teasing tongue that I knew so well how to do, would, I knew, bring him to a great fucking.

But—putting my mouth on Andy's cock would make It one with all the cocks I had sucked in high school.

"Come on," *Andy said impatiently.* "What's the matter?"

Still not looking at him, I said, "I can't stand the taste of It."

Andy reached one hand to expose my face.

"Hey, look, baby, this is Andy!" *he said softly.*

I wanted to turn away, but he wouldn't let me. "I don't care," *I said stubbornly.* "I don't like it, and I won't do it."

He stared at me. "You keep saying how much you love me. Have you been lying all along?"

My voice was soft. "You're the only person I've ever loved, Andy."

He was the inquisitor now. "You said you didn't like the taste of It. That means you've tried it. Right?"

I didn't answer. I was cold inside. I shivered with the cold.

"Have *you tried it?*" *he insisted.*

I couldn't tell him. The entire varsity football team? *he would say incredulously. How could I expect him to keep on loving me, knowing about that?*

The words had formed in my mind like stones. Yes, Andy, my love. I sucked every cock in my high school, starting with the football team. I bore that proud name, the Cocksucker of Clancy Street.

And then all of it: But I didn't do it in love, Andy. Not even in lust. I did it with hate in my heart for every man's cock in the world. Even while sucking It tenderly, I wanted to bite It off. It's a wonder I *didn't* bite when they filled my mouth with their come.

He would gaze upon me with contempt. How could the great Andy Glenn love some-one who would do what I had done? For whatever reason.

The words for lying were not in me. But I lied.

"Andy, I tried it once," *I heard myself saying.* "It . . . made me throw up."

His face cleared. Tenderly he stroked his hand against my shoulder. "But it's me, now, Alice."

I had to deny him. I couldn't let his beautiful Thing become only one more cock that had enjoyed the expert action of The Cocksucker of Clancy Street.

Stonily, I shook my head.

His voice turned urgent. "Just kiss It, that's all." *Again his hand was pressing me down.* "Maybe next time you'll want to kiss It, and then . . ."

"No!" *I said, struggling against him.* "I can't. I won't."

His voice was flat. "Well. If that's how you feel about it."

Turning his back, he lay still.

I sat huddled in on myself, waiting for him to come to me forgivingly. It was the first rift in our seamless web of love. And Alice had caused it.

When the silence got too long, I said, "I guess I ought to go home."

Without hope, I waited. Andy didn't say anything.

To get out of the narrow bed, I had to climb over him. Miserably, I got dressed, Andy watching every move, his mouth a grim line.

When I couldn't stretch it out any longer, I said, "I'm going now."

"Go," he said stonily. "If that's how you feel about it."

It was the only way I could feel about it. So I went.

Once he realized I hated the idea of sucking his cock, he wanted it so badly it inevitably became the central issue at the core of our love. In fucking, now, we had lost that first wild, wonderful freedom of our sensual selves. I could feel him holding back, watching me, testing me. And already my resistance was building against the moment when again he would try to make me go down on him.

Sometimes—but less and less often—we would get swept up into forgetful passion, and then it would be good again. With selfish calculation, Andy used those moments of brief goodness to coerce my reluctance.

He tried everything he could think of. Going down on me in the 69 position, he would thrust his cock within an inch of my lips. Gritting my teeth, I would stare at It as he made fucking motions toward my mouth. Sometimes, smelling its exciting maleness, feeling the thrill of his increasingly skillful tongue inside my pussy, I wanted to taste It. But I knew, as truly as I have ever known anything, that yielding to his perversely strong desire would destroy me as surely as it would destroy our love. Yet, every day, it was destroying our love.

I did not know how to escape the di-

*lemma. I could only hold on, with all my
strength, to the wonderful love that had
flashed between us. Hold on even as, in our
young and greedy hearts, it broke into desperate shards of itself.*

Awaiting us was a bottle of champagne, in a
bucket of ice, and two champagne glasses. Ceremoni-
ously Herb Gloss twirled the bottle, popped the cork,
and poured. Tulip glasses, I noted; at least Herb
knew that much. Those flattopped ones cause most of
the aroma to be lost.

Good champagne, too.

Herb touched his glass to mine. "Here's to us."

I sipped the champagne, looking about. A spectacular apartment, though small. Modern furniture,
all white cushions and steel tubing. The shag rug was
white, too, deep-piled. One or two of the paintings
were quite good; the others pretty awful. I remembered Herb had said that he possessed also the creativity of painting. Along with so much else.

Mirrors, too. I noticed; not, as I would have expected, for prurient purposes, but placed to lengthen
the vistas. The house plants, I noticed, were plastic.
In essence, a sterile place, looking like no one lived
there. The very model of backdrop for a creative life-
style.

"Get comfortable," Herb said. "I'll be right back."

He disappeared through a door. Not knowing what
he meant by "getting comfortable," I simply waited.

Herb was not gone long. He came back naked.
No brocade robe? I thought. I suppose brocade robes
are out of it.

I was picking up the language after all.

"You still dressed?" he commented in mild surprise.

He did not, I observed perforce, have even the
beginnings of an erection. His legs were short, thick.
His stomach was flatter than I had expected . . . he

must work really hard at that health club. Strangely, naked, he looked older. Middle thirties at least.

Unabashed by my staring, Herb crossed to the stereo and pushed a button. Soft rock music pulsed into the room.

He can choose the champagne and the music before he goes out, I thought, because, after all, he's creating a *personal* life-style. Another ego would only disturb the symmetries.

I realized, standing there still clothed, I was using irony as a defense against myself. You're here, Alice, I told myself, on your own initiative. You could have gone instead with that boy, if that was what you had wanted. So don't be so critical.

I took off my clothes, folding the pieces, placing them on a chair. Herb, busily pouring champagne, pausing to fiddle with the stereo to seek a precise balance and volume, didn't notice that I was naked until he brought the full glass.

"Hey, that's a good-looking bod," he said in a pleased voice. He studied me, head cocked to one side. "Give you a decent hairdo, more subtle makeup, you'd be something else."

"Thank you," I said. "Maybe I'll learn."

Walking behind me, he put his hand on my shoulder, slid it slowly down.

"I like your ass," he said with frank admiration. "Not many women your age can show an ass like that."

I laughed again. "How old do you think I am, anyway?"

He was in front of me again, appreciating my breasts. He wagged an arch finger. "I'm not prying into anybody's secrets. If you ask me, a person is as old as he feels." He exhaled expansively. "Tonight, looking at that fine ass of yours, I feel like I'm maybe twenty."

I finished the champagne, stood waiting. It was grotesque, two naked strangers standing about in a sterile area designed for fucking. I had not experienced the tiniest stab of desire. And Herb still didn't have an erection.

He indicated a place on the rug. "Right *here* is where you get the best stereo effect. Come on, let's lie down."

I laid down on my back on the thick white rug. He joined me. On his side facing me, he put a hand under my breast, shaping it, stroking upward toward the nipple.

"Nice breasts, too," he said. "But I like your ass best of all. I'm a connoisseur of asses. That's my thing, you know."

"What do you mean, your *thing?*" I was not stirred by the touch of his fingers.

He lifted the hand, waved it. "Well, there's tit men, and then there's leg men. Me, I'm an ass man. In my office—street floor, you understand, you'd be surprised how much walk-in business a street-floor operation will generate—I've got my desk situated so I can watch the girls walk by on Park." He smiled complacently. "Sometimes I sit there all day with a hard-on."

I looked down. Maybe just a hint that a hard-on might be possible. If I played my cards right.

I was tempted to tell him that the ass he admired so greatly—the entire bod, in fact—had been quite celebrated not too many years ago. I suppressed the impulse. No. Play it straight. Play it careful.

Taking my hand, he turned on his back. He let my hand drop on his cock.

"Give me some of that good head now," he said dreamily.

"I don't do that," I said.

He sat up abruptly. "Hey, now, that's not fair. You told me you give that good European head. That's what turned me on to you, didn't you know that?"

"*I* didn't say that," I told him. "You were the one talking about European head."

He looked disappointed. "If you want a real good

stiff one, you'll have to get down there and work on it," he said. "Like, I come from a long line of French ancestors." He had used that line before.

"I don't do that," I repeated.

His lips pouted for a moment. Then a gleam of interest showed in his eyes.

"You got a hang-up about it. Right?"

"I suppose so," I said.

He was involved again.

"It's amazing, the hang-ups people can get," he said. "You know, I had a girl up here last week wouldn't fuck except with a condom? I *told* her I had a vasectomy, but it didn't do any good. I had to go out to an all-night drugstore on Third to buy a condom."

"People can be weird," I said. "I'm certainly weird about giving head, I guess. I just don't like to do it."

"I count on a nice head job to get started," he said in an aggrieved tone. "Why, *everybody* gives head these days."

"Not Alice," I said.

He sighed. "All right. I have to respect your hang-ups." He looked at me. "You ought to work on it, though. You know? I got rid of *my* hang-ups. I set myself a primary goal of working through them, and I *worked* at it. I even did the gay thing a couple of times, just to prove to myself I wasn't totally hetero."

He was still watching me hopefully. "So just a taste. Take Him in your mouth, you don't have to do anything, just feel It grow."

"I'm afraid not," I said, almost regretfully in the face of his lingering hope.

"All right," he sighed. "I just hope you're not counting on a really creative lay. It takes two people without any hang-ups between them to create a really great lay."

Mercifully, he stopped talking. He leaned over my hips. Putting his nose against my pubic hair, he sniffed deeply.

"Nice," he said. "What's that perfume?"

"It's European. It's not sold over here."

"Thought I hadn't smelled it before." He raised his head to gaze at me. "Fine funky smell, Alice, but *clean*. My mouth is watering for a taste, now that I've got your funk in my head."

"That's nice," I said.

He quit talking. Carefully he parted the lips, touched the tip of his tongue to the clitoris. He flicked it once, twice, drew the clitoris momentarily into his mouth. The expression on his face suggested he was savoring a new wine. He smiled in appreciation.

"Ah, yes," he said. "You're going to get a great head job. One of my best."

He was expert, he was indefatigable, and very quickly he had me writhing. He concentrated totally on the stimulation of my sensuality, as though giving a great head job was the end-all of the universe. His tongue probed skillfully into crevices I wouldn't have believed it could reach. He practiced a delicate brutality with his teeth on the naked clitoris until he had me moaning in ecstasy and screaming in not-quite-consummated pain.

When he stopped, I was limp. Solemnly, as benediction, he kissed me. I could smell and taste myself on his mouth.

"Is that great head, or is that great head?" he demanded complacently.

I reached to grasp his cock. He had got to me so deeply that, half-limp or not, only a cock could complete me. It had been so long since Stavros; years longer since a different man.

In a way, I thought, I suppose Herb was right. I *am* divorced. Not from Stavros. From my island self.

Herb was gently fucking my hand. "You know, of course, that you're being quite ego-centered about the whole thing," he said. "You must realize you're not *giving* anything."

His cock was more erect, but still not very hard. But It was the only cock in town. At least for right now. I tried to pull him over me.

"You'll have to get on top," he said, judiciously. "He's not hard enough yet."

All right. I would get on top. And I would give him something, all right. I'd fuck him down to the bone.

Carefully I seated myself, holding It poised with my hand from behind. It curled softly, not even penetrating. I began to rock back and forth. He lay passively, his hands stroking my thighs.

I was, I realized, moving to the beat of the music. I began to vary the rhythm, off-beat and then on again. Pleasant, rather sweet, to feel his softness against my female softness.

His palms pressed against my thighs. The cock began to stiffen, going deeper with each downthrust of my loins. I felt It push through that inner doorway, stricking into hot softness. Herb groaned. His eyes were open now. The quickening was also in the eyes.

He remained passive, though good-hard now, the head more bulbous than I had expected. I could feel the swelling head; soon It would pump into me, and we would come together, rounded, finished, a creative whole. Herb dotes on creative wholes, I thought feverishly. Because, God, it was good.

Just when I was ready for orgasm, Herb, without withdrawing, rolled us over. He was on top, now, snugly in me, and he was stroking, not hard but deep, and It was driving me wild.

"Of course you know I won't be able to come," Herb said calmly. "You didn't start me right. But I'll get *you* off."

He got me off. He was as expert at fucking as at giving head, now that he had an adequate hard-on. A series of short strokes, teasing the bulging head against the entrance where once the hymen had been, until I surged frantically; then giving me the deepness I desired, as vigorously as anyone could have desired. When I began to come he slowed the stroke deliberately, stretching out my orgasm as he eased me down from the heights. When we lay quiet, he still had the hard-on because, as promised, he had not come.

He looked into my face with a faint smile. "Good?"

"Oh, God, yes," I said.

He laughed. He was pleased with himself.

"Fucking is one of the most creative things a person can do," he said. "If you don't fuck well, you really can't build much of a life-style."

"You're silly," I said fondly. "But I like you. And I *love* your creative style of fucking."

He slapped me on the thigh with the flat of his hand. "All right. Option time."

"Option time?" I was puzzled.

"I told you I was into ass. Ass is my ultimate bag. Turn over."

I turned over, thinking of the first time with Stavros. *If you fuck a Greek,* he had told me, *you get fucked in the ass.* So I held no resistance against Herb's ultimate bag. He slid it deftly in, my ass already soft to receive him. It felt so marvelous. I arched back against him. I heard him gasp. I arched again, feeling him stiff now at last, stirred to action.

Herb Gloss lost his vaunted control.

God, how wildly he plunged and thrashed, his cock blunt and fierce. I got on hands and knees, the better to take It fully. He came in one great spurt, then plunged briefly again, even more uncontrollably, before coming the second time. Finally, after a slowing, an easing of the violence, he came once more, and it was finished.

He reached a disbeliving hand to touch the curve of my buttock.

"I don't care if you won't give head," he said fiercely. "That's the greatest ass I've ever had." He nodded with decision. "I don't ask many of my women to come back. But you simply must."

Rolling over on my back, I looked up. I had not realized, until now, there were stars painted silver against a deep blue. I smiled at the preposterous ceiling. Alice's first adventure into Wonderland had been a good one. It only made me eager for more.

Andy showed a gloomy face when he opened the door. So alert to his moods, I said, "What's the matter?"

"Nothing," he muttered, turning away. "Everything's just hunky-dory."

I put my arms around his waist. His distress was so evident, I didn't experience the familiar stir of desire the mere touching of his body could arouse.

"Come on, now. Something's wrong and I know it," I said. "Tell Mama."

So often I cherished and coddled the little boy in him. Even when it was directed against me.

"I've just got to go out and get a job, that's all."

"But, why?"

"Dad's cut off my allowance, that's why," he said resentfully.

"Why would he do that? He agreed to give you an allowance for a whole year, didn't he?"

"Yeah. He decided to break the agreement, that's all. Says I'm just wasting my time and his money. He wants me to come into his real estate office." He looked at me defiantly. "I'll kill myself before I'll sell real estate."

"Well, it's not so bad," I said, trying to cheer him up. "Everybody else carries a job on the side."

Only true. I was lucky in that I could make good money at my profession. The other actor-aspirants ran elevators, worked as short-order cooks and messenger boys; one, an older man, was the superintendent

*of an apartment building. The jobs were
counted temporary, a mere tedious step on
the road to stardom. One day it would look
great in program biography.*

*My comment, designed to cheer his
gloom, only drove Andy from despair into
arrogant anger.*

*"That's all right for them. They don't
have the talent I've got. Andy Glenn can't afford to waste a minute doing menial work.
I've got to concentrate totally to become the
actor I can be."*

*I made myself pause. Then I said,
"You've always said Andy can do whatever
Andy Glenn has to do, and that's why they
won't be able to stop you."*

*More rebellious anger. "I'm not going to
waste eight hours every day just to eat!"*

*"It's either that, or make peace with
your father."*

*"Yeah," he said gloomily. "Wind up fat
and dumb like my old man, thinking about
nothing but selling, no matter how you have
to lie to do it." Violently he threw out both
hands. "Just get that holy buck, that's all."*

*I put my arms around him again. "It'll
work out, Andy."*

*He stood stiff against my embrace.
Pushing my hips provocatively against him,
I said brightly, "Listen, I came over to get
laid. So how about it?"*

*Churlishly he said, "I don't want to get
laid. I want you to suck me off."*

*Now he was using it as a weapon to
keep us separate. Unhappiness moved
through me like a dark cloud.*

"Oh, Andy," I said in despair.

*"Well, it's you that makes it such a big
deal," he said harshly.*

I knew from bitter experience that, once

started, he wouldn't let go, like a child being denied Christmas. I might as well leave now.

An idea struck at me. The solution to everything, including the bitter quarrel that loomed in the offing.

"Listen," I said. "Why don't you move in with me?"

My voice faltered as I realized that Paul would have to know about Andy Glenn. I had kept secret the glorious fact that I was in love because I knew Paul would disapprove.

I firmed my resolution. Andy and I would be together day and night, almost as though we were married. I wouldn't have to get up out of the sweet lethargy of sated sex to walk home alone through the dark streets.

Andy was waiting, a light of interest in his eyes.

I mustered enthusiasm. "It'll be perfect. You won't have to worry about rent, and I make enough money for both of us."

He put his arms around me. "It's sweet of you to think of it, Alice. But . . ." He tightened his mouth. "I won't live off a woman. Not even you, Alice."

"Even if it means the difference between acting and not-acting?" I said. "Which is more important?"

He nodded seriously. "That's something to think about." He shook his head decisively. "No. A damn good idea, and it's damned generous of you. But I can't do it."

He was still holding me. I knew now that we would fuck. My idea had broken us through the gloom and the anger and the pending quarrel into a new ground of being. With a stab of happiness that made me dizzy, I groped my hand into his crotch. He had an erection.

"Andy," I said, melting against him.

"Andy, I love you so. I'd do anything in the world for you."

A stab of fear. Because his inevitable line would be: "Anything. Except one thing."

He didn't say it. Instead he stooped, lifted me, carried me to the narrow bed. Laying me down gently, with quick hands he threw up my skirt and stripped off my panties. Not waiting to shuck off the trousers, he took out his cock and stabbed It into me with a fierce love that made my senses swim.

A beautiful fucking, reminiscent of that first time on the dusty sofa in the acting studio. Halfway through, he put his face into my pussy and ate me through one orgasm after another until I was utterly depleted. Then, my body limp, he fucked me all over again. Only after we had finished did we take off our clothes so that we could lie naked against each other.

For three days I argued with Andy Glenn before he would consent to share my apartment and my earnings—and then only after he had worked one whole shift as a busboy.

"Have a good time last night?" Mark Judson inquired.

The remark roused in me an inexplicable anger. "So you're spying on me," I said. "Is that part of your job, too?"

Ignoring the anger, he nodded seriously. "I figured you were just about ready to jump the traces." His voice hesitated. "So I . . . I thought I'd keep an eye out. In case the photographers got onto you." He did not smile. "That was a pretty good idea, using the kitchen exit."

I stared. "It bothers you, doesn't it?" I said. "What I . . . did last night."

His face tightened. "Not my business, Alice. You

know that. I know it, too." He paused. "But it *is* my business to protect you as much as you'll let me. That's why you're paying me a ridiculous salary."

I turned away. "I don't want to be thinking, every minute I'm with somebody, that you might be watching." I whirled. "Where *were* you, anyway?"

He grinned. Briefly. "I was there. I even saw you turn down the Italian kid."

"Then you must be the original invisible man," I retorted. "To my certain knowledge, you were not inside that bar."

He grinned again. "I happen to know the bartender. I was sitting in a straight chair behind the curtain that leads into the liquor storeroom. After you went in, I knocked at the back door."

"Pretty damned sneaky."

The left-handed compliment pleased him, for God's sake. I pressed on: "How long have you been waiting for me to kick over the traces, as you put it?"

He looked abashed. "Had you figured pretty good. This was only the second time I staked you out."

"Just don't overdo the Mother Hen bit," I said crossly.

A curious expression moved in his face. Unable to read it, I turned away from the direct weight of his gaze.

"At least I'm out of the cloisters."

"The next test is whether you can walk out through the lobby," Mark said. "Let's try it now. Nobody down there when I came up."

I was interested. "What shall we do?"

"Take a walk," he said. "I like to walk in New York City."

"Let me get ready," I said eagerly.

I put on the wig, made up as Prince Albert had taught me, dressed in the clothes I had worn last night. When I emerged, Mark Judson said, "Remarkable. I never thought you could look like an ordinary woman."

A left-handed compliment; it pleased me.

I put my hand into the crook of his elbow. "Let us go forth," I said gaily. "Let us explore."

Because he would surely be recognized by the press, Mark let me go ahead. Passing through the lobby successfully, I turned toward downtown, strolling until Mark had caught up.

"Did you see him?" he chortled. "Walked right past him, and he didn't flicker an eyeball."

"Really?" I said. "I didn't see anyone who looked like a photographer."

"Chauncey Sparks . . . we call him 'Chancy'," Mark said, a happy lilt in his voice. "He's a real bird dog. He was sitting in his car two spaces beyond the canopy." He laughed again. "He didn't even look at your legs."

There's no city in the world like New York; a quickness in the air, a sense of excitement and expectancy, a feeling that one is successful simply because one is in New York.

So many years since I had walked these streets; it was like a new experience. The city had changed while I had been away. I was fascinated by the changes.

People dressed more casually than in my day. Blue jeans and checked shirts, a marching display of boots and moccasins and heavy country shoes. The girls, in particular, looked comfortable in pants suits and leather skirts—and, so often, the ubiquitous jeans.

There were, of course, many traditional suit-and-tie men, and smartly dressed women. But the net result was a far more variegated scene. Rather than adhering to a uniform fashion, as in my day, people expressed their individual selves by their dress.

A friendlier city, too, it seemed. People were not so self-enclosed. That concentrated New York hustle remained evident, of course, people hurrying intently in an urgent need to accomplish, to *do,* to get there.

I was startled to see an old woman huddled in layered rags against the wall of an office building. Her legs were bird-thin in tattered stockings. Her lips moved silently as she muttered to herself. Beside her was a stuffed plastic bag, clutched by one hand as though fearful someone would steal her possessions.

"They're called bag ladies," Mark said, noting my startled glance. "They carry everything they own with them."

"There were always bums in New York," I said. "But they were men."

"Now we have down-and-out women," Mark said grimly. "There are shelters, but they prefer the freedom of the streets."

"It's so sad," I said. "Something ought to be done."

"It is sad," Mark said. "Especially the way people ignore them, as though that's not another human being inside that pile of rags." He looked thoughtful. "Somehow, we feel we have to protect ourselves by not acknowledging them. If one did recognize their humanity, one would also have to accept the fact that it could happen to you, too."

We were walking slowly.

"In New York, failure is the great sin," he said. "If you fail—even if you run through a bad patch— you become a leper, as though your trouble might rub off on your friends." He moved his shoulders. "So . . . you have no friends. Until you're on the rise again."

"You speak as if you know from personal experience."

His face changed. "Believe me, I do." He turned suddenly. "There's something down this block you ought to see."

I knew he wanted to change the subject. I accepted the change, saying eagerly, "What is it?"

He eyed me. "A topless-bottomless bar."

I was puzzled. "You mean . . . waitresses who don't wear anything at all?"

He grinned. "Better than that. Come on."

It was a shabby place, floor littered with debris,

the small bar showing worn plastic. Pausing to adjust
my eyes, I saw a long room dominated by three large
circular tables, around each table a ring of flimsy
chairs.

On each table was a naked girl.

Mark, taking my arm, led me to the table nearest
the door. As we sat down, a waitress plopped down two
cans of beer. "Three dollars," she said. Mark gave her
three dollars.

The girl on the table, buxom and blond, picked
up a robe, put it on, and climbed down. Another girl
immediately took her place.

She was a redhead, her lean body showing a prominent rib cage. Immediately she went into a series of
gyrations—one could scarcely call it a dance—her
bare feet moving in time to the beat, her hips thrusting
forward the prominent red thatch of pubic hair.

She was very young. Her face expressionless, she
leaned back, putting down one hand to the tabletop for
balance, and suggestively advanced her crotch close to
a customer's face. As vacant of expression as she, the
man gazed intently at her gyrating cunt. Still bent
backward, she shifted tantalizingly to the next man.
Reaching with her free hand, she stroked the air as
though masturbating, writhing in simulated ecstasy.

Except for me, the customers were all male. Those
wearing overcoats had not taken them off, but sat with
hands in pockets. They gazed glassy-eyed at the naked
girl, waiting their turn.

The scene astonished me profoundly. No attempt
at a showbiz atmosphere; not the least creation of
theatrical illusion. The girl herself, with not even a
dusting of powder, much less body makeup, looked as
ordinary as someone working behind a counter. She
scarcely pretended to artful dancing; she concentrated
on thrusting her naked bottom into one face after another, close enough to touch.

A crude presentation of the naked female sex
organ. That, and nothing more. And the barroom was

packed. I noticed a bouncer circulating, keeping a watchful eye. Maybe once in a while, I thought, a customer gets carried away and tries to touch a girl.

Impassively intent, they had not noticed that a female customer was now one of them. The girl had noticed; I caught the flash of her eye. Picking up the can of beer, I drank. Awful beer, a brand I had never heard of.

Suddenly the girl, skipping several men, was before me. The lips of her cunt were parted to show the inner structure, pink and healthy-looking. Suddenly, pushing it out, then rapidly sucking it in, she popped her cunt in my face. I was startled. She popped it again, only inches away, watching intently for my reaction.

Uncomfortable, wanting only to get out of there, I held still. She reached down her hand. This time she actually touched herself, trailing one finger through the gaping slit, writhing with fake passion as she did so. The bouncer was suddenly standing behind me. I looked up. He scowled at the girl. Perhaps she had broken a rule of the establishment by touching herself.

Shifting, she presented her bottom to Mark for his edification. A faint smile showed on his face.

"Nice," he said to her. "Nicest one I've seen all day."

Quickly she left him for the next man. Mark turned to me. "Seen enough?"

"Let's go," I said.

Mark rose, pulled out my chair. Immediately two waiting customers slid into the vacated seats.

At the door, I turned. The girl was standing erect now, grinding her hips slowly. When she saw me turn, she smiled. A secret, enigmatic smile, strangely disturbing. I followed Mark to the sidewalk. The sunlight was too bright.

"Well?"

"Incredible," I said. "How much do you have to pay to see her naked like that?"

"Pay?" he echoed. "The price of a beer. That's all."

I was incredulous. "You mean, not even an admission fee? You'd think it would be at least five dollars."

He laughed. "Buy a beer, see a cunt. They can't even sell liquor. The city is doing its best to close down those places, so they took away their liquor license."

I was thoughtful. "It would be better if they had to pay. I don't know why. But it would."

"I don't see what difference it makes."

I was intense about it. "Okay, maybe, given today's culture, a girl might have to exploit her body. That's nothing new. But so *nakedly,* without theatrical artifice . . . for the price of a *beer.* That's really reducing the female body to nothing. It should, at the least, fulfill a need. I couldn't see that the customers were even enjoying it, much less getting something out of it . . ." I stopped talking to look at Mark. "You go to those places, don't you? What do *you* get out of it?"

He began walking on. He was not dodging the question; he was thinking about it.

"Mostly, I think, my desire—my need—to know this town," he said at last. "Ever since I came to work on the *Times,* I've prowled these streets, frequented these bars. I go to Ryan's to listen to the old jazzmen, I go to O'Lunney's and the Lone Star Cafe for the country music, I frequent Carnegie Hall and Madison Square Garden. I'm in the Village at least once a week. I used to do Harlem, but it's too dangerous now for a white man. I go to literary cocktail parties, and artists' parties with cheese and Chianti." He laughed. "There isn't much I don't know about New York . . . though it's a city you can never hope to know in its entirety."

He paused, both in talk and in step. "Or maybe I'm just kidding myself. Maybe, like those other men, I enjoy looking at a naked cunt."

"It's all so sad, isn't it?" I said.

"Me?" he said. "Yes. I guess so. Whatever my reasons for doing whatever I do."

I had disturbed him. "No, I meant the bag ladies. I meant that girl displaying herself for the price of a beer."

"What's the difference between me and them?" Mark said. "Or *you* and them? It's only the pursuit of happiness that's guaranteed in the Constitution of the United States, not happiness itself."

"Would we be happy if it were?"

"Probably not." He paused. "I've even quit thinking of happiness as my birthright, like most Americans seem to do. I don't expect, anymore, to be particularly happy."

"I guess I do," I said softly.

We walked on silently for several very long blocks.

Safe again in the apartment, I challenged him. "So you claim to know New York. What are you going to show me next?"

Mark laughed. "Serendipity is sort of nice, you know. Just let it happen."

"No," I said. "Serendipity I can do on my own."

"All right." He considered. "For example only, I'm not recommending it, I know a very wealthy man with a very beautiful townhouse who holds a very splendid orgy every Friday night because he likes to watch people fuck."

I looked at him. "You've been there?"

"Several times."

The idea of Mark Judson in orgy was startling. Somehow I couldn't picture it . . . his countenance surely would remain sad, his eyes would yet be watchful. How could he participate and not-participate at once?

"I've never been to an orgy," I said. "Does one . . . have to take an active part?"

"It's everybody into his own thing," Mark said. "You can watch, or you can let it all hang out. Strictly off the wall. The only rule, no hideaway fucking; that's cheating."

I braced myself mentally. Somehow, I would rather have gone alone. But . . . I wanted to go.

"Will you take me?"

"Next Friday," he promised.

Friday was three days away.

Living with Andy was wonderful—except for the silent disapproval of Paul and Zella Riff. Neither of my two mentors said anything directly, though Andy and I were sharing an apartment Paul had let me have at a very low rental. The only perceptible change was that their boys no longer came racing up the stairs, yelling, "Alice! Alice! Are you home? We've come to play with you!" Quietly, Zella prevented her children from seeing me living with a man who was not my husband.

Paul ignored the presence of Andy Glenn. I suppose he considered my love life out of bounds even for his all-encompassing mentorship. Or, perhaps, he simply didn't know how to cope with the situation. However, he, too, quit coming upstairs for our strategy sessions; calling on the phone, he would ask me to come down instead.

Other than that small cloud, I wallowed in happiness. Waking in the night, I could put out my hand and know that my man was beside me. I adored his early-morning grouchiness—he always said actors should sleep till noon, anyway—and I quickly learned he awoke in a better mood with the smell of fresh-made coffee in the air.

And, dear God, the fucking! We shared love in all the flavors of late night and early morning, long, leisurely Sunday afternoon

fucks, urgent quickies grabbed between act-
ing class and a modeling assignment.

No longer, as in the beginning, that devastating feeling that this might be the last
one, so we had to grab it all at once in one
great dedication of lust and energy. He
was there. I was there. All the busy day I
could carry the internal message: at four
o'clock, five, whenever I get home, we will
fuck.

Andy wasn't the greatest roommate in
the world; he dropped his clothes where he
took them off and if I didn't pick up after
him, they stayed where they fell. He was always running out of clean shirts because he
couldn't remember to take them to the laun-
dry. Often I hastily washed out a shirt in the
kitchen sink, dried it in the oven and ironed
it, so he would look reasonably presentable.
And, one must admit, Andrew Glenn talked
interminably about Andy Glenn. It was as
though he had to spin out in words the
fantasies of fame in order to make them possible realities.

Not a good roommate. But a better lover with every passing day. He could be tender, he could be rough; small angers were followed by a boisterous rowdiness that often
left me breathless. Andy lived on a trapeze
of emotions. The smallest setback could put
him down, the least victory elate him into a
wild euphoria.

He loved to fuck. Sometimes he came at
me with the abruptness of a rapist, the hardness of his cock so swiftly into me it would
hurt in my unreadiness. Then again it might
go gently, Andy lying against me, his tender
hand stroking my breast, down my belly,
across the mount all the way to my knees,

*stroking until I would beg him to put It in
me before I died of longing.*

Sometimes he fucked silently. At other
times, he talked all the way through it:
"Where did I get a beautiful woman like
Alice, God, you're so lovely, you could have
any man you wanted, so how does Andy get
loved by Alice?" On and on, murmuring in
astonishment and pleasure as though he had
only in this moment discovered me, and as
he talked his cock stroked gently, persistently, until, fingernails clawing at his back, I
was drawn as taut as a bowstring. But I
wouldn't let myself come until I felt him
coming, even though I had to have it; then
he would come, I would come with him, and
it was so wonderful that I would have to cry.

There remained forever the continual
problem; when would I consent to go down
on the Thing I claimed to love so greatly?
But somehow, living in my apartment and
on my earnings, Andy didn't press the issue
in such reckless rages as before.

Money was another problem. It was tak-
en for granted by both of us that he didn't
need to seek a job because Andy Glenn, to
become the star he was destined to be, must
devote total attention to his career. After all,
we decided solemnly, I made our living at my
career, so it was all right for me to work. His
implicit assumption that I would never be an
actress caused me a deep and silent hurt.

But it was like pulling molars to get
Andy to take actual cash money. When I
asked if he needed money, he would reply
poutishly, "Oh, I can get along." If I pressed
it upon him, he would often become angry
enough to slap away my hand.

Finally I learned to put a few dollars,
every day or so, into his pants pocket while

he was asleep. That manner of giving he could accept without protest. As for his school expenses, prudently I made arrangements directly with Raskin Wells, so Andy wouldn't have to give it a thought.

Andy's wardrobe, when he came to me, consisted of three pairs of khaki pants, five pairs of dingy-gray Jockey shorts, and six shirts. Not a sock or a handkerchief to his name. I learned his sizes so I could buy new shirts to replace his worn ones, pocket handkerchiefs, socks, pajamas, once, even, a rather expensive suit and a tie to match. Even proud Andy could not refuse such gifts from such great love.

A wonderful time. Perhaps so marvelously idyllic in memory because it was so unmercifully brief.

For, too soon, the day arrived when I had to say to him: "Darling. I'm pregnant."

Though, in my soul, I was sure from the first indication, I nursed the secret for a week until there could be no doubt. I had never, like most girls, daydreamed about having babies. Now I contemplated in awe the miracle that Andy's baby was growing inside me. I hugged myself secretly, as I would hug the baby when it came, in a broth of delicious fulfillment.

I gave the news to my lover with great serenity. We would, I considered complacently, have to get married now. It would make things a bit tougher, naturally; but I would work as long as possible, to save enough money to tide us over. There's always, I thought smugly, maternity clothes to be modeled. I'd be absolutely beautiful as a pregnant woman. A pregnant wife.

"What?" Andy said, scowling.

"*I'm a week overdue,*" *I said.*

I couldn't read the expression in his eyes. It looked as if he were frightened.

"*What's a week?*" *he muttered.* "*You'll come around.*"

"*I'm* never *late,*" *I said.* "*Andy, I can feel your baby inside me.*"

Still scowling, he sat down on the bed.

"*I know about a guy over in Jersey,*" *he said.* "*It'll cost five hundred dollars. Have you got five hundred?*"

The words, so casual yet so brutal, struck death into my soul.

"*Andy. You don't mean it,*" *I said passionately.*

He stood up. "*We can't have a baby,*" *he said flatly.*

The words moved me to anger. "*We can't* not *have it, now that we've made it!*"

He stared at me. I stared at him.

I softened. "*Andy, I want to have your baby,*" *I said.* "*I want us to be married and have the baby and live together forever and ever. Can't you see how wonderful it will be?*"

His eyes were inscrutable. It was as though he had never seen me before, much less ejaculated into my receiving womb his living sperm. So much sperm, I thought hysterically, gallons and gallons of it, and just one brave little sperm, out of those millions, struggled successfully to fertilize the waiting egg. It was not only a miracle. It was fate, that could not be denied.

Andy Glenn denied it. Without another word, he walked out of the room. He did not slam the door behind him, but closed it gently.

I had an assignment. I got dressed and went to work. It was a long and tiring day, for I had nothing to carry me except the hope of seeing Andy again when I was through.

Even that sustaining thought was an illusion. When I climbed wearily up the stairs, it was only to find that he had removed all trace of himself from the apartment. Including, I saw without feeling, the presents I had bought so happily. It was as though Andrew Glenn had never lived there. Or in me—except for the irrefutable evidence of the foetus alive in my aching womb.

One week I waited for Andy to come back. Then I threw my pride into the garbage can and went to see Raskin Wells. His office was a tiny room, like something out of the eighteenth century with the wooden chairs and the rolltop desk.

I sat in the straight chair, hands clasped in my lap to keep them from trembling.

"Do you know where I can find Andy Glenn?"

A gleam flickered in Raskin's eyes; he had observed us holding hands in class.

He did not answer. Instead, he said accusingly, "You've been missing class. For a week."

"I'm sorry," I said. "But I need to know where I can find Andy."

It was a long time before he spoke. Then, turning away to his desk, he said, "He's gone."

"Gone?" I said stupidly. The single word rang in my head. "Gone where?"

"He told me he was going to Los Angeles," Raskin said indifferently. "A man walked up to Andy on the street, said, 'You're an actor, aren't you?' When Andy acknowledged the canard—" Raskin's lips

twisted wryly "—*the fellow handed him a card and said, 'When you get out to Hollywood, look me up.' Andy said he braced the guy with, 'Next week or next year?' and the guy said, 'Anytime you can make it, baby. Because you have got it.'*"

Raskin paused. "That's what Andy said *happened.* Not very likely, is it?" He moved his hands. "When he came by, he was on his way to get his clothes. He meant to hitchhike to the Coast."

I stood up. "Thank you, Raskin," I said, and turned to leave.

Raskin said from behind me, "Are you dropping the class?"

I looked back. "No," I said. "I won't skip again. I promise."

I could feel every ounce of my weight as I forced myself up the stairs to the empty apartment on the top floor. My key was in the lock when I heard the phone ring.

I knew it would not be Andy Glenn. And yet—I was gasping when I said, "Hello?"

Paul Riff. His voice was singing. "So you finally got home! Come down, come down, come down immediately."

Wearily I went back down the stairs. Paul waited in the open door. He was beaming.

"We've got it, kid!" were his first words. Behind him, Zella's kindly black face was showing a broad smile.

"Got what?" I said indifferently.

"The *assignment,*" Paul Riff chortled. "The big one that's going to make all the difference. Come on in so I can tell you about it. I thought you'd never get home!"

Numbly I entered. I sat in a chair.

Again my hands were folded in my lap.

Paul, so keyed up, didn't notice my still-ness; Zella, however, was eying me appre-hensively.

"Life *magazine,*" Paul burbled. "Includ-ing *a* cover. Alice photographed against the Great Bridges of the World, with Harris O'Brien, the great novelist, along to write great prose to go along with the great bridges and great Alice."

I sat mute.

Paul was nonplused. "Can't you see it? Life *magazine.* Halsband, the great **Life** photographer. Harris O'Brien. And Alice!"

I sat mute.

He was leaning toward me now in his eagerness. Looming behind him, Zella was quiet, foreboding.

"You'll be traveling for weeks, all over the world. And, once the spread appears, you'll be made. Everybody will know how beautiful Alice is, you'll be considered for all the big assignments, we can pick and choose, start thinking about a role in a play, maybe Hollywood . . ."

He stopped. "Alice. Don't you want it?"

"What's the trouble, girl?" Zella said quietly.

So I wouldn't have to see Paul's face, I looked at her.

"Your man's gone, ain't he?"

I nodded. I could not speak.

"I don't care about that," Paul said rapidly. "You can't let it throw you, kid. Not now, for God's sake!"

"Shut up, Paul," Zella said. "Quit throwing words at the girl like they were rocks."

Paul gazed at her in male bewilder-ment. Zella came to put her hand on my shoulder. "If your soul ain't warm for it, you ought to pass on it," she said. "You wouldn't be good enough."

I took a deep breath. I looked at it. Bleakly. But I did look.

"I want to do it," I said. "I will do it." I looked to Paul again. "But you've got to do something for me first."

"Anything, kid," he said fervently. "Just name it."

My throat was tight. It didn't want to let the words happen.

"Before I can take off around the world, Paul, you'll have to arrange for me to get rid of my baby."

Friday came. With it, Mark Judson dressed for an orgy.

The first time I had seen him without a suit and tie. He wore a soft blue cashmere sports jacket, an open-collared shirt, snowy white, slacks cut with slash pockets in the western style. The cut of the trousers made him look slimly cowboyish. On his feet were boots that looked as though made of glove leather.

"My, aren't we elegant tonight!" I said.

He grinned. "Keep working for you long enough, I might become the Beau Brummell of the seventies. Never owned a cashmere coat before in my life."

"I *love* the way those slacks look on you," I said. "Even though you've forced me to change my plans entirely."

He was alarmed. "Now, listen, you *can't* go as Alice!"

"I know. But I can do a *little* better."

I did a little better . . . and added a bit of prudent protection. A pants suit, quite plain, even rather mannish. But the fabric was soft enough to lay gently against my body.

Mark whistled softly. "I just don't know about that outfit," he murmured.

"Even with the wig?"

"Even with the wig."

"I refuse to be upstaged by my escort," I protested.

"All right," he said dubiously. "But . . . we'd better take the back way out."

An old brick townhouse, painted white, tall and narrow. The architectural details—the fanlight over the front door, the carvings on the façade—were superb.

The man greeting us was small-bodied, neatly built. His face so tiny under the great bald dome of his head, he looked like a pale-skinned gnome. Round thick-lensed glasses enhanced the effect. His hand felt both delicate and strong as he took mine, murmuring, "So glad you could come, my dear. I shall look forward to seeing you in action."

There was no formal presentation of names.

The interior was another surprise. Little real furniture; cushions were piled in what seemed to be random heaps. Random people, too, most of them lying in clusters on the cushions. I was disappointed that no one—at least within sight of the front hall—was naked.

The host gestured toward the stairs. "There are four floors of action," he said, chuckling. "Choose your own level. Bar's in the kitchen." He wandered away as casually as he had greeted us.

"Drink?" Mark asked.

"Yes, I think so."

Mark and I were rather clinging to each other, I thought as we went into the kitchen. Did he act like this when he came alone? He seemed rather shy. Or, I thought, maybe it's me clinging to him.

A barman in a white jacket gave us scotches. The host came hurrying back.

"I almost forgot," he said anxiously. "I hope you don't smoke. I can't bear the smell of cigarette smoke in the house. It lingers for days."

"What is *that* smell, then?" I asked.

A strong, acrid odor.

The host looked surprised. "That's pot," he said. "Pot's just fine, smoke all you want. But no tobacco, *please*, unless you have a real habit and can't help yourself."

I assured him I didn't smoke and, relieved, he hurried away. I looked at Mark. He was laughing.

"Anything else you want, too," he said. He indicated a small crystal bowl on the dining table. It held a few spoonfuls of a substance that looked like fine sugar. "How about a sniff of cocaine?"

"I think not," I said judiciously. "I *would* like to try marijuana, though." I felt a stroke of anxiety. "Or is that a good idea, under the circumstances?"

"Supposed to heighten sexual sensation," he said. "All it does for me is make me sleepy." He paused. "Want a joint?"

"I'll try anything once," I said bravely. Hastily I added, "Except the hard stuff."

"Come on, then."

In the living room, he took a lumpy cigarette, twisted tightly at both ends, from an ivory cigarette box. He indicated we were to recline on a set of cushions. I sat down, looking about the room.

Not a very exciting scene . . . quiet conversation in groups, and nobody had their clothes off. But nicely intimate. A decorous intimacy.

"Light up," Mark said. He put the cigarette between my lips and struck a match. "Inhale deep, and hold it."

I obeyed instructions. The smoke, unexpectedly harsh, cut acridly into the lining of my throat. I coughed, exploding the smoke out of my system.

"My God, it's bad!" I said. I couldn't stop coughing. Two or three people had raised up to look. Someone laughed.

"That, my dear, is the very best seedless leaf from Oaxaca," Mark said indignantly. "Thackeray West never has anything but." He reached up to the table. "Here. Try this."

A rose-colored plastic pipe with strangely placed holes. He set the cigarette upright in the tiny bowl, showed me how to stop the holes with my fingers.

"You can take in as much or as little air as you like," he said. "Ought to go better that way."

I tried it . . . carefully. Better, but I still coughed. Suddenly the smoke swirled into my brain, fogging it pleasantly. I could feel myself smiling at nothing at all.

My time-sense was altered, too. There was all the time in the world in which to look at my companion. *My paid companion,* I thought, giggling. I watched Mark pick up his drink, swallow from it. I hadn't noticed, before, that his Adam's apple moved when he swallowed. I was fascinated by the beautiful rhythm.

"Does my Adam's apple move when I drink?" I asked him. "Watch and see."

"You don't have an Adam's apple," Mark said solemnly. "But your throat moves. Everybody's throat moves."

I tried another puff. The pipe had gone out. Mark struck another match. I didn't take in as much air this time. I coughed.

"Drink again," I commanded.

While he drank, I put the tip of my index finger on his Adam's apple. "Don't stop," I said. "Let me feel it."

"Do I have to chug-a-lug?" Mark complained.

"You have a lovely Adam's apple," I said.

Mark looked at me. Mark looked away.

"Want a puff?" I asked.

"*Toke* is the word," he said. "No. That stuff just makes me sleepy."

Contentedly I toked on the pipe. We had closed in on ourselves. Remembering the others, I looked to see what they were doing.

"This is a very sedate orgy," I complained. "Nobody's naked."

"There are four circles to Thackeray's inferno," Mark intoned. "This is the first circle, for those who are chicken."

There was occasional kissing, the touch of a breast. One woman had her hand boldly on a man's thigh.

"Are you implying that I'm chicken?" I asked.

"No," he said. "I am."

"Well, I'm not." I got to my feet. Astonishingly difficult. Necessary to concentrate on balance. I swayed, my head swimming. "I'm good for the second circle, anyway." I looked down. "Come with me, Mark?"

"I told you. I'm chicken," Mark murmured. He laughed. "So I'm waiting for the *giant* chicken. Remember that joke?"

I didn't know what he was talking about. I threaded my way through the body-cluttered living room, stopped at the foot of the stairs to look up.

A very young, very naked girl walked carefully down the steps. She was red-haired, top and bottom. She was, I recognized immediately, the girl I had watched displaying her cunt in the bar. She didn't recognize me; her eyes were like the stone eyes of a statue. She had her hand on the doorknob when Thackeray appeared.

"No, dear," he said gently. "No nakedness in the streets, remember."

He put his hands on her hips, turned her around. Obediently, like a wind-up toy, she marched back up the stairs.

"Stoned out of her gourd," Thackeray said, watching her ass appreciatively. "Just out of it, that's all."

I gazed at Thackeray. His features dimmed, brightened, dimmed again. It seemed quite natural to ask the question.

"Do you really like to watch people fuck, like Mark Judson said?"

"It's lovely to watch people fuck," he said. "Don't you like my grass? I always have the best of everything."

"Don't you fuck yourself?" The semantics got tangled in my head. "I don't mean fuck-yourself, I mean . . ."

He looked at me as though I had issued an invitation. "I'm impotent, my dear," he said. "I haven't had It in a woman but once in my life."

"Oh," I said. "I'm sorry."

As if he had told me someone near and dear had died. Amazing how people, in this new New York, seemed anxious to talk about the most extraordinarily personal things. And willing to include the intimate details.

Which Thackeray West was now doing.

"My analyst explained that I have this guilt thing about fucking Mother," he said apologetically. "Fucking any woman, to me, is fucking Mother. With the guilt, it's impossible to maintain an erection." He gestured. "These little orgies were my analyst's suggestion, actually. Experiencing other people's sex lives, he thinks, will eventually make me realize, emotionally as well as intellectually, that fucking is a natural event. Under certain circumstances, like, for example, finding yourselves the last man and last woman on earth, with the duty of perpetuating the human species, it would be a virtue, actually, to fuck Mother. It's entirely situational." He nodded, savoring the word. "Situational."

"But it doesn't work?"

He shook his head regretfully. "Emotionally I can't accept situational ethics. But I will, I'm sure. He's a very good analyst. He loves these dos, himself. He's here tonight, as a matter of fact."

"But what do you *do?*" I asked.

It seemed a perfectly proper inquiry.

"I masturbate," he said quietly. "Quite a lot, actually." He smiled. "I'm a very highly sexed person, you see." He looked at me. "Are you thinking about participating tonight? I'd love to watch you fuck."

"I don't see *anybody* fucking," I said. "In the

living room, it looks like an ordinary cocktail party, except everybody's on the floor."

"People must be given an opportunity to adjust," he said seriously. "My analyst and I worked it out carefully. Actually, if I see somebody getting into action on the first floor, I shoo them right upstairs. There, on the different levels, a person can find everything his heart desires. Or, rather, his body." He peered anxiously. "But don't do anything you don't want to do, dear. That's a basic rule."

"I won't," I promised, and started to climb.

At the first landing, a man leaned against the wall. "Want a toke?" He thrust a half-smoked joint at me. Short, it was held in a sort of clip.

"Oh, yes, lovely," I said. Greedily I inhaled the harsh smoke. I didn't cough this time.

Reluctantly, I passed it to him. He toked deeply, held in the smoke, let it out slowly.

"Good stuff," he said. "The best."

"Yes, so I've heard."

He finished the joint. Politely he asked, "May I undress you?"

It seemed a perfectly reasonable request. "If you wish."

Careful not to touch flesh with his fingers, he unbuttoned the flimsy-textured coat and took off the blouse. He worked slowly, enjoying himself. He was put off by the bra. Leaving it, he knelt to take off my shoes. Then he unzipped the pants and, very slowly, pushed them down to my ankles. When he finished he was panting, as though he had run a long mile.

"Thank you," he said. "That was very nice indeed."

"Aren't you going to strip me naked?"

"Good God, no," he said, his voice shuddering.

I considered a new problem. "Where can I put my clothes so they'll be safe?"

"I keep them." He indicated a stack of female clothing folded neatly in a corner. "I'll be here to dress you when you're ready to leave." He scanned my face anxiously. "If I may."

"Yes," I said. "Of course."

I began to explore. This floor was three large rooms, furnished with mattresses and cushions. The striped mattresses looked plebeian.

People were naked here. People were fucking. First in view was an intricate triad, the woman on the bottom, lying on her belly, a man's cock thrusting into her arched cunt. On his back another man, fucking him in the ass. They moved in an attuned rhythm.

"Nice sandwich," Thackeray West said into my ear. "They always find each other. They often look for a fourth, but it doesn't seem to work out too well with another person."

He moved to sit on the floor near them, watching intently. His eyes were magnified through his thick glasses.

I walked on down the short hallway. A man, naked except for a cutaway coat with very long tails and a tall hat—both rusty with age—emerged from the bathroom. He presented an enormous erection for my titillation.

"I'm the Mad Hatter," he announced. "But I can't find Alice anywhere."

He was also enormously drunk.

"I'm Alice," I said.

Tottering heel-and-toe, he studied me with swimming eyes. "Then I'm supposed to fuck you."

I felt an impulse to touch his cock with my hand. A lovely erection he was showing, shiny, vein-ribbed, turgid.

"But you're awfully tall for Alice," he added doubtfully.

"Well, Alice gets smaller and Alice gets larger," I said. "Or is that the other book?"

"You *sure* you're Alice?" he persisted. "There must be no mistake. The Mad Hatter is *mad* about fucking Alice. That's the secret sexual fantasy Charles

Dodgson communicated through Lewis Carroll. *He* wanted to fuck Alice, so everybody in the book wants to fuck Alice. They do, too, each and every one."

"Not in the version I read," I said.

"It's all there," he said earnestly. "You only have to understand the secret code." He began stroking the erection with his left hand. "The Mad Hatter is saving this one for Alice," he said. "So I have to be sure, you see, before I let you have It."

"I'm Alice," I said. "So let me have It."

It was a lovely erection; I wanted very much to be fucked as Alice by the Mad Hatter.

He peered at me uncertainly. "You're pretty old for Alice, too," he said.

"Alice gets older and Alice gets younger," I said carefully. "Just like she gets larger and smaller. To fit the situation."

I held my breath, wondering if he would buy this editorial alteration.

He nodded soberly. "Yeah. I forgot about that. Come on."

He led me to a vacant mattress. I laid down. My head was swimming, but everything seemed sharp and real. He kneeled between my legs, his great cock thrusting. I put my hands on It as, catching at my panty hose with both hands, he stripped me naked.

He leaned forward. I arched my back, straining my lustful pussy upward, trembling to feel It enter.

He came, a great flood spurting on my belly.

"Shit," he said, "it happens every time." He looked at me pitiously. "Do you think the Mad Hatter will *ever* get to fuck Alice?"

I could feel the stickiness hardening on my belly. The terrible disappointment was like a heavy stone in my body.

"Not tonight, anyway," I said.

He stood up, cock dangling placidly, and took off the tailed coat. Folding it carefully, he placed it across my hips. He balanced the hat on top of the coat. He walked away.

I lay wilted, incomplete. This is really a bitch, I thought. A girl can't even give it away at this damned inept orgy. I wanted another marijuana cigarette. I didn't have the strength to go looking for one.

A muscular woman stopped beside me. Swinging one thick leg, she stood straddling my body. "Waiting for Old Marge?" she asked. I had an idea she was making her voice deeper than its natural pitch.

"Are you Old Marge?"

"Yes."

"I'm not waiting for Old Marge," I said.

She shrugged, walked away.

A wispy little man sat beside me. "Care for a sniff?" He proffered an elegantly chased silver snuffbox, a tiny spoon.

"What is it?" I asked.

He looked at me oddly. "Snow," he said. "Coke. What the hell do you think it is?"

Something funny about his nose; the flanges were red, and almost transparent. They didn't look as though they belonged to his face.

"What's the matter with your nose?"

He looked offended. "What business is it of yours?" he said nastily, getting up and walking away.

I sighed, rolling my head from one side to the other. People all about me were actively enjoying sex. But nobody seemed to be interested in Alice. I wondered if Mark Judson had yet risen above the first floor.

I said out loud, "If there's a man in the house, I'd like to get fucked."

No one looked at me. Sighing again, I curled on my side, pulling a pillow against my stomach. My head was still dizzy but I quickly became drowsily content.

"Before you mellow out completely, may I have my hat and coat, please?" the Mad Hatter said above me.

I struggled to sit up. The coat was tangled around my legs. I had somehow crushed the hat.

"What do you want them for?"

"I've found the true Alice," he said. Bitterly he added, "You weren't Alice, after all. You fooled me."

"I wish *I* could find the true Alice," I said wistfully. "Will you show her to me?"

"No," he said. "My hat and coat. *Please.*"

I hugged the coat with both arms. "You can't have them until you bring me some marijuana."

He stared petulantly. He went away. He came back, to hand me a joint already glowing. I inhaled recklessly.

"I suppose I really shouldn't blame *you*," he said. "Everybody gets fooled all the time."

"They certainly do," I said in a heartfelt tone. Tenderly, I added, "Sit down, share the joint with me."

He sat down. He took the joint, puffed awkwardly —apparently he drank instead of smoking—and coughed worse than I had in the beginning.

"Good boy," I said, and placed the crushed hat on his head.

He looked at me gratefully. "Can I have the coat, too?"

"You must pay a ransom first," I said. "Lie down."

He obeyed docilely. Leaning over him. I blew a mouthful of smoke into his mouth, sealed it in with my lips.

I drew away. "You're a lovely Mad Hatter," I said. "With a lovely mad cock."

I reached to grasp It in my hand. Limp as It was, It was still enormous. I teased the long foreskin over the head, pressed it back again.

"Don't do that," he said. "You're not Alice."

"I *am* Alice," I said. I took a deep toke. Again, mouth to mouth, I shared the smoke.

"With the true Alice, I wouldn't lose it too soon," he said dreamily. "I'd just fuck her and fuck her, and Alice's cunt would get small around me, then it would get big, and between small and large it'd last for hours. Because time changes in Wonderland, too, doesn't it? Time changes all the time."

"Yes," I said. I stroked It with my hand. "Yes." I stroked again. "Yes. Yes. Yes."

It was quickening mightily.

"I always know it's not Alice when I ejaculate prematurely," he said. "I realize I was fooled again."

"I wasn't Alice, that first time," I said. "But I'm Alice now. So everything will be fine."

"But I already lost it," he said plaintively.

"It's coming back," I assured him.

The joint was scorching my fingers. I crushed it out on the floor, then slid down the length of his body. I tilted his cock toward my mouth. Gazing upon It, I hesitated, remembering there was something about this. Sensually dazed as I was, I couldn't catch the memory. So I put my mouth fiercely, greedily, on It, sucking hard until he moaned.

Using one hand to tilt It into position, I threw one leg across his hips. Doubling both knees, he braced It up into me. I leaned forward, hands on his chest, and began fucking with a movement not too rapid; I was afraid he would, again, lose it too quickly. I can't stand it, I thought, if I don't get mine this time. The Mad Hatter gazed placidly into my face, giving me as good as he got. His cock thudded into me so huge and thrusting it made me gasp.

"Wonderful," Thackeray West said. "Wonderful."

Without breaking the rhythm, I turned my head. Squatting on his heels, Thackeray, his cock exposed through the trouser fly, was matching the beat of his fist to the rhythm of my ass. I quickened as the Mad-Hatter cock began to throb. All three of us came at the same instant, a quick, hard explosion like three separate masses merging to trigger a critical reaction.

The Mad Hatter dragged me down against his hard chest. His strong embrace was almost painful. I did not resist it, but lay peacefully exhausted.

Thackeray still squatted beside us, his hand now draped to hide his depleted organ. "I'm a terrible person," he said. "A very terrible person." Tears showed on his face.

"Thackeray," I said. "I'm not your mother."

With the other hand, he wiped his damp cheeks. He stood up, walked shakily away.

I looked into the Mad Hatter's eyes. "But I'm Alice, am I not?" I said teasingly, rolling my bottom against his soft cock.

"I don't know who the hell you are," he said in a perfectly normal voice. "But you're one goddamned good fuck."

I laughed in delighted surprise. "You were putting me on."

He grinned. "My gag for the night. I wasn't even more than moderately drunk." His eyes darkened. "Except . . . I wanted you so bad, that first time, I really did lose it."

I was rocking gently, feeling It sweet and tender and hot against my cunt.

"You son of a bitch, you really had me going," I said fondly. "I *felt* like I was in Wonderland." I had an inspiration. "You're Thackeray's analyst, aren't you?"

He gave me a quizzical look. "How did you know?"

"It just figured." Circling my open palm on his steamy belly, I added dreamily, "I'll look for you if I come to another of these things. Who will you be?"

"God knows," he said. "God knows."

I woke up alone, curled in on myself. I got to my feet, not knowing how long I had been asleep, thinking, There are two floors I haven't seen yet. Still on the marijuana high, I was compelled to climb the stairs.

The third floor showed a great mass of people piled into one huge touching mass. The idea of such massive togetherness unappetizing, I climbed on. Everybody was passed out on the fourth floor. They lay on mattresses, arms and legs flung out. There was the sound of stifled snoring, and, somewhere, someone cried out in a voice of terror.

Everybody was out of it. But one. In a corner, the tough woman, Old Marge, straddled the body of the red-haired girl. She was fucking her as a man fucks, pressing mount against mount, writhing upon her with a concentrated, maniacal lust. The girl lay inertly unconscious.

It looked like Beauty and the Beast.

I walked near. "Quit it," I said.

The woman looked up. Her lips were parted. "She likes it," she said. "She's just got to get stoned first."

"It looks like rape to me," I said angrily.

"She came with me. She'll leave with me." She hadn't even stopped fucking. "She's just got to get stoned first, that's all."

I gave it up. None of my business. I went down the stairs. In the narrow hallway, a middle-aged man, heavily built, turned himself sidewise to let me pass. He was wearing only a pair of bright green cowboy boots. As I turned sideways also, he put out both hands, pushing me against the wall.

"Wanta fuck?"

Without waiting for an answer, he squatted to push his cock against my mount. My legs opened to take It in. I braced against the wall, enjoying the rapid flick of his cock, like a narrow snake's head, inside my cunt. He came as quickly as he had entered, pressing hard to hold It angled tightly as he pulsed a single jet of come.

"I like it, standing up," he said, breathing hard. "Don't you like it standing up?"

Such a clean, uncomplicated fuck. "First time I ever tried it," I said, laughing. "But I guess so."

"The girls in England during the war, there was no way you could get them into a bed. But, standing on their two feet, they'd fuck till Kingdom Come. Somehow, that way, it didn't count."

"Really?" I said with polite disinterest.

"Really. Funniest thing I ever ran into." He wiped sweat from his face. "I was a bomber pilot, thirty missions over Germany, never lost a plane or a man. My wife, she don't like to do it standing up. Says it's too much of a strain."

"Maybe she wants it to count," I said, and walked on. Quite clearheaded by now, I was looking for Mark Judson. Not on the third floor. Or the second.

The clothes person still held station. "Don't tell me," he said quickly. "I know what you were wearing."

Searching in the neat piles, he triumphantly came up with my pants suit and blouse and shoes.

"You left your panty hose and bra somewhere," he said reproachfully, eyes averted from my nakedness.

"Sorry," I said.

Gingerly, anxious not to touch naked flesh, he dressed me. "You ought to find some panty hose somewhere," he said. "Indecent to go out in the street like *that*."

"I guess I'll have to, indecent or not."

The front door was snatched open as I descended the final stair. A black man stood looking at me with gleaming eyes. He wore a broad-shouldered mauve suit, a wide-brimmed hat of the same delicate shade, and lavender shoes. A symphony in purple.

"Hey, cunt, you can't leave now, Charlie Stud has *arrived*," he said enthusiastically. "Come on, now, let's truck upstairs and let me show you how the *man* does it."

"Thank you," I said. "I think not."

His eyeballs bulged in sudden anger. "What's the matter, you a racist or something?"

"No," I said, and went on into the living room. It was deserted—everybody had either left or gone upstairs. Except for Mark Judson; he sat exactly where I had left him. An empty glass in one hand, a burning cigarette in the other, he was half-drunk, half-asleep.

I spoke down at him. "Thackeray said you weren't supposed to smoke tobacco."

"Sorry, forgot about that." He made an effort to

stub out the cigarette in a crystal ashtray beside him on
the floor, but missed. I put my foot on the cigarette.

"Didn't you go upstairs?"

He shook his head.

"Why not?" I persisted. "Or don't you ever get
off the ground floor?"

He pulled himself together. "Not interested. Just
wanted to drink tonight." He lifted his empty glass,
made a futile gesture of drinking.

"Want another one?"

Gratefully he handed me the glass. I went into the
kitchen. Thackeray West was brewing a cup of tea. He
glanced at me shamefaced.

"Hello, Thackeray," I said. "Lovely party."

"Care for tea?" he asked, still not looking at me.

"I'd love some tea," I said. "Let me get my friend
a drink first."

I carried the drink to Mark, returned. Thackeray
was pouring into cups so delicate they looked as though
pressure of thumb and finger would shatter them.

"Beautiful teacups," I said, accepting it.

"They were Mother's," he said. His face reddened
as if he had said a naughty word.

"I've never seen any quite like them."

"Lemon?" he asked. "Milk? Sugar?"

"No," I said. The tea was very good.

"Your party wasn't at all like I had imagined it," I
said. "So . . . subdued, really."

"Sometimes it gets quite boisterous," he said. "Tonight, people were more into cocaine and pills than the
physical thing." He peered at me hopefully. "It might
get . . . livelier . . . later on. There's a very good feelie
group on the third floor. You never know how those
feelie things will end."

I looked at him across the cup. "If I stay . . . will
you fuck me?"

His face reddened again. "Really. I . . ."

"I think it would work," I said. I felt the words
truthful. I liked the pale little man.

He smiled. Bravely. "You've done quite enough

for me already." He gazed earnestly through his thick glasses. "I do hope you'll come back."

"Only if you'll . . . agree to try."

"Every woman I masturbate with wants to try it on with me. It's always a disaster." His mouth tightened primly. "I'm quite happy with the pleasure I can give others by staging my little orgies."

Putting my palm against his face, I kissed the other cheek. "You're a lovely person."

He drew away. "You feel sympathy for me," he said. "I can tell. Sympathy is the worst thing a woman can feel for a man."

"Yes," I said softly. "I suppose so. I'm sorry."

"More tea?"

"Yes."

"I'll have some of that," Mark said.

I wondered how long he had been listening. Maybe, weaving in his tracks as he was, he hadn't heard anything.

"Need hot something," he mumbled. "Got to get Alice home." He wouldn't look at me. "That is, if you're ready to go."

I laughed. "How long have we been here?"

He focused on his watch. " 'Bout two hours."

"My God, it's seemed ages," I exclaimed. "I guess the Mad Hatter was right . . . time does change."

"Mad Hatter?" Mark said suspiciously. "Who's that?"

"Someone I met upstairs."

Fearful that he would drop it, I watched Mark take the delicate cup. With great care, he drank the tea in two gulps, put the cup safely on the table.

"Ready if you are," he said.

I turned to our host. "Thank you, Thackeray. Good night."

"Good night," he said politely. "Do come again."

In the street, I shook my head. "Strange. Strange."

"How, strange?"

"They're all so determined to be someone else."

"You too?"

I nodded soberly. "Me, too."

"You liked the pot," he said. "No problem getting pot anytime you want it."

Surprisingly, I shivered inside. "I don't know. It makes me feel . . . unreal."

"Maybe, in this seventies world, unreal is the only way to be," he said. "God knows, enough people are trying it on. Hash, snow, pills, horse . . . anything and everything."

I looked at him carefully. "You don't sound as drunk as you did."

He swayed exaggeratedly. "Drunk enough. Whiskey does it for me quite satisfactorily. Unreal, I mean. Booze is the greatest unreality-monger there is. And just about the only one that's legal."

He sounded, suddenly, more drunk than ever. I took his arm and walked him to the avenue, where we could get a cab.

In the apartment, he said, "One for the road," and veered toward the sideboard. Carefully he poured brandy, as carefully poured it down his throat. I watched his Adam's apple.

"You're in no condition to go all the way to Brooklyn," I said.

He stared bleary-eyed, tilting precariously. He caught himself, wheeled, and began walking away from me. I followed him to the guest bedroom. He fumbled at the doorknob, pushed open the door, slammed his shoulder against the jamb as he tried to enter.

He grinned. "Hold the door still, I'll get through it." He got through it and collapsed promptly across the bed.

I stood in the doorway. "Get undressed."

He didn't say anything.

I came to the side of the bed. "Want me to undress you?"

He didn't say anything. He didn't move. I looked at him for a long time. Then I put out the light and retired to my room.

*London and San Francisco, Florence
and Venice, Brazil and Tibet ... the Ponte
Vecchio, the Rialto, the Golden Gate, and
London Bridge, a bridge made of grass rope
across the River Indus.*

There were only six of us, including
Halsband the photographer and his assistant,
and Harris O'Brien the writer. Clara was my
dresser, in charge also of the two wardrobe
trunks. A young man named Smith, an asso-
ciate editor of Life, was responsible for the
logistics; reservations, luggage, guides, and
permits where they were needed.

We began with the George Washington
and Brooklyn bridges, then journeyed to Niagara Falls for the Rainbow Bridge, to Dela-
ware and St. Louis, and on to San Francisco
and the world. And I did not care how long it
would be before I dragged my dreary soul
home to New York.

Much time alone in these strange places.
Halsband, a wispy man with enormously
large hands, was a meticulous artist. For days
he studied a bridge, in all lights and weathers
and times of day, before he began to shoot.
Even then he worked at first without Alice,
accumulating a hundred, two hundred pictures, which he would study for hours at a
time. When, finally, he called for me, he
worked quickly, knowing exactly what he
wanted.

Halsband was remote, totally professional. Harris O'Brien was totally personal.
The first moment he saw me, his eyes, his
face, his whole being, lit up in appreciation.

"I signed up because of all that cash
they kept waving at me," he said enthusiastically. "But the money is going to be the
least part of it!"

Harris O'Brien was a bandy-legged

little man with a broad chest and arms like a stevedore. The lilt of Erin in his voice, though he had been born in New York. I heard much conversation in that charming voice. Too much conversation, all dealing with one topic.

"We shall pretend to be newlyweds," he informed me in the Niagara Falls motel bar. "In fact, if you insist on sanctified sex, I'll even arrange a ceremony sufficient to tide us over the week."

He did, at least, make me laugh. "Harris, you're a dear," I said. "But you're the last man in the world I would marry."

Fervently he wiped his brow. "Thank God! What could have got into me, to make such a decent proposition?"

His eyes were green and lively, his hair a deep auburn. There were freckles on the backs of his hands, as in his face. He was the novelist everyone said would win the next Nobel prize to be given an American author.

"You should know, darling, I am not prone to make proposals of marriage. My mind runs in deeper gutters than that." He paused for effect. "Shall we fuck, then?"

The way he had phrased it, somewhere between intent and humor, it was impossible to take offense. Still, the idea of another man, after Andy Glenn, moved in me darkly.

"No." I said it honestly, because I did like him. "Not now. And not ever."

He finished his scotch. He ordered another one. He lit a cigarette.

"I should have told you at the beginning," he said gently. "Women don't say no to Harris O'Brien."

I smiled. "This woman does. And no it will remain."

Firmly he shook his head. "Sorry, dar-

ling. That's not how it's going to be. It's simply the question whether we waste half the
trip before getting into bed." He laughed,
his eyes bright. "A pity it'll be for every hour
that passes."

I cast about for a means to lighten the
conversation. "You started out talking about
honeymoons. Now, suddenly, it's 'the trip.' "

He nodded. "The deviousness of Harris
O'Brien, darling. You can fuck your way
around the world with the great author and
know to your heart's ease that, once we land
in New York, you'll never see me again."

A tightening inside me. Andy Glenn
abided still, his memory lit with candles of the
love, the tenderness—and the passion—we
had shared. All right; so the love had been a
shabby thing after all. But, having had it, I
couldn't imagine making love without love,
as Harris O'Brien was so adroitly suggesting.
I couldn't imagine being the Alice I had been
before Andrew Glenn had come into me.

"Do I look like the kind of girl to go for
a deal like that?" I said, a tinge of anger
showing in my voice.

Harris was watching me closely. "With
the right man at the right time, every girl is
that kind of girl."

I looked at my drink. "It's certainly not
the right time."

He put his hand on mine. "Ah, the dear
lass has suffered a disappointment in love.
Tell Harris about it."

I took away my hand. "It's none of
your business."

"The lust of O'Brien has eased many a
painful memory."

Abruptly, I had had enough of his sly
persistence. I stood up, saying, "I'm going
to my room," and walked away.

After hastily paying the check, Harris caught up with me in the corridor. I stopped at my door.

"Shall I come in, then?" he inquired.

As though nothing I had said—nothing that I *was*—had made an impression on his impervious self.

"Not now and not ever," I said coldly.

His eyes regarded my face. They roved over my body. Elaborately, he sighed. "All right, darling. I'll allow you to waste this good day. But not many more, I assure you."

He walked away, whistling faintly. I watched him go. Certainly in his thirties, maybe over forty, I thought. He walked the way he talked, with a certain lilt.

I decided to avoid being alone with O'Brien. In St. Louis, however, he came directly to my room. I was lying down for a nap; Halsband had indicated he wished to shoot at sunset. Thinking it was Clara come to dress me, I got up and opened the door.

Harris O'Brien promptly stepped into the room. "Darling Alice. You've been avoiding me," he said reproachfully.

I was wearing only bra and panties. I turned away to put on my robe. I went to the window. High up over the river, it was a lovely view. I had not bothered to look at it until now, when I needed a buffer

"I thought we had it all sorted out, Harris," I said without anger or impatience.

I kept on not looking at him.

"I need a friend, not a lover," I said. "I'd like to be able to talk to you, Harris. Not about sex, not about me-and-you, not even about personal troubles and ideas. Just ... talk."

I could sense that he was close behind

me. He said, "That all comes after, darling."

I listened to the tone, not the sense of the words. I wanted acceptance, an understanding.

"You are a sensitive man," I said into the empty spaces beyond the window glass. "You must be, to write the books you have written. Sensitive enough to realize what I must have."

His tone changed. "Alice. If I'm to be your friend, you'll have to help me get past this terrible lust for your body. I must possess you, legs and breast and belly and cunt. All of it." His voice was trembling. "This is not Harris O'Brein's usual style with a woman, Alice. I freely confess it. I capture, I don't get captured. But . . . you have captured me."

He cupped both hands against my ass. I could feel the strength of his hands through the filmy robe.

I let him touch me. After a while, he took away his hands. Only then did I turn. Great beads of sweat stood on his forehead.

"Then you refuse to be my friend."

He made an attempt to recover his persona. "Harris O'Brien will be the greatest friend you've ever had, darling."

"But you won't give your friendship without the prior condition of becoming lovers," I said steadily.

"I can't," he said. "And that's the simple truth."

"I have a simple truth, too," I said. "When your hands were on my ass, I didn't feel a thing."

He nodded soberly. "I noticed."

I felt sad. For Alice. For Harris O'Brien. For the whole world.

"So . . . there's nothing to be done."

He remained still for a long moment. I had been aware of his erection. It was gone now.

Harris sighed. "Nothing."

He left me as abruptly as he had appeared.

I lay down across the bed. I wanted to cry, but I didn't dare; any moment, now, the call would come to pose for Halsband's camera.

Harris O'Brien would not possess Alice's body. Alice would not possess Harris OBrien's soul.

In San Francisco, and at the Hawaii stopover on the way to Japan, Harris left me alone. Then, irrepressible spirit that he was, he began again with the same old O'Brien-the-great-novelist act, glib, self-assured, enjoying as much as I the funny, insinuating sexual talk that rhapsodized the sheer physical aspects of good fucking. He developed an elaborate theory of the spiritual qualities inherent in pure physicality. I had the feeling he was formulating the skeleton of some future novel.

I could sense, in his elaborate wordplay of idea and suggestion, a detachment that had not existed in the beginning. He no longer expected to talk me into bed. A playful game for the sake of the game; no score when playing time was over.

Halsband, working so intensively on each phase of the project, might as well have been alone. Harris O'Brien, to all outward appearance, did not work at all. Seldom did he spend as much as an hour looking at the current bridge. He did not study the histories of design and construction. Wherever we were, he staked out a corner of the most hospitable bar, immediately gathering a court of fans and admirers to applaud the anecdotes and ideas that became ever more extravagant with each successive drink order.

During our stopover in Hawaii, Harris disappeared with a lovely wahine *with black hair and golden skin who performed the hula in a nightclub. At the last minute he got on board, and slept all the way to Tokyo.*

I began to worry about how he would fulfill his contract to produce an essay complementary to the photographs. When, imprudently, I revealed my concern, he immediately introduced into the sexual game the concept that my intransigence was creating in him a massive writer's block. How could he write about Alice in any meaningful way until he had possessed her?

"No other way a man can truly know a woman," he insisted. "It's a professional obligation, darling, that you cannot continue to ignore."

I refused the responsibility

Halsband, with each passing day, liked more and more the way I appeared in the view-screen of his camera. So often, now, he chose the filmiest garments in the wardrobe. He liked me to pose with the wind molding the sheer fabrics against my limbs. He would not let me wear anything underneath.

"Ethereal," he'd say with the tenderness of a lover. "Ghostlike, unreal; as though you might float away from your foothold on the bridge. Lovely, Alice, lovely."

He fretted about the earlier work, wanting to do it over again. When we got back, he decided, he'd have to talk the magazine into repeating the earlier phases of the assignment.

"They must have some respect for ar-

tistic integrity," he insisted. "I'll simply inform them I'll never again work for Life if
they deny me the opportunity." He gazed
dreamily upon me. "Because you're a different Alice now. More different with every
passing day."

In Tibet, he tried first with the gossamer
garments. Then, taking the clothes off, he
draped them over my body with his own
hands. Still he was not satisfied.

We were alone together on the rope
bridge; the others watched from the bank.
Halsband commanded them to go away.

When he returned, he said, "It is necessary to do it in the nude."

"For Life magazine?" I said incredulously.

Solemnly he nodded.

"I've never posed in the nude," I said.
"Underwear, sure, but—"

"But you must," he said.

I shook my head. "Paul Riff would have
your head, and mine, too."

"I will fix it in the darkroom so all will
accept," he said. "The Life people, also."

"No."

He looked at me with a steady gaze. He
said quietly, "Then I quit. We'll go home,
tell them it's impossible to complete the assignment."

"You can't do that, Halsband," I cried.
"Your work is too beautiful."

He nodded. "Yes. But without making
the artistic whole, it isn't worth the film I've
burned."

Overwhelmed by his instinct for perfection, his dedication, I said, "How do you
want me?"

On the grass-rope bridge over the River

Indus in Tibet, Halsband posed me on tiptoe, with a single wind-blown white scarf in a lifted hand. The wind was so strong, it flowed my long, straight hair across my face, streaming away wildly. Captured by the patterned tangle of ropework, yet dominating it, my nude figure touched the bridge so lightly I might have been floating on air. Later, in the darkroom, Halsband added a mistiness that removed all eroticism, as though my body were seen through a veil, though the bridge itself was starkly, meticulously real. Alice was the essence, the crystallization, the ghostly embodiment, of Woman, captured by, yet capturing, the primitive bridge-aspiration of Man.

When he was finished—he only made three shots—Halsband enfolded me in his arms.

"You have given me the greatest photograph of my lifetime," he said emotionally. "I thank you, Alice. I thank you forever." It was the first and only time he had touched me physically.

The shot made the cover of Life. It became the definitive Alice-photograph. Yet, so ethereal, so unreal, it was as though Alice was not in the frame of reference.

Having finished in Venice, we would fly home to New York the next day. The job was done, except for the early shots Halsband wanted to repeat.

New York tomorrow. For so long, now, I had been enclosed within a cocoon of time and place. Surrendering Alice to Halsband, nothing had existed outside the unreality he had created for the sake of the work.

Now the cocoon had ruptured, exposing

me to the chilling reality of going home where home no longer existed.

New York would be New-York-without-Andy. Walk alone the blocks we had walked together, holding hands. Sleep in the bed where we had made love so many times I could not count the tears or the orgasms.

I couldn't bear the thought of returning vulnerable to memory and desire. I must go home a different Alice from the Alice who had departed. Without pause or hesitation, I picked up the telephone to ask the switchboard for the number of Harris O'Brien's room.

His eyes lit up when he opened the door. But then, gesturing toward the paper-strewn table, he said, "You came at exactly the worst moment, darling. Half an hour ago I began the writing."

I came into the room, shut the door behind me. "The writing will be better now," I said. I went to my knees to zip open the fly of his trousers. With both hands I tenderly unveiled his already-rampant cock.

Not a remarkable Thing. Average in size, average in eagerness. Nevertheless, I cherished it with my eyes; tenderly the tip of my finger caressed the rosy bulb until It thumped eagerly in my hand.

I looked up into O'Brien's face. He was gazing down, his expression rapt, bemused. I transferred my concentration to the instrument of his desire. And mine. Delicately I warmed It with my breath, inhaled It into my mouth. His hips thrust hard, demanding that I take all. With all the expertise I had garnered from Iowa schoolboys, I did everything that a loving mouth can do to a man's Thing. Harris, without urgency to enter, allowed me all that I wished. Only when I rose of my own volition to undress and lie down on the white iron bedstead did he make himself naked.

He cupped his palm over my mound. "You are the darling Alice of the world," he said with charming sweetness.

He put himself inside me as I opened my legs to allow It to slide smoothly home, joining our bodies with the hard nail of his cock.

From the volatile Harris O'Brien I had expected—sought—violence. He was, instead, gentle and persistent, moving for a long time with only the tiniest of thrusts, opening me petal by quivering petal.

When he came it was long-lasting also, meted without loss of control. He sighed, resting his leonine head on my breast. With both arms, I held him for a moment before stirring to get from under

"No, darling," he whispered. "O'Brien is only beginning."

I realized, then, that his cock within me was still hard and sure. And when he began again he had such skillful control that he manipulated my responses as though I were a puppet. I yielded the event, riding at his chosen pace on the tide of his lustful energy. I was in the hands of a master.

I had not meant to come. But Harris made me come; not once but again and again, until it merged into a deep, tender fucking that I would not have believed could exist without love.

Only after his sixth or seventh orgasm— I had long since lost count for both of us— he quickened into ultimate release, groaning deeply as he flooded me with the long-delayed *culmination. Promptly going limp, It slipped out of the great wet warmth he had made of my vagina.*

Harris swung his legs to sit on the side of the bed. "We should have had it around the world, darling," he said. He spoke without reproach, but with infinite regret.

Dreamily satiated, I put my hand against his rib cage. He was not breathing hard, as though he were a world champion who had just gone fifteen easy rounds.

"You will be in New York," I said. "And so will I."

He shook his head. "No, darling. In New York you will not be my bridge-Alice. In New York, I will no longer be the Harris O'Brien you surrendered to at last in beautiful Venice."

"We can be friends," I said. "I like you very much, Harris O'Brien."

His eyes were suddenly dark, somber. "I don't trust your liking, Alice," he said. "No more than you trust my lust."

He leaned over, reaching for his striped boxer shorts. He stood up to put them on.

"The writing is waiting for O'Brien," he said.

It was a dismissal. "Will it be a better writing now?" I asked wistfully.

He smiled tolerantly. "Alice! has been in my head since Tibet," he said. "I was only waiting for you to come ripe."

I got up, got dressed, and left him. A new Alice-butterfly, freed from the cocoon, I was now brave for New York.

Prince Albert came, prancing with eagerness and bursting with news. I was just up, still on my morning coffee.

"What's the great news, Albert?" I said, laughing.

He couldn't contain himself. "Alice! I'm in love! I'm getting married!"

I stared. "For God's sake, Albert, what poor girl is sacrificing herself to the idea that you might change?"

It wasn't a smile; a grin of pure joy.

"Don't be silly. Of course I wouldn't marry a *girl*. I hope I know myself better than *that*."

I was bewildered. "But . . ."

"It's done nowadays," he said earnestly. "I never thought it could be for *me*. But it *is* done." He began to laugh at my bewilderment.

"Sit down, have a cup of coffee, and explain it to me." I smiled at him. "If it makes you happy, I'm all for it."

"Oh God yes, I'm happy," he said. "I had given up all hope of having a stable relationship. But now . . . marriage!"

Over coffee, Prince Albert told me how he had met an attractive man in a gay bar.

"Not a pickup," he said earnestly. *"Conversation.* Bruce is the minister of a gay church—gay himself, of course—and he was cruising the bars for God, not to inspect the meat on the rack."

"You've never struck me as a religious person."

"I'm *not,*" he said. "At least, I've never been. After all, you know, the church has never welcomed the gay person. According to Christian doctrine, as long as you remain what you *are,* you're a *sinner."* He sighed. "But Bruce Walcott is different. He's been there himself, he knows what a gay person goes through, always having to *try* to hide his real self. Even now, we are truly comfortable only when we stick to *ourselves."*

Gently I said, "You're quite serious, aren't you?"

He nodded. "You see, I began to attend Reverend Bruce's services. His church is nondenominational, so one doesn't have to worry about doctrine. Simply love and understanding, and a chance to feel that God is near."

He looked at his hands spread on the table.

"I've never expected *not* to be lonely." He looked up. "Reverend Bruce has made me realize that God loves and understands the gay person as well as He does the straights. After all, if God is *everything,* He's got to be gay, too." He took a deep breath. "God simply . . . *encompasses.* Do you understand, Alice?"

"I think I do," I said softly.

"There—at church—I met him. Tom Faith." Albert chuckled. "Not his original name, of course. He took it when he accepted Jesus as his personal savior."

Prince Albert had never been a shy sort of person. He was shy now.

"Tom was strung out when Bruce found him. His body was dying, his soul was already dead. That's Tom's own description of himself." His voice was soft. "Bruce took Tom home, cold-turkeyed him, got him clean of drugs and healthy as a horse. But, Tom Faith says, his soul was still dead."

Albert gazed at me. "Tom began working for Reverend Bruce, janitoring the church, ushering at services, learning how to keep the books. It was not a sexual relationship. I know, because Bruce and his lover have been married for five years, and they are completely faithful. To him, Tom was simply another lost soul."

Albert's eyes were shadowed, as though he himself had lived the experience. "Reverend Bruce had done all for Tom Faith one man can do for another. Now it required—the intervention of God."

His voice dropped to a whisper.

"It was a religious experience, Alice. Tom was resting on the back steps of the church after cleaning up for Sunday services. Just sundown, and he was tired and hungry. He's young yet, you know, eats like a teenager." Prince Albert sighed happily. "I don't know how I'm going to feed him, as much as he eats."

His face was lighted with the talking.

"As Tom tells it, without any warning he *experienced the universe*. Not experienced . . . *felt*. A rhythm, he says, a pulse beating through every atom of matter. Including Tom himself."

Albert took a deep breath. "Such a simple thing, Tom says. He felt it, he looked up, and he said, 'Yes, God. I understand now.' "

Prince Albert wiped at his cheek. I had never seen him so vulnerable, yet so real. All the self-defensive campiness had vanished.

"It must be wonderful to have something like that happen," he said. "But you can't *count* on it happening. You know?"

"I know," I said.

"He went to Reverend Bruce. 'I have been given faith,' he told Bruce. 'Now I am Tom Faith.'

"He was baptized at Sunday service. Tom still takes care of things at the church. But he spends most of his time carrying his faith to others."

"He sounds like a good person. But how did you . . . ?"

Prince Albert laughed. "At church service. Where else? He . . . caught my eye. There's a *pure* look about Tom, he's very handsome, you know, and gentle . . ." Albert stopped. "I looked at him. And I was in love."

He paused again. He was being very careful.

"In his former life, Tom had been more *trade* than gay. Anything to support his habit." A flicker of the old Prince Albert showed in his grin. "Of course, you know what they say: Today's trade is tomorrow's competition."

We laughed together.

"He used to have violence in his soul, Tom tells me. He liked to beat up on people. But Tom *Faith* . . ." He sighed a heartfelt sigh of love.

"You know, Alice, gays are so *frightened* of love. We turn love into blatant *sex*."

His eyes were bleak.

"You know how it goes. A couple of fellows meet, feel an attraction, they give themselves to each other. Then—they can't wait to betray their friend before their friend betrays them." His mouth was bit-

ter. "It's happened to me a hundred times. A thousand."
He spread his hands. "So how can one hope to establish
a real relationship? No way."

His voice turned soft.

"I . . . invited Tom. He consented to see me." His
mouth twisted again. "We're all so *physical*. His body
was all I cared about. A week, I thought, two weeks,
maybe a month, and then it will end like it always
does: *Who's hustling who around here*."

He didn't look at me.

"I *expected* Tom to hustle me. Hell, I'm used to
it. Time was, I was the beautiful young man. I'm not so
young anymore. Not so pretty, either."

"You're one of the handsomest people I know," I
said.

He flashed a look of gratitude.

"Anyway. I *accepted* being hustled by Tom.
After all, I am quite celebrated in my own sphere. I
have money and style. Tom had, I considered, only his
poor self."

He looked up at me.

"I didn't realize he was rich with Christ in his
soul," he said quietly. "I didn't touch Tom. He told
me, with the simple truth in his eyes, that if it happened between us it would have to be love."

He spread his hands. "Suddenly, as real as Tom's
religious experience, it *was* love. We realized that we
wanted, more than anything else, to be together." He
took a deep breath. "So we're getting married. Of
course, Reverend Bruce can't *legally* marry us. But . . .
it's what takes place in your heart that counts."

He was shy again.

"We still haven't . . . touched each other. We
decided we'd rather wait until after the ceremony."

I put my hand on his hand. "It's beautiful, Albert," I said.

"Beautiful?" He shook his head. "Miraculous.
There's just one thing: Tom wants me to confess
Christ." He moved his shoulders. "We both realize we
can only hope it will happen. You can't *force* it." He

brooded. "Tom is bringing God to our life together. I ought to be able to bring God, also. Or . . . maybe Tom's faith will be enough for both of us."

"I'm sure it will be," I said warmly.

He smiled. He laughed joyously. "I never thought I would say such words. But, Alice . . . will you come to my wedding?"

"I wouldn't miss it for anything in the world!"

A lovely wedding. Mark didn't want to escort me, but I talked him into it.

Unworthily, I had expected a certain campiness: how could gays resist the opportunity? But I underestimated the commitment involved here.

It was spring, so the church was decorated with lilies. An impressive building, once an Episcopal church; austere with its old wooden pews, yet ornate due to richly embroidered altar cloths and lovely old stained-glass windows. Reverend Bruce was a slim man of serene countenance. He wore a black turtleneck sweater, vaguely clerical.

Prince Albert and Tom Faith rose from their places in the congregation to stand before him. Prince Albert wore a severe suit, a white flower in the buttonhole. He was as glowingly beautiful as any bride on her wedding day. I studied Prince Albert's lover. Slim, yet sturdy in build, he wore black slacks and a black, short-sleeved shirt, open at the throat. He was fair-skinned, with hair the color of straw. Tom's face, so young, showed, beneath the peace he had achieved at such great cost, the ravages of his history.

Reverend Bruce lifted up his voice.

"These two men, Prince Albert and Tom Faith, having declared their love, have come forth in our midst to receive the blessing of God upon their relationship. Let us pray that God be with us on this day, in this church and in the hearts of us all."

He bowed his head to pray silently. I looked about the congregation. No more than thirty or forty, a few couples, most of the men solitary. I glanced sidewise at my escort. Mark Judson looked distinctly uncomfortable. I felt a twinge of annoyance.

Reverend Bruce raised his head.

"Do you, Prince Albert, declare here in the presence of God and this congregation your heart's decision to cleave to this friend and lover, Tom Faith, with all the sincerity and devotion your soul possesses?"

"I do," Prince Albert said in a firm voice.

Reverend Bruce repeated the words for Tom Faith. There was a pause, in which Tom turned his head to look at Albert before he spoke.

"I do," he said, so softly one could scarcely hear the words.

There was a champagne reception in the church basement. Still no campy extravagance. Simply Prince Albert glowing with happiness as he told me, "We're going to Fire Island for our honeymoon, Alice. It'll be *deserted* this early in the season."

Mark Judson insisted on leaving as soon as we decently could. But not before I had kissed Tom Faith on the cheek, and embraced Prince Albert, whispering into his ear, "Albert, stay as happy forever as you are now."

We gazed upon each other with fondness. Such old friends. I knew about Prince Albert as no one else did. As he knew about Alice.

He smiled, the tears glistening in his eyes. "God willing, Alice," he said fervently. "God willing."

Strangely enough, returning to New York, I was vulnerable to love. Perhaps it was because Alice had truly changed.

Changed also was Alice's New York. The bridge sequence for Life *magazine accomplished everything and more that Paul Riff had envisioned. In the professional term,* Alice! *was suddenly a hot property. Even before the photographic spread, with Harris OBrien's classic essay on the beauty of bridges and the loveliness of woman—in which, with genius-inspiration, he added the spectacular exclamation point to my name forever—had been published, it was known to be a great success.*

The week Life *appeared on the newsstands with the cover showing Alice! eerily beautiful on the rope bridge over the Indus, I moved into my new apartment. Now I had New York, figuratively and literally, at my feet. The penthouse on Central Park West was worthy of a star of the first magnitude; a flagstone terrace, a bedroom of pure white that was promptly featured in* Town and Country.

Paul Riff now devoted himself full-time to the management of my career—and to working sixteen hours a day to capitalize on the situation. Money from modeling assignments flowed in, along with scripts and offers from Hollywood. I left it all to Paul in the sublime confidence he would make the right decisions.

And . . . love.

Paul took me to Sardi's, one evening, to discuss a new idea; a Broadway musical in which I would be featured, not starred. Paul liked the idea because I wouldn't have to carry the show by myself.

The tables, as always at Sardi's, were jammed too close together. I couldn't help but notice the man at the next table. He was practically in my lap—and, though accompanied by a beautiful woman, he gazed boldly.

Male attention has always dwelled lustfully upon Alice! Nevertheless, something within me thrilled under the impact of this man's gaze.

He was tall, handsome, with distin-

guished wings of gray at his temples. His face was smooth of flesh, yet strong-featured, with firm, controlled lips. And beautiful eyes. They were almond-shaped, lambent black, with extraordinarily long lashes. Yet he was totally masculine.

I tore my eyes away to appraise his companion, recognizing her immediately as a reigning queen of Broadway. She was intense, sexy-looking . . . and annoyed at the attention he gave me. Possessively, her hand rested on his arm.

"I'm sorry," I said to Paul. "What did you say?"

Paul patiently repeated his remark. When I looked again, a faint smile showed on the man's face. And, in his eyes, a recognition. I felt suddenly jubilant.

A new Alice!, in a new world. No longer hopelessly in love with a shabby, ego-ridden actor. Sharing a shabby apartment, fucking madly on a semen-and-sweat-soaked sheet. I belonged in these glamorous surroundings, attractive to, and attracted by, men of power and substance. Successful men, to match Alice!'s success.

His companion departed haughtily for the ladies' room. Promptly, the man leaned closer.

"Give me your phone number."

Paul, startled, started to say something. But, seeing my face, he held his peace.

"What's my new phone number, Paul?" *I asked calmly.* "I can't remember it yet."

Paul spoke the number. The man nodded. Soon after his companion had returned, they departed.

"You sure you wanted to do that?" *Paul asked quietly.*

"Yes," I said.

He studied me for a moment. "Do you know who that was?"

"No," I said.

He smiled. "Peter Able. The producer."

"Oh," I said. Then I said a strange thing. "We're going to mean a great deal to each other."

When Peter called at two o'clock that morning, his first words were the identical ones I had spoken to Paul.

"You know, don't you, that we're going to mean a great deal to each other?"

He had not announced himself by name. No need; I had been waiting, still inside, for the phone to ring.

"Yes," I said. "I know."

I heard him breathe deeply; he knew I had sensed the same vibrations.

"Shall I come over? Or do you want to come here?"

"Now?" I said.

"Of course," he said.

"You'd better come here," I said. "I'm already in bed."

"Ten minutes," he said. "Be ready."

I was ready.

The doorman called up, so I had the door open. He put his arms fiercely about me.

"Thank God you recognized it, too. Without playing games."

A warning flickered across my brain. Perhaps this intensity was fake, his accustomed method of conquest. But I didn't care. I was holding him fiercely, also, as he kissed me.

"Come on," I said. "Hurry."

I led him to the bedroom. He only

glanced at the enormous white bed. He looked at me.

"Out there," he said, gesturing toward the flagstone terrace. Obediently I opened the glass doors. Peter stooped to grasp a white bearskin rug by the jaws, dragging it outside.

No stars above, because this was New York. But summer air was soft against my skin as I stripped off the nightgown. He hoisted the bearskin onto a chaise longue. He laid me down on it, the fur-bristles harsh against my skin. My head rested on the bear's head. He made himself naked, tossing his expensive suit aside in careless haste.

No preliminaries. He thrust into me like a lance of fire. I held on desperately as our bodies merged with the violence of great love and great passion.

Never had a rampant cock so overwhelmed my senses. Love and lust mingled, one inextricable from the other. I could only ride the whirlwind of soaring ecstasy; there was not the phenomena of come and not-come, only one continuous, never-ending sensation of a perfect blending of body and heart and soul.

Spent, we washed up on the shore of ourselves.

"Peter," I said. My voice trembled. "Oh, Peter."

He was kissing me, his mouth warm and hungry, saying between kisses, "You are my new love, you're all the love I'll ever need," and it was not strange to hear from him these words of commitment.

We went to sleep holding each other. I came awake, somewhere near dawn, to feel his tongue in me. I opened my legs, my en-

tire self, to his need to taste me deeply.
When, finally, he brought his mouth up to
mine, it was fragrant with the odors of me. I
kissed him avidly, with lips that had never
been so softly giving.

We fucked again as dawn came over the
city. Not a gentle fucking this time either,
though I had anticipated it as a gentleness,
but sweeping as quickly as before into a
striding passion.

Over breakfast, we talked for the first
time. Or, rather, Peter talked, in a manner of
meaning that left me as breathless as the
ardent lovemaking.

"We'll have to work together, too, after
we're married," he said. "We mustn't let our
work separate us. Too many show-business
marriages have failed for exactly that reason."

"Married?" I said.

"You do want to marry me, don't you?"

"It doesn't matter," I said contentedly.

"Married," he said firmly. "I've never
been a husband. You've never been a wife."
He smiled. "So, obviously, we've been waiting to marry each other." He laughed softly.
"I've never even proposed to anybody, before now."

I was struck by a realization. "I've
never been proposed to," I said. "Nobody
has ever wanted to marry me. They've just
wanted to fuck."

"The work," Peter continued. "I've
been thinking about getting into films. I've
only produced plays until now." His voice
expanded. "We shall do the kind of films
that aren't made anymore, with beautiful
people, beautifully costumed, living lives of
romance and adventure. Sheer make-believe
magic, like our love." He took a deep breath.

"I will star Alice! in a film with the eerie, lovely quality of that Life *cover. Will you do it for me?"*

"Yes," I said.

"Was that your manager with you last night?"

"Yes. Paul Riff."

He nodded. "All right. We'll work it out." He looked at his watch. "Alice!, I want nothing more than for us to spend the day together. The week. The rest of our lives. But . . . I've got to go."

"Come back as soon as you can," I said serenely.

He looked at me anxiously. "Actually, I have to fly to the Coast for three days. I can cancel if you think I should. But it is important."

Trustingly, I took his hand. "Call from the airport when you get back," I said. "So I'll be ready."

Three days, in which I was in love as I had not been in love. Even with Andrew Glenn. That green love had been adolescent, powerful but flawed. This was a ripe love, with a full man.

Peter called, as promised, from the airport. His voice was harsh.

"Alice! I deeply appreciate the dose of clap you were so kind as to give me."

I was numb.

"What?" I said.

He repeated the bitter message. Then he hung up, leaving the words curdled in my heart.

Harris O'Brien. Of course.

I had experienced no symptoms. Then I remembered; a girl at the acting school had told me, once, that a woman can have *gonorrhea without knowing it. But, she said, there was no way a man could not know.*

Harris O'Brien had known.

Oh, God, I thought, I had his diseased Thing in my greedy mouth.

Remembering how, cherishing his cock, I had lavished upon it all the well-known expertise of The Cocksucker of Clancy Street, I wanted to vomit.

Then—the bitter memory. In the dawn following that night of great love, Peter Able had gone down on me.

That, I realized, was how he must feel about it, too; his mouth on my cunt, tongue probing and licking at the diseased tissues, humidly tender, not with desire, but with the horrible, infectious disease.

I did vomit then. I barely made it to the bathroom before it came spewing forth, a projectile vomiting that racked my body in its vain effort to get rid of the poison.

But the flesh could not be so easily cured of the venereal disease. I imagined I could feel the insidious germs multiplying, spreading through my body like a fifth column of destruction.

I could not bear to live inside this diseased envelope which the world had always regarded as so desirable. I had never been able to think of myself as truly beautiful; yet until now I had not been ugly. Horrible to know Alice as ugly, diseased. Never again, I thought, will I feel clean.

I didn't give up without a fight. Not this time. I knew, for the truth, that I had never in my whole life fought for what I wanted. I had accepted the reputation of The Cocksucker of Clancy Street. I had fled from the Daddy-revelation. There had been no

*opportunity to fight for Andy Glenn; one
cannot fight a coward who runs away.*

This time, numbly, almost without feeling, I fought for the happiness that had
flowered so briefly, only to be snatched away.

First, I did what had to be done. Unable to face Paul's kindly old doctor, who was
the only medical man I knew, I picked a
doctor at random. The nurse-receptionist insisted on knowing my problem before she
would let me see the doctor.

Painfully I said, "I have gonorrhea."

The nurse, looking wise and sympathetic, pulled out a form and asked my name
and address. Filling it in, she said, "Do you
know who infected you?"

"I just want to be cured," I said. "Do
we have to go into all that?"

She looked at me across the desk.
"Dearie, the Public Health Service has a
major drive on. The only way they can hope
to stop the rising rate of venereal disease is
to trace the vectors of infection. So they've
asked private doctors to cooperate."

I was numb. I didn't care.

"There's no way I can force you to supply the pertinent information," she went on.
"But . . . do you want that man to do to
other women what he did to you?"

"What happens if I give you his name?"

"A Public Health Service worker will inform your exfriend that he has been reported as a carrier of venereal disease, try
to persuade him to seek treatment if he
hasn't already done so."

I liked that idea; Harris O'Brien being
harrassed by the Public Health Service. I
liked even more that he would know Alice
had reported him.

"Harris O'Brien," I said.

The name didn't mean anything to the nurse. Writing, she said, "Do you have an address on him?"

"No," I said. The nurse looked up in surprise. "We were traveling together on assignment at the time," I added.

She nodded as though she understood the situation entirely. "Is he a resident of New York City?"

"Yes. He's the famous author," I said. "You can find him easily enough."

She made an additional note, saying, "I hardly ever read anything but magazines, myself." She nodded again, briskly. "No need to see the doctor. I'll give you a dose of penicillin massive enough to knock it right out."

I was grateful I wouldn't have to see the doctor. Another man.

She frowned slightly. "We are running into new strains, these days, that have become penicillin-resistant. So we'll have to do a follow-up, make sure you're clean." She stood up. "I must take some blood, now, for the Wassermann."

"Wassermann?" I said, my heart sinking.

"Syphilis and gonorrhea often go hand-in-hand."

Despair. I hadn't thought of syphilis.

The nurse took blood, injected me with a shot of penicillin that left a nauseating knot on my rump. Finished, she slapped me on the other cheek, saying cheerfully, "Well, girl, I suppose you'll pick your man a little more carefully, next time."

I could not see even Paul Riff during those agonizing days of waiting for the results of the Wassermann. Sleepless, scarcely able to eat, I could only stalk the apartment,

imagining that I could feel the germs crawl-
ing dirty in the cells of my flesh. I was so
convinced I was still infected, I couldn't be-
lieve the nurse when she told me the Wasser-
mann had come back negative, that I didn't
need another shot of penicillin.

Walking back to the apartment, I could
only think: But they have left scars; not only
in my flesh. Scars that will always be a part
of Alice.

Only then did I try to call Peter Able.

I was put through to the private secre-
tary, embodied in a pleasant voice. A voice
that, after a small wait, had changed to ici-
ness.

"I am sorry. Mr. Able will be in con-
ference all day."

"Will you ask him to call me?" I said
miserably.

"Does he know your name and num-
ber?"

I gave it to her. Peter Able did not call.

Two days later, I tried again. This time,
no waiting while she checked with the mas-
ter.

"I'm sorry. Mr. Able is out of town."

"Do you know when he'll be back?"

"I really couldn't say."

A day later, when I called yet again, the
voice nastily informed me: "Look, dear, it's
no use to keep calling him. So don't give me
a hard time. All right?"

I went to the building where Peter Able
had his offices. Stationing myself near the
newsstand where I could watch the elevators,
I scanned the home-going throng flowing
out of the elevators. My heart lurched when
I saw Peter. He came late, after the crowd

*had thinned to occasional laggards, walking
slowly, engrossed in conversation with two
other men.*

*Approaching close enough that he
could not ignore me, I said, "Peter. May I
talk to you?" Startled, his head jerked
around.*

*Alone, he could have avoided the con-
frontation. In the company of his associates,
he could only say, "Catch up with you fellows in a minute."*

*His companions, with curious glances,
went on.*

"Peter, I didn't know," I said numbly.

*His face twisted. Briefly. But his voice
was cold.*

"You know now, though, don't you?"

*Filled with hopeless despair, I was still
fighting.*

*"I'm clean now," I told Peter. "I can
. . . bring you a certificate from the doctor if
you wish. Can't we . . . go on?"*

His eyes had flinched.

*"I went down on you," he said in a
trembling voice. "Don't you know I'd remember, every time, how I went down on you?"
He shuddered. "A body so beautiful, but,
on the inside, ugly, ugly . . ."*

*He stopped talking. He looked toward
the men. They were waiting near the outside
doors. He looked at me.*

"Don't bother me again."

*Numbly, I watched him walk away.
When he joined the others, one man, glanc-
ing toward me, said something. Peter Able,
laughing, shook his head. All three were
laughing as they went out the door.*

*Standing in the deserted lobby, a truly
terrible thought came to dwell in me.*

I shouldn't have been so quick to cure my body of the clap. I should have nurtured it, a just reward for every man who lusted after Alicel's beautiful shell of flesh.

The United States Public Health Service would beat a path to my door.

I shuddered. Not at the thought. At the knowledge I could entertain such hatefulness.

Numbly, I went on alone.

I hadn't intended to see any man twice. That was, after all, the basic idea of the singles bit, wasn't it? One-night stands, no commitment on either side.

Physically, however—and rather surprisingly—a certain itch for Herb Gloss remained. Whenever the memory of our episode floated idly across my mind, I felt a distinct twitching in my vagina, a lust for a repeat performance.

Inexplicable, really. The farthest thing from my mind was taking a steady lover. And Herb Gloss! A silly man in so many ways. Laughable in his earnest jargon that skated so glibly across the surfaces of feelings and meanings. Obviously trying too hard to capture the youth he had missed out on . . . and, beneath it all, so desperately lonely.

Yet Herb Gloss, taking so seriously the art of fucking, had dealt with me so expertly that the memory could put into my flesh a deliciously reminiscent shudder.

Quite late one night, after having retired early, I suddenly got out of bed, put on my tacky wig and outfit, and departed for Lord Harry's in search of Herbert Gloss.

Only a few people remained; some couples in booths, one customer, the predatory Italian boy who had briefly attracted me that first night, leaning on the bar brooding over a glass of beer. And Herb.

He sat in a booth talking to a baby-faced girl with that earnest air of imparting the wisdom of the world. Seeing me enter, he smiled. Then, frowning thoughtfully, he glanced at the girl beside him.

I slid up on the same stool I had taken before. Pete Regalado smiled, saying, "Nice to see you. One more time, we can start calling you a regular."

"Doesn't twice make one a regular?" I asked.

He shrugged, laughed. "How you like it is how it'll be."

It was late enough to think about waiting for closing time. Pete was an attractive man.

I sipped at my white wine, thinking how pleasant to pursue one's sexual whims. Even if only in the mind.

Herb Gloss slid onto the stool beside me. "You should have let me know you'd be around," he said reproachfully. "I *asked* you to phone."

"I didn't know, until a few minutes ago, that I was coming out tonight," I looked at him. "I was already in bed, but I got to thinking about you, Herb. Remembering how good we were together." My voice was deeply inviting. "So . . . here I am."

Herb looked troubled. "Well, there's this girl, you see. The one over there."

I looked over there. She was watching us, lips pouting. Scared she'll lose him, I thought. I felt recklessly selfish. Whim time. Right?

"Dump her," I said ruthlessly. "That is, if you want to fuck me again as badly as I want you to."

"You've got to understand, Alice," Herb said earnestly. "I have *committed* myself. Emotionally, physically, creatively." He almost blushed. "She smells like apples."

"An apple a day keeps the doctor away," I said.

He looked puzzled. Then he laughed. "You really do have your act together, Alice," he said appreciatively. "I'd *hate* to know that I had done anything to stir jealous anger. It's so *destructive*. There's quite enough destructiveness in the world, don't you think?"

"I am disappointed," I said.

"Next time, we must *plan*," he said. "We can be

ready for each other." He regarded me anxiously. "Or is not-planning your life-style? I wouldn't want to ask you to go against your life-style."

I put my hand on his. "Herb," I said, "we'll just let it happen. Right?"

He laughed happily. "You're right. Spontaneity can be the most creative thing of all."

He lifted himself off the stool.

"After all, Alice, I remember you, too. Most pleasantly. That lovely ass. "You *were* a bit passive at first, maybe all the way through. You could have been a *bit* more active. And you don't realize the importance of really creative head to get a fellow started."

I couldn't be offended by such earnest criticism. Nevertheless, there was a tiny hurt. I had given him good ass, hadn't I? I said it out loud.

"I gave you good ass."

He brightened. "You certainly did. You're very creative with your ass." Surprisingly, he thrust out his hand, shook mine.

"Got to go now. See you when it happens."

"See you when it happens," I said solemnly.

Watching him walk away, I wanted to laugh and wanted to cry. Silly man. And a great fuck.

On his way out, Herb Gloss smiled at me with gratitude and friendship—even a sort of loving. I watched him depart with the girl who smelled like apples, turned back to my solitary glass of wine.

I was not to be alone. The Italian boy slid onto the stool vacated by Herb. "I don't know what all you women see in that turkey," he sneered. "Every time I'm in here, I see him walking out with another piece of ass on his arm."

"Maybe it's because he fucks good," I said sweetly.

Wonderful to say precisely the thought in one's mind instead of suppressing it in favor of something decently polite. I've censored myself all my life, I thought. Not anymore.

"You don't know what good fucking is," he said. "You ain't fucked me yet."

Without attempting to reply to such arrogance, I laughed.

He stared challengingly. "Buy my a drink? I came in here with the price of one beer in my pocket."

"Sure," I said indifferently.

He mentioned to the bartender. "I'll have a—" his voice hesitated "—a Manhattan."

The bartender looked at him flat-eyed. "Let me see the color of your money."

The boy jerked a thumb. *"She's* paying."

Regalado wordlessly began to mix the drink. Sliding the glass across the bar, he looked at me, faintly but unmistakably shaking his head.

Uneasiness swarmed up like a hive of disturbed bees. Along with it, a tiny rebellion. Pete meant to warn me away from the boy. He was also trying to censor my activities.

I turned to my guest. "What's your name?"

Sipping gingerly at the drink, he made a face.

"Tony Saprito," he said. "Just call me 'Tony the Sap' if you want to get your teeth kicked in."

The automatic belligerence had the paradoxical effect of warming me toward him. Can't be more than twenty, I thought. Good-looking, too, with that arrogant Roman nose, the thin, bitter lips. And the scar on his neck, making him look both tough and vulnerable.

"Did they call you Tony the Sap in school?" I couldn't keep the softness out of my voice.

"They didn't call me that name but once," he said unforgivingly. This time he made the face before tasting the drink.

"If you don't like the Manhattan, order something else," I told him.

His glance was pure gratitude. "Don't see how people drink that garbage. Hey, down there. Bring me a depth charge."

I was fascinated. "What's a depth charge?"

"You'll see."

The bartender brought a mug of draft beer and a shot of whiskey. I watched as Tony delicately dropped the shot glass into the beer. It went heavily to the bottom. Tony picked up the mug and drank deeply. He smacked his lips.

"Now, that's what I call drinking!"

"My God!" I said involuntarily. "How can you keep it down?"

He sneered. "My Dad's a construction man. All the construction workers drink depth charges. Or boilermakers." He grinned. "Want to try it?"

I shuddered. "I should think it would make you very drunk, very quickly."

"It does." He leered suggestively. "But it don't take no edge off me. If you know what I mean."

"What do *you* do?" I asked. "Work in construction, too?"

His mouth twisted. "Me? Work? I'm strictly on the street, baby."

"My name is Alice."

He grinned meanly. "I don't need your name," he said. "To me, you're just another old cunt."

"You didn't have to say that."

He straightened. "Said it, didn't I?" He paused to stare at me. "You took it, didn't you?" He nodded affirmatively. "That's the way it is, baby."

"Why are you on the street?" I said carefully.

"Whaddaya want, my life story?" he demanded.

"Yes."

With a flourish, he drank the beer-and-whiskey down to the dregs, waved the mug. "Hey, fill 'er up here. Don't you know how to do your job?"

He watched Pete belligerently as he drew the beer.

"Another glass of wine, too, please," I said.

Pete didn't look at me. He put the wine before me, went away to the end of the bar where he sat reading the *Daily News,* ostentatiously demonstrating indifference to my fate.

Tony Saprito drank deeply.

"All right. My old man kicked me out when I told him he could take that old bricklayers' union and stuff it up his ass. I ain't gonna carry bricks for the next forty years till I get a slipped disc in my back—he can't straighten up for half an hour after he gets out of bed. He beat me up and threw me out of the house just to prove that, bad back and all, he was a better man than I am."

The words were hard-edged.

"I got three older brothers, they're already working with him. I don't know why he had to have me in the union, too."

"What did you really want to do?"

He looked away. "I was always good with math," he said. "You know? Wanted to go to college so I could get into that higher math." He jerked his shoulders. "I'd have settled for a course in accounting. Anything to do with numbers." His shoulders jerked again. "The old man had to have it his way or nothing. Said they'd turn me into a queer off at some college."

His mouth moved grimly. I remembered Herb Gloss had said he hustled gays as well as women.

Tony jerked his head around. "Had enough soap opera?" he demanded. "If you want some more, I'll cry you another lie or two. If you don't, let's go fuck."

I stood up. "All right, Tony. Let's go fuck."

Tony finished the depth charge, then reached for the unfinished Manhattan, pouring it down in one gulp.

"Keep the change, Pete," I called, laying a ten-dollar bill on the bar. He barely glanced up.

"That's a hell of a tip," Tony said harshly. "What's the matter, you got the hots for that Puerto Rican dude?"

"No," I said camly. "I've got the hots for you, Tony."

On the street, Tony hesitated. "Got a place we can go?"

I hadn't thought about that. I hadn't intended to take him to the apartment. Dangerous, I had realized without thinking about it, to let Tony Saprito know where I lived. Too late now, however, to withdraw.

"Come on," I said. "It's only a block or two."

The street was empty of people. At the head of the alley, Tony halted abruptly. "Down this way?" he said suspiciously. "Who lives on an alley?"

"I have to go in the back way," I said.

He looked at me. "What's your game, cunt?" he demanded. "Got somebody laying for me down there?"

"My game is getting laid," I said evenly. "Are you coming along to do the job or not?"

Reaching down into his boot, he brought up a knife. He flicked his wrist and the blade shot open, a silver flash under the streetlight.

"All right, lead on," he growled. "I'm ready for anything."

The sight of a knife in Tony's hand sent a cold shiver down my spine. It frightened me to think of walking into that tunnel of darkness with this violent boy. But, I thought in sudden realization, he's afraid too. As afraid as I am.

I reached to take his free hand. "I'm always scared when I come this way."

Tony gripped my hand firmly all the way to the door of my building. In the other hand he carried the knife.

I used the key, pushed open the heavy door. The kitchen was empty, utensils gleaming under overhead lights. Tony surveyed the place carefully.

"Hey, you work here?" His voice quickened. "I got an idea. Let me in some night when you know a couple apartments are empty. We'll split the loot between us." He was excited by the prospect. "I got a guy you can dump anything on, TV sets, silverware, even jewelry. Ought to be some rich pickings, building like this."

His eyes were hard. "Are you game?"

"I can't do that," I said. "The security is too good."

"You come and you go, don't you? That's good enough. Just slip me in, I'll do the rest."

"Tony," I said, smiling, "I want you to come often. But not to steal." Thinking about the knife he had returned to his boot, I kept on smiling. "Let's don't mess up our little playhouse. All right?"

Grudgingly, he said, "I guess you're right." He looked wistful. "I'd sure like to hit some places in a building like this, all right."

I was watching him. "Tony. Are you a thief?"

"I'm anything I have to be," he said in a hard voice. He jerked his head. "You taking me on upstairs, or are we gonna stand here jerking off all night?"

I was cautious in switching from the service elevator to the penthouse express. I didn't want the security men to see Alice! with this street boy.

Emerging into the apartment, Tony let out a low whistle. "Man, this is something!" He turned to me, a certain respect in his eyes. "You must be the maid."

My silence let stand the lie.

He studied me shrewdly. "When your people are away, the maid gets to play. Right?" His eyes cast about. "Where's your room? Or . . . hey, hell, let's fuck in *their* bed." He grinned fiendishly. "Lead me to the master bedroom, cunt."

I led him to the master bedroom.

In the bathroom, I realized that I was trembling. I was as frightened as I was hot, as hot as I was frightened. But—I meant to be fucked by that fascinatingly unpredictable boy.

When I came out, Tony stood naked before the full-length mirror. He swung around. "How you like that cock?" he demanded. "Ain't never seen nothing like it, have ya?"

Surprising. With his slight build, his hips were nonexistent, and I could count the ribs framing his chest. But his balls hung so heavy I thought it must be uncomfortable to wear blue jeans as snugly as he affected. And his cock, standing rigidly upright against his belly, was so long and thin it looked grotesque on his undernourished body.

He measured himself with his hand. "Nine inches. Queers go crazy when they see that Thing," he boasted.

"Women, too. So come get it, cunt. Sharpen your teeth on it, then I'll fuck you up the wall."

The trembling was deeper now, undeniable. As I watched, he thumped It deliberately against his belly. Seeing the glow in my eyes, he grinned delightedly.

"Don't be bashful," he said. "It's all yours."

I put up my hands. I took off the wig, tossed it to the floor. He stared as the real hair cascaded to my shoulders. Walking past him, I went to the dressing table, where, with a handful of cold cream, I took off the bad makeup. Deftly I touched on lipstick, eye shadow, making up my face in the accustomed way.

I went next to the closet. With back turned, I took off my clothes, put on a filmy, golden-transparent gown. I turned. Tony Saprito stood goggling. In his astonishment, his proud flag had drooped to half-mast.

"You don't work here," he breathed. "This place *belongs* to you." His eyes widened. "I seen your picture," he said. "You're . . ." He fumbled in the clutter of his mind for the right name.

"Alice!" I said. "And Alice! is mad for that cock of yours."

Gliding toward him, like a queen in a dream, I laid my crotch against his thigh. My fingertips touched the pink head of his cock, moved on to peel back the foreskin, exposing the shaft. It throbbed with violent eagerness.

No finesse, no foreplay, simply ruthless young energy exploding inside my vagina. His narrow hips drove in short, hard plunges, as though he meant to beat me into submission.

With such violence, I was afraid it would be too quick. Greedy to get mine, I began straining immediately for orgasm. I got it. Tony didn't come with me, but kept on fucking at the same headstrong pace. Still he didn't come. Forced into a second and a third orgasm, finally a helpless fourth, I was used up. I lay still and trembling under the drive of his cock, thinking he would never be through with fucking me.

Suddenly, he stopped.

Speared deeply into me, he gazed into my face. His eyes were no longer predatory; there showed, instead, a sense of wonder.

"I'm fucking Alice!" he whispered in awe. "It just now got through to me. I'm fucking Alice, the most beautiful woman in the world."

"One of the *five* most beautiful women," I murmured. "But you didn't come."

He grew sullen. "I don't come all that much. It gets so hard it *hurts* to come, and then I can't. All I wind up with is the stone ache."

"Because you don't really like women?" I whispered.

His face was naked now, the young vulnerability showing through the belligerence. Yet he was still hard inside me; I could feel in his cock the beat of his heart's pulse.

"I like *you*," he said. "Because you're the most beautiful woman in the world."

"You're a sweet boy," I said in his ear. "So sweet and hard inside me."

I put both hands on his narrow ass, pulling him snugly into the cradle of my loins. As I did so, my vagina melted upward on the shaft of his cock. I felt Its head penetrate the final barrier of resistance to touch the cervix. It hurt, and it felt good, so I moved again, the same way. I could feel myself sucking hungrily with my innermost cunt, enfolding the feverish head. I did not will it; it happened of itself, when in all my earlier fucking I had not known it *could* be willed into such delicate action.

He began to come. He didn't need to move, because his cock was gripped so tightly, the stroking muscles of my cunt milking the come out of his balls and down through his penis, sucking it out to overflow moistly on the sheets beneath us.

When he was finished, I would not let him go, but held him in my arms, turning so we could lie side by side. His cock, now limp, rested sweetly in Alice!'s pussy.

"Hey, I gotta get outa here! It's nearly daylight."

The harsh words rousing me from slumber, my arms clutched instinctively to hold his restless body. Even sleeping, the flesh remembered, and did not want to let him go.

Bursting out of restraint, Tony sat up.

"I told you. Gotta get out. Don't want me walking out in broad daylight, do you, let everybody know Alice! has been fucking Tony Saprito?"

His usual sneering tone. As though the night had never been.

As he got dressed, he kept his back turned. I lay watching, savoring in my mind the new discovery. Like riding a bicycle, I thought dreamily, I'll never forget how.

"Tony, you're a love," I said in a voice as languorous as my body.

"Yeah, sure," he snarled.

Armored now in blue jeans, he could look at me. Curiously I studied his crotch. How did he get It all in there?

Marching over to the dressing table, he picked up the clock, yanking its cord out of the socket.

I said, "What are you doing?"

Ignoring me, he picked up my wristwatch, placed it beside the clock. He turned, surveying the room. He yanked loose the plug of the small Sony television, unscrewed with deft fingers the cable connection, and put it on the floor with the other things.

I lay still, watching. He snatched up a pillow from the bed, flipped the pillowcase empty and put the watch and clock into it, along with my silver-backed brushes.

Alarmed, I sat up. "What do you think you're doing, Tony?"

Not the sweet kid I had cherished during the night; the eyes were predatory again. Stooping quickly, he came up with the switchblade.

"Just stay where you are, and keep quiet. I don't want to have to cut that beautiful face."

"Tony. You don't have to do this."

"Who's to stop me?" he demanded. "You?" He looked contemptuous. "I'm gonna walk out of here with everything I want. Make a complaint, you got to tell the cops you been fucking Tony Saprito. Right?"

I stood up. "Tony," I said tenderly. "How long have you been on the street?"

The movement, the tone of voice, disconcerted him. He took a step backward.

"Nearly a year, but what business is it of yours?" he muttered. Then he added, "Cunt!" spitting out the word like a bad taste in his mouth.

I was closer now, getting closer still.

"And you're hungry and you're scared most of the time, and more than anything else you want to go home to your brothers and your father."

He waved the knife menacingly, "I don't *want* to cut you, Alice! Don't make me do it." Then he said, "I told you, I ain't gonna lay bricks with a bad back all my life, like my old man."

Close enough to touch, now, but I was not quite brave enough. The violence was in him. The knife was there.

I went on past him. Opening the drawer of the dressing table, I took out my checkbook and a pen. I sat down on the vanity bench and made out a check with meticulous care.

Tony watched warily. He flinched when I handed him the check.

He looked at it. Stupidly, he said, "That's a check for five thousand dollars."

"Yes," I said. "So you won't have to steal the television set, and my silver-backed hairbrushes."

He kept on staring at it in disbelief.

"Five thousand dollars ought to be enough to get you through college, if you're careful," I said. "It's another choice between home and hustling, Tony."

He thrust it violently at me. "I can rip you off. But I can't beg."

"You're not begging," I said. "I'm giving it to you. In the trust that you'll use it for college."

"I don't even know I can get *in* college," he muttered.

I was thinking, with a secret satisfaction, that with one quick move of his hands he could have torn it up. He had not done so.

He dredged up a suspicion. "How many times I got to fuck you?"

"You can fuck me anytime you like, Tony," I said serenely. "If you'd rather not, you don't have to see me again."

"Listen," he said hoarsely. "You *deserve* to be ripped off, letting somebody like me into a place like this. But I can't take this kind of money."

"Then consider it a loan," I said. "Once you're through college, earning enough to afford it, you can pay me back. All right?"

"You're just putting me on, anyway. A rich woman's joke. This check will bounce like a rubber ball."

"It's the Chase Manhattan just around the corner," I told him. "They'll probably give you some trouble about cashing it . . . though, if I were you, I'd open an account, not risk walking around with so much money in your pocket. If they question it, tell them to call me."

He began to believe it. "I didn't expect anything like this," he said hoarsely. "I just expected another cunt hot to get Tony in the sack." He studied me. "You do this all the time, don't you? Put on that ugly wig so nobody will guess who you are, go pick up somebody to get laid."

I laughed. "As a rule, I don't hand out five-thousand-dollar checks." I paused. "You'll keep my secret, won't you?"

"Sure," he said expansively. "I wouldn't rat on your cute little caper." He tried to look scornful again. "Wouldn't nobody believe it, anyway. Tony Saprito from the Bronx, fucking Alice!"

He was out of words. The check in one hand, switchblade in the other, he leaned suddenly to plant an awkward kiss on my mouth.

"You better get me outa here."

I took him down through the kitchen. Just dawn, fortunately the staff had not begun to arrive. I unlocked the outside door. Tony stepped through, turned, made an effort to curl his lip.

"Ah," he said, waving a negating hand. "It's just chicken feed to you, anyway."

Rapidly he walked away down the alley. He did not look back.

> *I was numb. Not just temporarily but forever. Going through the paces of life and career like a programmed robot, I smiled when it was time to show a smile, dressed the beautiful body at the time for the beautiful body to be dressed, posed at the time for posing, gave sparkling interviews when it was time to sparkle.*

> *When the time came to fuck, I laid down the beautiful body and let it be fucked.*

> *One would have thought, with soul and body so scarred by Alice!'s experiences of love, I would have retreated into celibacy. It didn't work that way. Being asked to fuck is programmed into the life and career of a professional beauty. Whenever any man's gaze lighted on Alice!, his groin ached with desire. It had always been so—including Daddy—and so it would always remain.*

> *When Alice! was implored or commanded or charmed or challenged into bed, I accepted the necessity of performance as I accepted the assignments arranged by Paul Riff in exploitation of my burgeoning fame.*

> *I have no idea how many men fucked Alice! during that year. There's no individual*

*memory of an individual man. A faceless
procession of parading cocks, in all the infinite variety of cocks, into and out of my
flesh awkwardly or skillfully, impatient with
ardor or cool with expertise. They came too
quickly, or lasted too long, they demanded
response or passivity, they needed cherishing or simply a warm hole.*

*In all their variety, they were the same.
They were* Them.

*In my numbness, not once can I recall
looking at a cock, robustly ready to thrust
into me, and wondering if this man, like
Harris O'Brien, was conscienceless enough to
fuck me in full knowledge that he would leave
me with a souvenir of his passage through my
flesh.*

*Though truly indifferent to all event
and circumstance, I did not lie passive, allowing them the use of Alice!'s beautiful envelope of flesh. No; like a robot I writhed my
body through the responses demanded by titillation and fulfillment. My pussy quickened,
eager to accept the erection. Tissues engorged
themselves with blood, flowered and warmed
and became moist. If the man was good
enough, lasted long enough, I would have the
requisite orgasm. But the orgasm reached no
deeper into my cold self than a failure to
achieve orgasm. Either/or, I remained unaf-
fected.*

Numb.

*Fifty. A hundred. Two hundred. I never
knew the number. Because Alice! never said
no.*

*Paul Riff was concerned about my be-
havior. I made no attempt to enlighten his
puzzlement. I only did what Paul Riff told me
to do. Alice! had complete confidence that
Paul would do the right thing at the right*

time for her career. Even, if that was possible, for her happiness.

Paul Riff was a man. He was my friend. His wife Zella was also my friend. But, as numb to him as to the bellboy or the company president who had fucked me last night, if Paul Riff had requested the boon of a piece of ass from the lovely Alice!—I would have fucked Paul Riff.

He had never even hinted. He did not ask now. But—Paul Riff did a far more terrible thing.

Paul was uneasy, that day, when he entered the apartment. In his friendship and dedication, the man was so transparent I said immediately, "What's the matter, Paul?"

"What makes you think something's the matter?" he said jerkily.

I smiled. "Because something is the matter. So you might as well tell me."

He turned away, muttering. "So it was going to be the biggest deal of all. Who needs it? That's what I say." He forced himself to look at me. "We're doing great, aren't we? A year ago, could anybody have guessed Alice! would be where she is today? Just tell me that's not true!"

I was still smiling. "Paul. I'm not arguing with you. You're arguing with yourself." I paused. Then I made a shrewd guess. "It's the TTM contract, isn't it?"

The TTM contract had dropped on us out of nowhere. Not just a film; a career in films. Though the first project alone was spectacular enough by itself. It was presented to us by Reid Ulric and his associates as a multi-million-dollar film, a panoramic portrayal of the Alice!-body in a dazzling series of historical fashion creations, from Cleo-

patra's Egyptian style to Dolley Madison's
inaugural gown. The costumes were to be meticulously researched and recreated by the
great Paris designer, Fauchard.

The character role bodied forth in those
elegant fashions was equally fascinating; a
reincarnation epic, the history of that eternal
female spirit whose destiny it was to become
embodied in a catalytic Everywoman of each
historical age from Cro-Magnon man to the
Kennedy Camelot. Alice!, as an actress,
would have the glorious opportunity to create
the avatars of that enduring soul which
dwelled within the temporal envelopes of
beautiful flesh. The challenge awed my soul,
excited my spirit.

"Woman The Great" was only the first
film. Beyond . . .

"Reid Ulric is convinced that the only
way motion pictures can meet the challenge
of television is to do on the big screen what
the little screen cannot do," Paul had told
me on first bringing the proposed contract
to my attention.

"Alice!, it's the deal of a lifetime. Ulric
wants to put you under personal contract for
a period of seven years. He will operate, ex-
clusively for Alice!, like the old studios used
to operate with their stables of stars. He'll
take charge of everything; the studio will
dress you, display you, manage your publicity. A total package." He paused, gazing
earnestly. "He intends to build a studio complex, complete in all phases, devoted ex-
clusively to the exploitation of Alice! as an
international star. He's putting millions into
it. Millions."

"But, Paul," I said. "Where does that
leave you?"

He nodded enthusiastically. "That's

*what makes it absolutely perfect. I will be-
come Vice-President for talent. In other
words, I'll be Vice-President in Charge of
Alice!"*

*He frowned. "I won't be in complete
control, you understand. No way, in a pro-
duction company of that size, headed by
Reid Ulric, who is a take-charge guy if I
ever saw one. But I will have my influence.
And you, Alice! You'll be the greatest star
in the history of show business."*

*Paul was so enthusiastic on that first
occasion. Then, of course, the negotiations
dragged on interminably. "It's for seven
years, Alice!," he kept saying, warning himself as much as me. "We have to think of
everything!"*

*His spirits rose and fell with the prog-
ress, or lack of progress, in the negotiations.
Never, however, had he reached the dispirited
depths he now displayed.*

*"You told me the other day everything
was bolted down except for a few inconse-
quential details," I said.*

*He nodded morosely. "It was. But then
. . . a whole new concept was injected into
the discussions." His eyes avoided mine. "By
Reid Ulric himself. In a . . . private conversation."*

*I stared at Paul Riff. I sat down on the
white sofa, arranged my hands in my lap.*

"You'd better tell me."

*Paul fidgeted as though he had found
himself standing on a hot plate.*

*"I'm changing my mind," he pro-
claimed. "The whole deal is too grandiose.
It's bound to fail, leave us with egg on our
face. One man can't single-handedly recreate
the old studio system. Not even Reid Ulric."*

He glared defiantly. "TTM could sur-

vive a failure. Alice! can't." He moved his shoulders. *"Doing so great the way we're going, why take a big risk?"* He looked at me pleadingly. *"Seven years, Alice!. You'd get to hate it. Tight control of every phase of your life, being made to do things you didn't particularly want to do . . . It's not for you."*

"I do things now I don't particularly like to do," I said, *"because Paul Riff tells me it's right for Alice!"*

He firmed himself. *"I say, tell, Reid Ulric it's a flat-out no. To the whole deal."*

I looked at my hands. *"Tell me. What is the new . . . idea . . . Ulric injected into the negotiations?"*

He wouldn't look at me. His tone was flat. Dead.

"Ulric says a personal audition is necessary before the final signing. Goes by instinct, he claims, and he can't trust his instinct about Alice! without a personal meeting."

A very long pause. Then, somehow, Paul made himself lay it out.

"He wants you to be his houseguest for the weekend at his hunting lodge in the Michigan woods."

At the beginning, Paul had declared the basic principle: Alice! would not fuck her way to fame and fortune. No moral judgment; simply Paul's conviction that such means, revealing a lack of class and style, would be detrimental to the successful creation of the persona to be known as Alice!.

The denial of such demands, he felt, created a greater respect and regard. But the prospect presented by the great contract had seduced my mentor into a greediness I would not have believed was in him. Paul Riff wanted me to fuck Reid Ulric.

Reid Ulric had discovered Paul Riff's price.

So I looked at Paul Riff for a long time before I spoke.

He wouldn't, I knew, tell me I must do it. He wouldn't even ask me to do it, for his sake and mine. But—he was willing to put me on a plane for Michigan. He might even pretend forever after that it had not happened.

But Paul Riff would know. As Alice! would know.

All right, I told myself. Paul knows that I fuck. With utter promiscuity. He can tell himself, What difference? So she fucks Reid Ulric this weekend instead of somebody insignificant and accidental. If it helps to smooth the path, well and good. So what is lost?

Except Paul Riff's basic principle: Alice! will not take the easy shortcut to fame and fortune. Alice! will be respected for her integrity as well as cherished for her beauty.

That was all.

What about me?

Dead inside already, a small death more couldn't matter. But how many small deaths can a soul endure?

I had already died again in that moment when I saw the greed in Paul Riff's soul.

Again: If I had met Reid Ulric in an elevator, at a cocktail party; if he had suggested that we make love, numb-Alice, whether or not I knew who he was, would have numbly accepted. Because the dead-inside Alice! never said no. Numb-Alice was indifferent to Them.

Again—what difference?

"*It's against your own principle, Paul,*" I said.

The shrug involved his whole body, writhing its gesture of ultimate indifference.

"*That's what I said. So we forget it. Too big a risk, anyway. Fall on our face with Reid Ulric's grand ideas, we'd never get up again.*"

He wanted me to do it so badly he was aching inside.

"*All right,*" I said, standing up. "*When does the plane leave?*"

Paul's face was stricken. He had hoped beyond hope, even in the clutches of greed, that I would deny his betrayal.

"*Alice!*" he said brokenly.

Putting my arms around him, I held him as one comforts a baby. Breaking down completely, he cradled his head in my arms.

"*They always get to you sooner or later, don't they?*" he said, his voice crying out the words. "*I'll make it up to you, Alice!*"

I didn't say anything. I was numb inside, even as I comforted him for his own betrayal.

He made an attempt to pull himself together. "*It's a tough world, Alice!*" He was quieter now. "*The higher you get, the tougher the world gets.*"

Better now. He disengaged from my embrace.

"*You're a great woman, Alice!*" he said earnestly. "*You'll go all the way, because you've got what it takes. It's a privilege to be associated with such a great woman.*"

Sure, I thought, I've got what it takes. A cunt.

A private plane, and I was the only passenger. At the small airport, a chauffeured

*limousine waited. We transferred to a motor-
boat for a swift ride across wind-choppy
water to Reid Ulric's private island.*

*Until this moment I had not known a
person could own his own island.*

*The island was evergreen-wooded down
to the water's edge. The trees grew close to
the walls of the hunting lodge, making it
darkly secretive. The only sign of civilization
was the single building, blending into the dark
green of the trees, and an unpretentious
wooden dock.*

*The boatman, carrying my weekend
bag, escorted me directly to my room. It was
furnished in rustic, masculine style. The outside light from the one large window was
screened to dimness by the evergreen boughs.*

*I found a message on the bedside table:
"I will expect you for drinks and a get-ac-
quainted session at five-thirty. Ulric."*

*Only three-thirty now. I unpacked my
suitcase, laid out my toilet articles, took a
bath. I lay down on the bed. The flight from
New York had lasted just long enough to get
fucked by the pilot and the co-pilot.*

Alice! was ready for Reid Ulric.

*But only when I emerged at the ap-
pointed time did I discover that I was in
competition with two other beautiful girls
for Reid Ulric's favor and patronage.*

*Time was of the essence, it seemed, for
we arrived simultaneously in the living room.
A huge room, it was sparely furnished in
natural woods and leather, decorated with
graceful, antlered heads and bearskin rugs
with claws and grinning teeth.*

*No time to register the unexpected pres-
ence of the competition before Reid Ulric
came in unto us.*

"All right, girls, here we are!" he said, beaming and clapping his hands together. *"First we've got to get acquainted. Get to be friends. Right?"*

The three of us stood silent. We did not look at each other. We were giving our full attention to Reid Ulric.

He must be, I thought, close to seven feet tall. He was large in proportion, with long, brawny arms, hands like hams, a bullet-shaped, completely bald head. Apparently having just come from a swim, he wore a pair of still-wet trunks and a white terry-cloth bathrobe. His chest, his forearms, were extraordinarily hairy.

His face was bold in feature, a large, bulbous nose, a generous mouth. Scar tissue prominent in the eyebrows made his brow a lowering shelf even when, as now, he smiled. The black brows were thick in one line.

So ugly, so scarred—yet so magnetically powerful that it emanated in waves—he was a fascinating man.

"A drink first, then I'll fill you in on the deal." He slapped his hands together again, like a camp counselor inciting enthusiasm. *"What'll it be? Name your poison."*

"Bourbon," I said. I had never drunk bourbon.

The other girls made theirs a Tom Collins and a daiquiri, respectively. When Reid Ulric became occupied with mixing drinks, we had time to study each other.

The small, neat-bodied girl was red-haired, with provocative, slanting oddly green eyes that lent her a look both innocent and wicked. Dimples in her cheeks, a cute dusting of freckles across her uptilted nose. She wore a simple green frock that revealed the petite lines of her body.

The other girl was bigger, with a broad-shouldered frame ample to support her spectacular breasts. The breasts, in subtle motion from her breathing, were outlined by a sleek black blouse. They thrust out nobly, the nipples taut under the fabric as though she were in heat. Her hair, falling straight to her shoulders, was sleek and glossy black. The rich black fabric of her skirt molded her loins boldly. A pale complexion, with sensual lips. Her eyes had a strange, brooding quality in the still face, as though dreaming of the last time she had been fucked. Or the next.

Alice! was the blonde.

Ulric came with drinks, returned for his own. He, too, I noticed, was drinking bourbon. Jack Daniel's, the label read. I tasted it. Smooth and heavy in my mouth, warm in my belly.

I wondered why, here on this island, I had decided to drink bourbon, when I had never tasted it before.

"This cute little thing here is Terry," Reid Ulric announced. As he passed, he slapped her lightly on the fanny. Terry smiled.

"This big beautiful woman is Marlene," he continued. Putting one hand under a massive breast, he lifted it appreciatively. *"Ain't them the most beautiful tits you ever saw?"*

Marlene smiled.

He turned. "And this . . . is Alice!"

He did not touch me.

Alice! smiled.

He moved one hand in a hospitable gesture. "Make yourselves comfortable, girls, and I'll tell you what this little shindig is all about."

We sat in a row on the long leather sofa,

so dominated by Reid Ulric's presence, none of us had spoken a word.

"Now, girls, I'm going to give you in a nutshell Reid Ulric's philosophy of life."

He had centered a straight wooden chair so we could pay him our undivided attention. He sat leaning forward, his legs apart, the glass braced in his hand on one knee. His great thighs overflowed the narrow seat.

"That philosophy is . . . competition." *He repeated the word, watching each of us in turn.* "Com-pe-TITION!"

He leaned back expansively. The muscles in his hairy belly rippled. A lot of fat now, I thought. But also strength.

"I started out as a football man," *he said.* "I was a star in high school, an All-American in college. For ten years in the pro ranks, I was the greatest center professional football has ever boasted."

He paused impressively. "When I signed with the pros, Reid Ulric had never played in a losing game. The first time my pro team lost, I cried like a baby."

He slapped his knee, his voice leaping out at us. "Competition! That's what it's all about!"

He smiled widely. "Good, clean, healthy competition. I had my nose smashed so many times I lost count. My left leg was broken in three places from a beauty of a block, and before my third year in the pros I didn't have a tooth left in my head." *He grinned reminiscently.* "You know, one of the great locker-room pranks, somebody'd go in during the game and mix up everybody's teeth into one big pile. Man, you ought to have heard the cussing as the guys tried to find their own dentures!"

His laughter was loud, booming. Be-

*cause the other girls were laughing with him,
Alice! laughed also.*

"To me, competition is the most American thing about America. It's made us the
great nation we are today."

He was serious now.

His brows knitted together, he said,
"I dreamed up this great project to restore
the motion picture to its former glory as the
greatest entertainment medium in the world."
He was leaning tensely forward again. "You
want to know something? I hate that little
box that's dominating the life of every man,
woman, and child in this great nation. Hate
it! And I'm going to rescue the movie industry—my industry—from that goddamn
idiot box if it takes the last breath of my
body, the last cell in my brain, and every
dime I possess in this world."

*His great hand pounded instantly
against his knee.*

"To do what I mean to do, I need a
woman. A sex symbol, and girl-next-door, a
movie queen and a mysterious goddess, all
rolled into one. A STAR to capture the
imagination of the world!"

He leaned back, breathing heavily.

"All right. I started looking for a woman possessed of those capabilities—the beauty, the talent, the soul and the spirit and the
courage . . . not to mention the will!—to become all things to all men."

Quieter now. "I searched. For months.
I didn't delegate the task to an underling. No
sir. I devoted my own energies to finding that
woman. Because nobody could do it but Reid
Ulric."

*I drank deeply of the bourbon. The glass
was nearly empty. Reid, the gracious host,
noted it and rose to replenish the drinks.*

He resumed in a conversational tone.

"I found Terry first, dealing blackjack in Las Vegas." *He grinned at her.* "You probably don't remember, but I dropped a grand on your table one afternoon, in about twenty minutes. You deal a wicked hand of blackjack, girl."

Terry gave him a conspiratorial grin in return. "I remember. I had to ask who you were."

Ulric nodded. "An agent brought Marlene to my attention. She was playing the role of an exotic dancer, down on her luck, in a bus-and-truck show that was a Broadway hit ten years ago. I flew to Butte, Montana, to look at her."

"God, do I remember Butte," *Marlene said, nodding.*

I had heard them speak now. Terry's voice carried a happy lilt, Marlene's throaty, intimate quality.

"I didn't see *Alice!* in person," *Reid said, looking at me.* "I don't look at magazines, I don't read books, I don't even read scripts. No time for that sort of thing. But somebody happened to leave a copy of Life magazine on my private plane. The issue with a Halsband photograph of *Alice!* on the cover."

He nodded soberly. "I had an embarrassment of riches. Looking for one great woman, I had found three who showed enormous possibilities. No way could I make the final choice."

He placed his broad palm on his scarred forehead. "Then it came to me. Competition. The only way to decide. Reid Ulric's way. The American way."

He smiled as if in gratitude for the inspiration.

"Girls, that's what this weekend is all about. We're entirely alone on the island; I gave the staff a vacation." He stared at us in challenge. *"I want you to understand one thing very clearly. Each and every minute— from the moment you walked into this room —you are in competition with each other. The winner will become the greatest star the world has ever known."*

Ulric signaled a break for fresh drinks. I stood up and went to look out a window. The water beyond the trees was black under the late-afternoon sun. This was farther north than I had ever been.

"Alice! will you join us?" Reid asked politely.

I returned to my seat, accepted the third drink. The other two had not moved.

"I have a program definitely mapped out. I won't go into it in detail, because one important element of the competition is not knowing what's coming next."

He leaned forward, his voice exploding.

"Don't get me wrong, girls. This is not playacting. It's for real. I intend to put pressure on you. You'll be putting pressure on each other. The first one to break is out of it!"

Breathing hard again, he went on, *"But I guarantee you. You won't leave here wondering whether you've won or whether you've lost. That's the American way . . . compete . . . keep score . . . and crown the winner!"*

He subsided. *"All right. Are you willing?"*

Such sheer drive, utter concentration, could not be other than compelling. Simultaneously, the three of us nodded our compliance.

"You're going to be naked to me," he warned. "Your heart, your soul, your body. When I say 'naked,' I mean it both literally and metaphorically." Calmly he added, "Stand up and take off your clothes. You will put them on again when you leave the island."

As though mesmerized, we rose and began to undress. When we stood naked, we did not look at each other. We gazed at Reid Ulric.

"First of all, I will fuck you. It's one of my deepest convictions that, to be a great star, a woman must be a great lay. Beyond that, it is necessary that I know the texture of your skin, the temperature of your pussy, the smell of your body. I must know you—and fucking is the basic communication between a man and a woman."

He raised a hand.

"Don't misunderstand. I didn't dream up this weekend to avail myself of some lovely ass." He snapped his fingers. "That's all Reid Ulric's got to do when he needs a woman. As a matter of fact, I have a friend who's not half the beauty you are, but since the first time I laid her, eleven months ago, I haven't touched anybody else. Lucy performs a very simple and profound function in my life. She satisfies Reid Ulric."

The heavy line of his brows drew down. "This is serious business. If it could be delegated to someone else, I would have delegated it. But only Reid Ulric can gather the data necessary for a final decision."

He concentrated on us one by one; Terry first, Marlene, then me.

"If you don't want any part of it, now's the time to say so." He turned heavily in the chair, pointing. "I'll pick up that telephone and tell them to bring the boat to take you back to the mainland."

He turned again. Now the finger was pointing at us. "If you stay, you are consenting to each and every phase of the competition I have devised." His voice heavy now, the words as solid as stone. "Clean competition. Hard-hitting but fair. No cat-fighting, no back-biting, no bitchiness. Fair and open and aboveboard. Anybody displaying bad sportsmanship gets disqualified."

His voice sank into a compelling softness.

"But understand one thing, girls. If you quit now, you'll know for the rest of your life that you refused the greatest opportunity for stardom that has ever been offered in the history of show business."

It was very still in the big room.

"We got any quitters here? Speak now, or hold your peace."

Nobody spoke.

Startlingly, he again clapped his hands. "That's the spirit I expected to see!" Surging massively forward, he put his arms around all of us at once. "You're great girls, and I love you. In my book, you're all winners."

We were much too close in his collective embrace. My thigh was pushed against Marlene's thigh; I could feel the trembling of her muscles. I was trembling, too, with nervous excitement. It was like being in the huddle before the start of a football game.

Reid Ulric, releasing us, fixed new drinks all around. As he returned, Terry said in her merry voice, "Reid, if we have to be naked, you ought to take off your clothes!"

Provocative, insinuating, a purring be-

hind the words. Terry, I decided, had a marvelous instrument of a voice.

Reid, grinning, took off his bathrobe and flung it at a chair.

"I'll let you remove the trunks," he said to Terry.

Eagerly she knelt, her hands reaching to push down the knit fabric. Marlene and I stood watching. When the cock and balls emerged into view, involuntarily I looked at Marlene. She looked at me. It was the first eye contact between us.

I wondered if her reaction contained as much surprise as mine. Such a huge man, one would have expected a penis to match. Instead It was quite small, with neat balls snugged underneath. It looked, indeed, like the equipment of a boy not quite adolescent.

Maybe It's really quite normal in size, I thought, but on him It looks small.

Only then, with Reid Ulric naked too, did I realize that the opportunity for withdrawal from the competition had not tempted me.

Instead, I felt compelled. The power and intensity revealed in his driving words had created an atmosphere in which it was impossible not to compete. And win, I thought fiercely. Win!

My attention was drawn abruptly to Terry's activities. From her kneeling position, she rose with her crotch pressing against the tree trunk of hairy leg. She moved slowly, making him feel her pubic mound. Putting both arms around his massive belly, she shivered against him.

"Will you fuck me first, Reid?" She giggled in an irresistible burst of sound. "You've made me so horny!"

He smiled benevolently. "All in good

time, my dear." His arm around her, his hand patted her shoulder. "I haven't decided who I want to fuck first, last, or in the middle."

His eyes swept speculatively over me and Marlene. Then he looked down at Terry.

"Seems to me you girls ought to be thinking about getting me horny," he said. "Then I'll know who I want to fuck."

Before he had finished speaking, Terry's small hand had crept down to cup his balls. I looked at Marlene. Marlene looked at me.

Simultaneously we moved in on cute little Terry's sexual monopoly.

Because Terry's hand had captured his balls, and Marlene, leaning her rose-nippled breast against his arm, was kissing him with languorous thoroughness, my only recourse was to take his Thing in hand. It was like touching a delicate flower, watching it bloom in one's hand. The pink head peeped out of my fist with a shy boldness that made me want to—want to—caress It with the tip of my tongue. As I watched with avid eyes Its stiffening response to our tripled caresses, a bead of moisture formed in the eye. If we had been alone I would have supped it delicately, as a bee probes for nectar, with the tip of my tongue.

Why, or how, or when it had happened, I didn't know. But the numbness had dissolved as winter's ice melts under the breath of spring. Inside me, something came flutteringly alive. I feasted my eyes on the monstrous body, desiring to encompass his ugliness as I was encompassing with my hand the singular beauty of his delicately immature cock.

Reid Ulric looked down into my face.

For a long moment, our eyes clung. Marlene, her mouth on his nipple, was sucking as greedily as a baby. Terry, her hand touching my hand because she still caressed his balls, nibbled at his häiry thigh with quick little kisses.

For that long moment, Reid Ulric and I were alone with each other, drowned in the ocean of our seeing, and again the butterfly wings fluttered. Involuntarily I gave him a secret-sharing smile, intimate and real. In acknowledgment, the corners of his mouth quirked.

The other women were closed out. Sure now of their power, the wings fluttered once more.

Had the numbness in which I had dwelled so long vanished simply because Reid Ulric had aroused a competitive spirit in my soul? I had counted on the numbness to carry me through the three days of Ulric.

A man of diabolical power, I thought. He's done it to all three of us; shattered our womanly reserve, reduced our egos to the non-ego of a slave, aroused in us hungers and appetites we didn't realize existed.

I knew it now. I hated Marlene and Terry. I was also afraid of them. Passionate to be chosen for the first fucking, the fluttering inside me was no longer the delicate beating of a butterfly's wings. It had grown into a fierce dragon of hate and desire, its savagery to be tempered only by victory.

Desperate to build upon the shared moment, I moved downward, ravenous for the taste of Reid Ulric's cock.

Reid, however, was heaving himself to his feet. He stood with legs braced conqueringly apart, looking down as we gazed up at him. The small cock was rigid.

Ulric held out a hand. "Come."

Eagerly, all three reached. But it was to Marlene he had spoken. Taking her hand, he pulled her to her feet. A black wave tossed rebelliously through me. It's not fair, a being greedy for victory screamed inside me. We looked at each other.

Sportsmanship. The single word rang, a warning bell, in my head. No crying foul, I told myself sternly. Not in this game.

Rising to my feet, I watched Marlene walk victoriously before Reid Ulric. Aware of his eyes, her body undulated seductively. At the door to his bedroom she turned briefly, her look across the room at me and Terry a blaze of triumph. Then, as though her legs had weakened under voluptuous anticipation, she swayed against Reid Ulric. Clapping a hand over her breast, he smiled down at her.

They disappeared together.

Terry snapped indignantly to her feet. Her face was furious.

"He really wanted me," she said with a toss of her red curls. "He chose her deliberately, because he knew he wanted me before anybody else."

She was cute even in anger, prettier than ever with the lambent eyes glowing in fury.

She turned to me. "If Ulric's a tit man, we're dead, you and I."

She was offering an implicit alliance against the temporary victor; a sympathetic sharing of misfortune, a mutual girding of our loins to recapture the lost ground.

"We've both got nice boobs," she said generously. "But hardly a dairy farm, like hers." She spat out the two emphatic words

as though they were pebbles in her mouth.

She nodded conspiratorially. "And so fleshy. *Call it voluptuous if you want to,* but to me it looks like fat."

I didn't say anything.

"Fat!" Terry said again, savoring the word even as, looking down at herself, her hands smoothed the flat lines of her belly.

She looked at me challengingly. "Well, why don't you say something? Don't try to hide it. You're as mad as I am about being second choice. Or third."

A shrewd thought filtered through my mind. Reid Ulric had not revealed every aspect of the competition. Somewhere a silent reel might be turning, recording our every word.

"There had to be a winner and two losers," I said calmly. "There'll be a lot more losing in this game for all of us. And the victories may be harder to handle than the defeats. I want another drink. What about you?"

Going to the bar, I poured from the square bottle with the black label. I tasted the bourbon. Too strong. There was a pitcher of spring water. I added from it and tasted again. Good.

"You'd better be careful about drinking so much," Terry said spitefully. "He'd probably hate it if you got drunk on him."

Without reply, I took another swallow. Jack Daniel's will be my drink from now on, I decided. I'd have Paul put in a clause that TTM Productions would be required to supply me with the good bourbon throughout the seven years of the contract.

I knew, then, that I meant to win. Would win.

Terry, aggressive defiance showing in

*her face, came to the bar, made a drink with
practiced deftness. Not the delicate daiquiri
she had requested of Ulric, but a salty dog
. . . heavy on the vodka, light on the grape-
fruit juice.*

*She inhaled half of it in one gulp. "If he
thinks he's going to put It in me still dripping
from her cunt, he's got another think coming," she said viciously.*

*Regarding me, she smiled with sudden
friendliness. "Now I wouldn't mind so much
if it were you." She giggled. "In fact, I'd
sorta like the idea."*

*Her tilted eyes were glowing. She fin-
ished the drink in another swallow, expertly
fixed another.*

*"You ever been loved by a woman?"
she asked.*

"No," I said.

*"We might have to get into some of that,
if he likes to watch things." She nodded
judiciously. "So you'd better be prepared."*

*"Have you made love with a woman?"
I asked curiously.*

*"I had a terrible crush on the Phys Ed
instructor at my boarding school." She giggled. "We got caught in her room. She was
fired, and I got sent home."*

*She brooded, her eyes shadowed by ten-
der memories.*

"But not since?"

*"I still had my cherry then, I was just a
child. First time I got laid by a man, I knew
that was where it was at." She giggled irresistibly. "But, with her, you know, it was
sorta nice."*

*"Your first boy must have been very
good, then," I said politely.*

*"Well, I've certainly been queer for men
ever since." She added matter-of-factly, "Ac-*

tually, it was rape. My uncle, and he was about fifty years old, with a paunch out to here." Her eyes were remembering again. *"I loved it, after I got through being scared. I pestered him for months, begging him to do it to me again. But he wouldn't."* Her tone turned scornful. *"He wanted to pretend it didn't happen. You know?"* Her voice was inquisitive. *"You ever get raped?"*

"No. I suppose I have a rather limited experience, actually."

"Limited? As beautiful as you are?" She was matter-of-fact again. *"A man couldn't look at you without getting a hard-on."* She added complacently, *"Just like me."*

"Do you really think so?"

Her mouth twisted. *"A good body like ours, you're just a cunt to any man in the world. They don't care whether you're smart or dumb, a nice person or a bitch. They just want to shove It in there and get theirs."*

She paused. I had noticed a slurring in her voice.

"The hell of it is, you can't help but like it. You know? It's so easy." She giggled again. *"When you like to have a man panting after you like a stud dog, like it when you let him have it finally, what the hell can a woman do?"*

She finished the drink, promptly made another.

Matter-of-fact again. *"But you have to learn to use it."* She swung her hips provocatively. *"To get what you want. Like now."*

"Did you know it was going to be a competition?"

"Sure. Didn't you? I jumped at the chance."

She drank again. Deeply.

"Terry," I said, *"keep on drinking like that, you'll knock yourself right out of the competition."*

Her eyes were wavery. She put down the glass with a decisive gesture, as though she meant to take my advice.

"Yeah, got to keep a clean mind in a clean body," she said. *She giggled, delighted with herself. "Good clean sportsmanship!"* she cried. *"A clean mind and a clean cunt to please the man and win the big prize!"*

"Terry," I said warningly.

Coming close, she laid a confidential hand on my arm. "Listen," she said, *"if he makes us get into that lesbian bit, I'll go down on you and you go down on me. That way, we won't have to touch that cow. All right?"*

Repelled, I moved my arm. "Let's see how it works out."

"Well, now, how about some steaks?"

Reid Ulric's voice, accompanied by an enthusiastic clapping. Gratefully I turned to the interruption. Even as I thought, Well, she didn't keep him busy very long.

He stood beaming, Marlene clinging to his arm. The small cock was limp now, pinker than before. Marlene seemed half asleep, so languorous were her eyes, her body. Like a well-fucked cat, I thought.

Reid strode into the room. "Fix myself a drink, then I'll throw the steaks on a fire. I hope everybody likes 'em bloody, because that's the only way I cook 'em."

He poured straight bourbon, drank gustily. "What you girls been up to?"

"Just talking," I said. *"Getting acquainted."*

"Fine, fine," he said. *He clapped his*

*hands again. Like a cheerleader, I thought.
Cheering us on. "But I'll tell you something
I think you ought to know. You're going to
have to go some to beat Marlene in the sack.
She is something else!"*

*Marlene was not looking at us, but at
Ulric. "Fix me a drink, too, Reid?" she said
in her throaty voice. Throatier, now, because
it contained a memory.*

*"Sure, baby, anything you want," Reid
said generously. His eyes were on me, then
on Terry. He clapped his hands again. "How
lucky can a fellow be? Three lovelies to fuck
in one night. I just hope my friend down
there is up to it." He laughed like a gusting
gale. "Come on now! Who's hungry?"*

*On the sun deck, Reid fired up a gas-
fed grill. I stood looking toward the west.
The sun was just down, a twilight spreading
across the western sky. This far north, I
knew, it would linger long.*

*Reid's exhorting voice reached out. "All
right, now. Who's good for a salad?"*

*"Me!" Terry said eagerly. "I make a
great salad."*

*"You'll find all the ingredients in the re-
frigerator. Alice!, Marlene, you can peel potatoes. I want about a bushel of French fries
to go with these fine steaks."*

*We busied ourselves, first in the kitchen
slicing potatoes into French fries, Terry
meanwhile working cleverly with lettuce and
celery, wine vinegar and olive oil, to create
her contribution to the meal.*

*When we were done, Reid took four
thick slabs of meat from the refrigerator and,
admiring them loudly, led us to the grill.*

I had never eaten meat so bloody. The

*first bite revolted me. Realizing how hungry
I was, I gritted my teeth and cut the second
slice. It was surprisingly tender and tasty.*

*Exhorting us meanwhile to eat up, a
good plain training-table meal, he said, that
would give us strength and spirit, Reid Ulric
wolfed down two of the great steaks and ap-
proximately a bushel of the French fries.*

*After we had put the dishes into the
dishwasher, Ulric led us to the poker table in
a corner of the living room.*

*"Card time, girls," he announced, slap-
ping the green felt. "What'll it be? Gin rummy? Pinochle? Stud poker? Name your
game."*

"Blackjack!" Terry cried eagerly.

*Reid Ulric leaned close into her face.
His voice was as heavy as a bludgeon.*

*"No, dear. Draw poker. Table stakes.
No limit."*

*Terry, squelched because she had
guessed wrong and he had let her know it,
turned white. Reid Ulric, ignoring her
stunned reaction, knelt to open a small steel
safe concealed behind woodwork, and took
out thick packets of money.*

*He placed the money around the poker
table. "This is your money you're gambling
with. Understand? You start with five thousand apiece. Somebody can leave this island
with fifteen thousand dollars clutched in her
hot little hand."*

*Terry, her eyes bright, riffled a deck of
cards expertly. "High man deals," she said
crisply.*

*Reid Ulric, acting as cashier, sold us
chips. I thought about it, then asked, "Will
we play poker every night? Or is this it?"*

*His eyes flickered at me. "Play cards
every night. Not necessarily poker."*

I indicated the money. "But this is our stake?"

"That's right, dear. When you run out of money, you're out of the card games. Of course, that doesn't necessarily mean you couldn't still be the ultimate winner." He nodded ponderously. "It's not just winning or losing; it's also how you play the game."

I knew very little about poker. Gin rummy would be the best game for me. I decided finally to take a thousand dollars' worth of chips.

"Table stakes," Ulric warned as he dealt them out. "You can't go back in the pocket."

I nodded my understanding. Terry recklessly changed all her money into chips. Marlene, rather bewildered by the whole idea, hesitated for a long time before she bought two thousand dollars' worth.

Deciding to survive rather than take chances, I began cautiously, folding when my cards showed a weakness, keeping the bets as low as possible. Quickly it became apparent that Terry was in her element. Playing deftly, she also revealed a streak of recklessness. But, as though by instinct, she knew when to plunge, when to hold back. She was not only very good; she had exceptional luck. Cards she needed seemed to gravitate to her draw as though by God's grace.

Marlene was inept. At her turn, she shuffled slowly, dealt badly. She seemed to bet by impulse, first overplaying her hand, then underplaying it. One could not tell by her betting pattern what kind of cards she held. Consequently, her pile of chips melted rapidly, Terry winning most of the pots. I picked up a scattering of smaller pots. When her chips were gone, Marlene, with a sigh of relief, retired to the leather sofa.

Terry looked at Reid Ulric. "Draw poker with two people isn't a very good game. Why don't you sit in?" *She grinned.* "I'd like to take some of your money, too."

He shook his head. "I want to see you go head to head."

We went head to head. I played the cards even closer to my chest, knowing fatefully that Terry would win most of the hands. I kept the pots as small as I could, but steadily she wore me down. Quiet now, intense, her eyes gleamed as she studied my face.

I still had half my chips when Reid Ulric looked at his watch and stood up, saying, "That's it, girls. Eleven o'clock. Up early in the morning for everybody."

I was glad for the game to be finished. With every hand, it seemed ordained of God that Terry would get her cards, while I would just miss mine. The continual flow of luck in Terry's favor had made me so angry I could scarcely contain my feelings. I didn't blame Terry for being both good and lucky; I was simply irate at the inexorable fate that consistently, hand after hand, denied me an equal share in the draw.

Reid placed his great hand on Terry's naked shoulder. "I do like a winner," he said. "Let's go fuck."

"Oh yes," *Terry breathed, rubbing her cheek against his shoulder.* "Cards always excite me. I've got to do something."

My turn will have to wait until tomorrow, I thought with a sinking feeling.

"Wait till we get back," *Reid ordered as they departed.* I wanted only to retreat into sleep. But I knew that I must obey.

The moment Reid and Terry were gone,

Marlene whispered tensely, "Alice! Come here."

I joined her on the couch. Fervently, she grasped my arm.

"Listen, we've got to do something about that little bitch, or she'll kill both our chances."

She glanced nervously over her shoulder, as though fearful of being overheard. Reminding myself that the room might be bugged, I didn't say anything.

Marlene's voice pressed at me. "She's vicious, Alice! She'll do anything to win. She was cheating at cards."

"You should have called her on it, then," I said carefully. "I don't think Reid would have stood for cheating."

"I know she was! Nobody could possibly get such good cards without cheating." She breathed deeply. "I can't stand girls like her, anyway, who think they're just the cutest thing that ever came down the pike."

"Reid knew that she had dealt blackjack. So of course he would watch her." I shook my head. "She's just good. And lucky."

Resentment at the fates burned in me even as, for the record, I made the careful statement.

Marlene would not be deterred. "Let's make a deal, Alice! We'll declare a truce, and work together at getting Terry disqualified." Her eyes were sharp on my face. "Then . . . we fight it out between ourselves."

"How could we possibly get her disqualified?"

"Remember what Reid said about bad sportsmanship? Down under all the cutesy-pie stuff, that girl's got a temper. Gig her just right, she'll blow up."

*I drew away. "As far as I'm con-
cerned," I said firmly, "it's every woman for
herself. That's how Reid Ulric laid down the
rules. That's how I intend to play it."*

*Marlene stared resentfully. "She'll win,"
she insisted. "I know she'll win. We've got
to gang up on her."*

*"I don't want to discuss it," I said. I
looked at her straightly. "Maybe you can
talk Terry into ganging up on me instead."*

*She was indignant. "Do you believe I'd
do that?"*

"Yes," I said.

*I got up and left her. At the bar, I fixed
a light drink—we had had nothing after dinner—and, anxious to calm myself, sought
solitude in a corner of the living room. I
still burned with resentment from the card
game. And from knowing, even as I sat
alone that Terry was reveling in Reid Ulric's
arms.*

Alice! hadn't had a winner yet.

*Terry was shy and bright, her eyes
flashing surreptitious glances of wondering
adoration at the huge man who had so re-
cently possessed her.*

*I got up from where I sat, crossed to
Reid Ulric, stood on tiptoe to kiss his cheek.*

*"Good night, Reid," I said. "I'm very
tired. I'm going to bed."*

*He smiled a benevolent, fulfilled smile.
"That's a good idea for everybody."*

*"Good night, Terry," I said. I turned
to call across the room. "Good night, Marlene."*

*"Good night, love." Terry's eyes on me
were level, a small smile showing on her face.
"Sleep tight."*

Marlene did not respond. I went on.

In my bedroom, I put on a nightgown. If I had to be naked all day, I could at least be clothed for sleeping.

Reid Ulric's voice. "Alice! Come in to me."

He was not in my room. "Where are you?" I said into darkness.

"The last door down the hall."

Wide awake, I put on the light and looked at my watch. Only two o'clock.

I went into the hall. The lodge was very quiet. I moved stealthily, not wanting Terry and Marlene to discover that I had been summoned. It would be a secret stroke against them if they didn't know.

A vast bedroom, windowed along the side facing the lake. Beyond the open drapes, the stars were very bright, and, bright as a new penny, a sliver of a moon.

Reid Ulric was propped up in bed, his body a great mound under the covers. Documents were stacked beside him. He pushed black-rimmed reading glasses up on his forehead and smiled in greeting. I still had on the nightgown. I stooped to catch the hem, preparing to strip naked.

"You can keep it on," Reid said quietly. "My little friend is pretty well used up for the time being. I just don't like to sleep alone; I have bad dreams."

I felt a thud of disappointment. Was it a victory or a defeat? I didn't know.

He patted the bed. "Just get in with me," he said invitingly.

I slid under the sheet, moved myself against his great frame. Putting my arm across his chest, I could feel the beating of his heart.

"Maybe I can get your little friend interested," I suggested, sliding my hand down the slope of his great belly.

He yawned mightily. "No need." He put his great hand between my legs. "I love a nice morning fuck, anyway. A woman feels different when she's been sleeping." His hand dwelled on me without restlessness. "So just turn out the light and go to sleep touching me. To keep away the bad dreams."

His voice had changed. Gentle now, the words flavored with a comfortable intimacy as though we had spent a hundred nights in the same bed.

Cozy. The butterflies were in me again. I wanted to fuck. I desired this great gentleness, the underlying power that yielded such an intense feeling of security.

I leaned to turn out the light, came back to him. I slid my hand down the vast slope of his belly to his small Thing. It was warm in my hand, limp.

"Wouldn't do you justice now, sweet Alice!" Reid murmured in the darkness. "That Terry fucks like a mink. Drained me dry."

"It's all right," I said. "I just want to hold your friend."

The huge body generated an awesome amount of heat; like lying beside a banked furnace. I fondled his friend sweetly, thinking contentedly, In the morning.

"Don't stop, that feels good," he murmured, shifting his bulk slightly to give me freer access. "Just don't expect Him to get excited."

"I can wait," I said quietly.

Turning toward me, he took his hand out of my crotch to fondle my breast. His head rested on my shoulder.

"Talk to me until I go to sleep."

"*Is it fair to ask who's ahead?*" I said.

The wrong thing to say; he stirred fretfully. "*I'm keeping the only score card,*" he said. Then, more gently, "*Tell me about yourself.*"

I said the thing that was in my mind.

"*When I was a very little girl, my Daddy used to hold me high in his arms, with my legs tight against his chest. I could feel his heart beating against my thighs. I thought it must be the strongest heartbeat in the whole world.*"

Reid Ulric didn't say anything.

"*When I laid my arm across your chest, just a moment ago, I felt your heartbeat, Reid,*" I said. "*I wished you would pick me up like he used to, holding me high against your chest. Because you're strong, like Daddy was strong.*"

His voice was a murmur in the darkness. "*Did you love your Daddy?*"

"*Yes,*" I said. "*Until I began to hate him.*"

"*Why did you hate him?*"

I couldn't keep the harshness out of my voice. "*Because he wanted to fuck me.*"

A silence. I wondered if Reid had gone to sleep. He spoke again. "*If you had to hate him for that, you must have wanted to be fucked by your father.*"

I had his balls in my hand now. They were small, smooth, very warm. They were the core of his body heat. Somehow, here in this darkness, so cozy with his balls in my hand, I could say it.

"*Yes. I wanted Daddy to fuck me. As badly as he wanted to do it.*"

Reid nestled his head deeper into my shoulder. "*There's more incest than people realize,*" he said. "*In Egypt, incest was a*"

royal prerogative. When you play the Cleo-
patra-avatar, you will have to portray emo-
tionally that royal prerogative. Because Cleo-
patra was married to her brother."

"I can play it," I murmured. "It won't
even be acting. Because I know."

Moving my hand upward, with two fin-
gers I stroked delicately the small Thing.

"Oh, yes, that feels good," he whispered. "You're a very gentle person, Alice!
I'm glad I chose you to sleep with me tonight."

"You are the gentle one," I said.

"I can't afford to be gentle. Because I
must do what I must do."

"Yes," I said in complete understanding. "Alice! must also do what she must do.
But, down under the strength and the drive,
there is in both of us a great gentleness."

I stopped talking to listen. He was
breathing more deeply. I smiled in the dark-
ness. Reid Ulric had gone sweetly off into
sleep.

But, holding the warmth of his tiny
cock cupped in my hand, I did not sleep for
a long time. Because I did not know which
part of the truth, spoken into that secure
darkness, had come from that deep-laid core
of competitiveness, said only to win points
in the contest.

I came awake to the touch of his thick
finger stroking my pussy. Sensing the stir of
response, he whispered, "Open your legs.
But keep your eyes closed."

Eyes shut tight as commanded, I spread
my legs. The mattress shifted as he heaved
himself ponderously to bring his massive
body upon me. I felt smothered, as though a
great bear had come to oppress my flesh.

Covered completely, I had to turn my head to one side to breathe.

An imperative need, in that first moment, to fight my way out from under the great weight of flesh. But then, feeling his stiff cock probing at my pussy, I held myself still.

Dry from sleeping, my vagina would not accept It. But suddenly, as he made a mighty thrust with his hips, forcing his Thing into me, the dragon-butterfly came alive. Instinctively I tried to draw up my legs to surge in rhythm with his fucking. But, pinned so thoroughly, I could not move.

No man, before or since, has ever given me that sensation of utter helplessness as did Reid Ulric in our early-morning fucking. He did not seek a response. He only wanted me open. Helplessly, I was open, whether I wanted to be or not. Astonishingly agile for such a huge man, he was not even breathing hard as he fucked me with rapid thrusts, the small cock licking hotly inside me with each surge and withdrawal.

A rebellion arose in my flesh against such forced surrender. My body wanted to do, as well as be done to. It was also a rebellion of the mind; Reid Ulric was robbing me of the chance to prove I was the best, that I deserved to become the Star.

Without warning, all such considerations vanished. Somewhere deep inside, I surrendered body and soul to the power of Reid Ulric. My very bones seemed to melt, and as my pussy dissolved he seemed to sink deeper into me, depths without end, the tiny sword flicking ever more keenly into my flesh.

Then there was a response, so deep it did not manifest itself in the flesh. Or per-

*haps it did, a tidal rolling that both engulfed
him and bore him along, and still Reid was
not breathing hard, still he moved his body
with that enormous vitality I could not hope
to contain. He would destroy me, he would
use me up completely. As I lusted to be
used.*

*I didn't know when, finished, the great
weight rolled away. I lay sprawled in the
bed, only realizing when I dizzily opened my
eyes, that I had kept them tightly closed all
the time Reid Ulric had been fucking me.*

*Twice I had to make the effort before
I could move. Reid lay on his side, watching
me intently. Placing my fingers against his
lips, I said, "Reid. You destroy a woman."*

*He grinned. "I've always said, it's not
how* much, *but* how." *I could feel his lips
moving under my fingers. Chuckling, he
touched himself. "I've had to say that."*

*"I thought those two were faking it
when they came back from being fucked by
you," I said. "They weren't faking."*

*"Some women can't let go," he said. "I
thought you weren't going to."*

"You could feel it when I did?"

He nodded. "Absolutely unmistakable."

*I wanted to explore the experience. But
a small fear intervened. With a faint frown,
I said, "But you didn't let me show what
Alice! can do."*

*His grin broadened. "Now's your
chance. If you want it."*

I raised up. "It's my turn?"

*"Your turn," he agreed. "Ought to warn
you, though. I'm not likely to come again."
He chuckled. "Lot o' fucking, last night and
this morning, for an old man."*

"You'll come," I said with grim humor.

In one lithe movement, I slid across his barrel, laid my pussy tight against his chest. I sat upright, my hands cupping my breasts, thumb and finger stroking the erected nipples. Watching his face, I began with slow insidiousness, to work my pussy downward on the balloon of his belly. I was so wet I made a moist track in the thick body hair.

Quickening the rhythm as I reached the final slope, I held my breath, waiting to know if It was ready.

It was ready. I stopped dead still, body tilted above It, looking intensely into his face. Leaning slowly forward, I fastened my mouth to the hairy right nipple as I let my pussy enfold, inch by tiny inch, the stiff little cock.

Before It was fully socketed, he was coming. I let him come until I was sure he had passed the point of no return. Knowing I had to have it, too, quickly I writhed into crescendo, bearing down on It, taking the last drop of semen It had to offer.

I laid down, then, on that enormous, ugly body, as totally surrendered as when I had been captured underneath.

The huge hands reached to cradle my head. "Great, Alice!" he whispered. "Just great."

When we rose to wake up the girls for Reid Ulric's proclaimed tennis-before-breakfast tournament, he stooped suddenly and lifted me into his arms.

He grasped me just above the knees, so that I had to hold onto his bald head with both hands for balance. My bare thighs were tight against his chest; I could feel the beating of his heart.

He laid his face against my belly. "Alice!, you're just about the best fuck I've ever had," he murmured.

"Better than Terry or Marlene?" I asked jealously.

With his free hand, he playfully slapped my naked ass. "Better than anybody!" he said jovially.

"You did to me . . . things nobody's ever done," I said with hesitant sincerity.

But then, walking ahead of Reid into the corridor, I suffered a touch of paranoia. He had evoked me, all right; but had he done it out of tender regard for Alice! as a person, as it had seemed? Or was it a coldly calculated ploy to make Alice! reveal herself? If so, how successful it had been! Alice! had melted. Alice! had surrendered.

Somberly, I began to wonder about myself.

Had it been calculation on my part, also, the verbal and physical response shrewdly modulated out of the inherent competitiveness he had aroused? I shivered. I didn't know.

"Reid," I said.

He turned. "Yes?"

"Paul Riff," I said. "Did he know about the . . . competition?"

His eyes were sharp on my face. "Didn't he tell you?"

"No," I said, feeling the dullness weighting my voice. "He didn't."

Involuntarily his mouth moved in what should have grown into a smile, except that it didn't.

"You mean you walked into this thing blind?"

"I guess I did," I whispered.

You don't have to remember in total detail, I told myself. Just the last part. That all-important last part.

There was stud poker and gin rummy and, finally, Terry's cherished blackjack. At blackjack she triumphantly cleaned us out of chips, bringing the card games to an end.

We played tennis and swam races. Though I had always been good at tennis, Terry had such a strong serve I had to fight back with precision placement. But, after a hard struggle, I beat her.

Marlene was scarcely a factor in the sports competition—though she did reveal herself as a surprisingly strong swimmer. She possessed an ingrained laziness that forestalled those final stretching efforts so often necessary to win. In tennis, in two-on-one volleyball, she displayed greater interest in appearance than in performance.

Maybe, I thought, Marlene is right; after all, the name of the primary game is Sex Goddess. And who had won? When Terry and I came off the tennis court, Marlene was sitting on Reid's lap, wriggling in ecstasy against his cock thrust into her from behind. And, that night, Marlene was invited to help Reid Urlic make it through the night without bad dreams.

Before retiring, though, Reid Ulric fucked us communally as we lay side by side on bearskin rugs. Terry first, then Marlene, and last me. Though I had endured their squeals and moans of passionate ecstasy, I concentrated silently on seeking the surrender I had given Reid last night. But not getting it, so that he looked down into my face with a quizzical expression. He did not come, nor did I. I was too proud to fake it.

Next, we fucked him, Reid lying on his back with one on top and one on each side. Marlene's wetness was on him when I took my turn in the saddle. This was something I had not done before, so I fucked with great energy, seeking not for submission but striving, instead, for dominance over the great body. I was determined to make him come this time, willing it with my flexible ass and my stubborn mind.

He came, so much against his will that as he started he pushed me rudely aside, exclaiming hoarsely, "All right, who's gonna grab it?"

Terry, her head moving as fast as a snake strikes, fastened her mouth to the come-belching head like a leech. Sucking greedily, her eyes dilated strangely as she swallowed Reid Ulric's semen.

Reid got to his feet, leisurely fixed himself a drink, returned to sit on the couch.

"Girls, you've used this old man down to the nub," he said plaintively. "From now on you'll have to play with each other."

It was a command. Obediently, Terry put a prompt hand on Marlene's mound, at the same time fastening her mouth to the thumb-like nipple. With an unavoidable reluctance, I curled tightly against Terry's backside. I got through it by willing myself numb for the necessary length of time. But, in spite of all determination—even after Terry's agile tongue had given me an astonishingly intense orgasm—I couldn't make myself lick a female organ.

I went to sleep that night wondering what the ultimate day could hold that we had not already demonstrated for the edification of Reid Ulric's artistic and entrepreneurial instinct.

That last terrible day.

It began, quietly enough, with a long walk in the woods. Marlene, as inept as with all other athletic endeavor, gave up all pretense, complaining about being naked in the woods, suffering the assaults of vicious nature upon her civilized woman-flesh. Terry, as with everything else, was tirelessly cute, darting about, like a schoolgirl on an outing, discovering endless wonders.

I enjoyed the walking. It provided a space in which I could be quietly within myself. I needed a quietness, because I no longer knew the person the competition was making out of me.

The afternoon was separate; Ulric had decreed that we should rest from our strenuous activities.

Though I had never been one for afternoon naps, I slept profoundly because I had decided that, at some indefinable point, a winner had been declared. And, I told myself, Reid Ulric's choice was not Alice!

Sleeping so hard, I was groggy when I joined the others.

"Ah, there you are," Reid Ulric said at my belated appearance.

I sat down, accepting the Jack-Daniel's-and-spring-water he had already prepared for me.

"Girls, we've got a problem," Ulric said, his big right hand sweeping to outline its dimensions. "It hasn't happened. Understand what I'm saying? Reid Ulric has not clicked."

He was deadly serious. "It should have been decided long before now," he said heavily. "But it is not decided."

Again he moved his hand broadly. "We've swum and we've fucked, we've played tennis and gambled; we have com-

peted. *All in good clean fun, like competition ought to be. And, I've got to say it, you girls have shown great sportsmanship."*

He lowered at us. "Oh, I've listened to tapes of some conversations I'd rather not have heard. I will tell you that in all frankness."

So I had been right about the bugging. I glanced at Marlene and Terry. Their faces were studies in dismay.

"But the fact is this," Reid Ulric said violently. "We've just been wasting our time."

Hard breathing. Eyes glaring.

"So let me tell you something. We're starting all over again." His voice emphasized each word. "Nothing up to now has counted."

Terry sprang to her feet. "That's not fair!" she cried indignantly. "At cards, I won every chip!" She whirled to glare at us. "And you told me yourself, Reid, I fucked you and sucked you better than anybody."

Reid Ulric's voice curled against her like a whip. "Shut up. Sit down."

Terry sat down as abruptly as she had risen.

"Who said anything about fair?" Ulric spoke calmly. "I make the rules around here. If I say go back to square one, we go back to square one." His arm thrust suddenly out. "We've got to get deeper than we've got so far. Up to now, we've been playing games." He breathed hard. Once. Twice. "But we're not playing games anymore. This is for real." His arm was still thrust out, massive and hairy, the fist pointing one stern finger. Slowly, the finger turned to point downward. "There's a basement under this house. We're going down into that basement. And I give

you fair warning. Don't go down there unless
you're ready and willing to lay it on the line
once and for all. Because we're not coming
up until we have a winner!"

Stunned, we sat silent.

He bellowed at us. "ARE YOU
READY?"

Simultaneously we jumped at the snap
of his voice. I looked at the others. Their
faces were white. I felt a foreboding terror at
the thought of going down into that mysterious basement. I yearned for Terry, Marlene—one or both—to protest, complain, refuse. But I had no intention of quitting. And
neither did they.

The basement, as large as the living
room above, was outfitted as an exercise
room: weighted arm-pulls along one wall, a
heavy and a light bag, an exercycle, horses
for tumbling. A stark, utilitarian room, the
floor a shiny hardwood covered with mats,
the walls antiseptic-looking tile. The lighting was harsh and uncompromising.

"We'll start easy, with a battle royal,"
Reid Ulric said grimly. "Every girl for herself."

We stood unprotesting while he laced
on boxing gloves as big as pillows. I could
only think that I must not show my fear.
Must not, whatever came.

"Don't want to run the risk of ruining
those beautiful faces," Reid remarked, bringing out mouthpieces and protective head-
gear.

Reid Ulric also put on us grotesque har-
nesses designed to protect our breasts. A
stroke of cold knowledge moved inside my
terror. The basement was not a desperate
improvisation; it had been on the agenda all

along. Otherwise, how could Ulric have been prepared with all this apparatus?

I wondered if Terry and Marlene realized it also. I couldn't tell. Terry, demonstrating a brave eagerness, was gleefully slapping her gloves together. Marlene, looking blank, stood with arms at her sides.

"Have at it," Reid Ulric said. "And may the best girl win."

We remained still for a long count. But women don't fight, I was telling myself. Not physically. Women don't . . . Without warning, Terry hit Marlene in the stomach. Hard. Marlene went down squalling. Terry spun cleverly, aiming the next blow at my belly. Ready for her, however, I parried and retreated. Rigid with fear, I moved clumsily.

Marlene was on her feet again, squalling and slapping like a madwoman, assaulting Terry from behind. I attacked Terry from the other side in a momentary alliance with Marlene against the aggressor. Terry, crumpling under the combined assault, went to the mat. Marlene, turning on me, clubbed her right arm straight down on my head. Ducking too late, it caught me on the ear, knocking me on top of Terry. We both sprang to our feet and took out after Marlene.

It was a terrible battle. Furiously angry, yet deeply ashamed of such physical violence, we surged back and forth in a whirling mêlée of bodies and fists. My head was aching, my eyes felt as though they were starting from their sockets, a gasp of air was like fire in my lungs.

Ease up, I told myself. *Let them fight it out.*

I became wary, circling watchfully, striking a blow only when the victim was too

*involved to retaliate. Terry and Marlene
were forced by my sly withdrawal to concentrate on each other. Flailing away, squalling with each blow, they stumbled in a mad
dance. Marlene was twice the size of the
small-bodied Terry. But Terry whipped her.
Marlene, slapping and cuffing, used the
gloves like a club. Terry struck cleaner blows
that left red welts on Marlene's ribs.*

*Going down finally out of sheer fatigue,
Marlene refused to get up again. Terry
leaned over her, ruthlessly hitting her shoulders and back, until Reid Ulric pulled her
away.*

I was resting, hands at my sides.

*"You've got one more to beat," Ulric
said, turning Terry toward me.*

*She stood glaring, as though she
couldn't believe she had to go on fighting.
But Terry had guts. Moving flat-footed, she
began stalking me with grim determination.
I circled cautiously, hitting her in the side,
twice, as hard as I could. She took the blows,
wading in, her fists thumping solidly against
my midsection. The shocks numbed my
flesh. I had to retreat to give myself breathing room.*

*I could not have beaten Terry if she
hadn't already expended most of her energy
on Marlene. Chasing me, her movements
quickly became leaden. When she succeeded
in getting close enough, she could scarcely
lift her arms, the blows so feeble they were
not difficult to parry. But she wouldn't quit
trying, and I became increasingly desperate.
Because the gloves were like pillows, and our
heads and breasts were padded, I couldn't
inflict enough damage, in my own exhaustion, to make Terry quit.*

Finally, after I had taken the offensive,

she couldn't even lift her arms to defend herself. When I realized she couldn't strike back, I stopped pounding on her, looking to Reid Ulric.

Smiling grimly, he came between us. "That's enough," he said. "Now to the next phase."

Reid Ulric had divested us of the boxing gear.

"You whipped Marlene's ass," Reid said to Terry. "Now Marlene gets her revenge."

Grabbing her by both wrists, he pushed Terry against an upright rack of bars. Terry, breathing hoarsely, struggled to escape his brute strength. Holding her pinned with his massive body, he tied her hands high above her head.

Reid Ulric opened a locker and took out a whip, three broad strips of leather bound to a foot-long stock. He put it into Marlene's hand.

Marlene stared uncomprehendingly at the whip.

"Punish her naked ass. She can't fight back this time," he said encouragingly. "Like this." Gripping her wrist, he swung her arm, flicking the triple lashes lightly against Terry's buttocks.

Terry's terrified face showed whitely over her shoulder. "Don't hurt me, Marlene," she begged. "Please don't hurt me."

A look of malevolence moved across Marlene's face. Reaching her arm backward, she snapped the whip forward. Terry screamed. Three broad welts showed suddenly on her suntanned rump.

"Please, Marlene." Terry began to gibber. "Please, please, please."

Marlene braced for the second blow.

Then the third and a fourth, striking harder each time. Her face was a twisted mask of gratified revenge.

Terry writhed under the beating. Her voice was a scream. "You can have it, Marlene, I don't want it, I'll go away, I don't want to be hurt, please, please, please!" On a rising crescendo, the words merged into a wordless hysteria of sound.

Reid Ulric grabbed Marlene's wrist, saying, "Enough, Marlene. That's enough now."

Terry, released, collapsed sobbing into Ulric's arms. "I want to go home. Please let me go home, Mr. Ulric, I don't like it here anymore, please, Mr. Ulric, just let me go home."

Tenderly he touched a big hand to her backside. "It's all over," he assured her comfortingly. "And you're not in all that bad shape." He shook her gently. "Now it's your turn. Do you hear me, Terry? Your turn."

She turned a tearstained face.

"Alice! whipped your ass, didn't she?" Reid said. "Don't you think you ought to have a chance to lay it on her?"

Terry looked at me with narrowed eyes. "Yesss . . ." she whispered. "Yesss . . ."

I didn't move until Ulric's hands touched me. Then I said sharply, clearly: "No."

Ignoring my protest, he led me to the rack. I stood cold and tight against the bars, silent inwardly and outwardly, as he tied my wrists. There was a trembling in my flesh.

I knew what Terry would do to me. As I knew, deeper and colder, that this, too, had been planned by Reid Ulric. What was he doing to us?

To me?

I didn't look to see it coming, as Terry had done. A lash of fire licked across my buttocks. Despite myself, I moaned through clenched teeth. The muscles in my buttocks were writhing, now, in anguished anticipation of the next blow. And the next.

So deep inside I hadn't known it was there, I thought: Daddy whipped me. I endured it. It can't be as bad as when Daddy whipped me.

Terry flayed my body in a deliberate rhythm, talking to me now, telling me how much she hated me, I thought I was So Much, didn't I, but she'd show me, by God. In her voice again a rising note of hysteria, but in a different tone; she was enjoying her pleasure and her revenge. With each reckless sentence of the diatribe, the blows fell more heavily. My head began to swim, my vision blurred; I knew she wouldn't stop until I was a flayed piece of dead flesh.

Reid Ulric stopped Terry, finally, and, releasing me from bondage, laid me down on a mat to examine my back. Gritting my teeth against the pain, I rolled over and sat up. It couldn't have been as bad as I thought, I told myself. There isn't any blood. Daddy whipped me until there was blood.

I looked up at Reid Ulric. "Is she through now?" I could scarcely speak through a throat made raw by the screams I had not uttered.

"Yes." He did not smile. "Your turn now."

"What?" I said.

Putting his hands into my armpits, he lifted me to my feet. "You get your choice," he told me. "Terry or Marlene."

"Why do I have to choose?" I said dully. "I don't care which one."

He looked at them. "Marlene deserves her taste of the whip, too, don't you think?"

At the words, Marlene began to run. Not with graceful sexiness now, but lumbering, her heavy breasts bouncing. When he captured her, she squealed like a small animal caught in the jaws of Death.

He gave me the whip. "She's all yours."

I stared at the fleshy rump, the broad back. Her skin was too white. I imagined red, three-lashed welts against that whiteness of skin. A stroke of—something—speared through me. I had seen in her, when she had whipped Terry, the joy of inflicting pain. She had hated Terry. As Terry had hated me.

As, I realized, I hated both of them.

That something motivated the muscles, swinging my arm back slowly. I could sense the vicious contraction, the merciless follow-through. Yet, in spite of myself, the blow fell weakly, the lashes only brushing against her straining flesh. She screamed as though I had brought blood.

The whip dropped out of my hand. "No," I said. "I won't do it."

"Marlene did it to Terry," Reid Ulric said. "Terry did it to you. So you can do it, Alice!"

"I didn't say I couldn't do it. I said I won't."

We stared at each other. He took a step forward. "You want to win, don't you?"

"No," I said. "Not that badly."

My hand was already free of the whip. All I had to do was turn, walk out of the basement.

I walked out. I climbed the stairs. I went through the living room. I opened the door to my bedroom. Inside, I reached into the closet, found clothes, dressed my aching body. I packed the rest of my clothes into the small bag.

Finished, I realized, suddenly, that I was still at Ulric's mercy. No way to get off the island unless and until he summoned the motorboat.

I sat down on the bed, waiting. I waited a long time.

"But you can't quit," I said to Mark Judson. "I won't let you."

He was holding himself very still. "Sorry," he said.

I kept on looking at him. "You come to me out of the clear blue and tell me you're quitting. There must be more to it than that."

His eyes avoided my direct gaze. "I just don't like this job anymore, that's all."

I held my voice level. "Not enough, Mark. I won't accept it."

Upon entering, he had refused to sit down. He stood before me in an elegant sports jacket I had not seen before. He wore a fine new pair of boots, white-and-blue striped trousers for the spring.

My money on his back. And now he meant to quit me.

I put away the thought as unworthy. The money didn't matter.

"I simply won't accept it, Mark."

"All right," he said grudgingly. "I'm getting divorced. So things aren't like they were when I hired on."

"What difference does it make whether you're married or not?" I said. "Though I'm sorry to hear about it. You didn't want a divorce, did you?"

"It's her idea," he said. "First she wanted out of the house. Now she wants to be . . . free."

"Free?"

His face moved. "It seems she met this nice fellow who's a long-haul trucker, like she wants to be. Between them, they can put together the money for a down payment on their own rig. A Peterbilt, that's what she said, the very best. They'll travel together, live together, be partners in every sense of the word."

"I'm sorry, Mark," I said sympathetically.

"I knew it was coming sooner or later," he said stoically.

"Seems like that's all the more reason to stick with the job." I tried to laugh. "At least you won't have to make those long trips to Brooklyn anymore. Get yourself a nice apartment in Manhattan."

He looked at me. I could not fathom the pain showing in his eyes.

"Mark," I said.

He shook his head. "No. I don't want this job."

"Think of me, Mark. Prince Albert is on his honeymoon. Even when he gets back, you know I won't see much of him. There's no one else. I'll . . . I'll be alone."

"That's the way you ought to like it," he said inflexibly. "You can do as you like, without well-meant advice from anyone."

"But the photographers . . ."

"They haven't bothered you all that much. Except when you first arrived."

"But I rely on you, Mark. More, I think, than you realize."

"Sorry," he said, the word abrupt.

"Mark," I said. "Please."

"I don't want to discuss it anymore."

I couldn't let him go. But he went. He looked down at me for a long moment, his face as stony and enigmatic as his eyes. And then he was gone.

Alice was alone.

It was what I should want, he had told me.

But not the Alice that I now was. Please, I begged silently. Not ever alone.

I heard the motorboat coming, a distant growling that became quickly louder. Good,

I thought, he has summoned the boat for me.

I could only wait.

The motorboat sound curled in toward the dock, died into silence. I kept on waiting. A long ten minutes; then the motorboat started up again. I arose in agitation. It couldn't leave without me!

It faded into the distance. Sitting down again, I looked at my hands folded in my lap. I didn't know, now, what I was waiting for.

Suddenly Reid Ulric stood in the doorway. I rose. "Why did the boat leave without me?"

"He's taking the other girls to the mainland."

"But . . . the competition."

His voice had a curious flat quality of emptiness. "The competition is finished. You won."

The response came solidly out of the greatest depth of Alice! "No."

"Yes." He nodded soberly. "We return to New York, we sign contracts, we go to work." His body shifted in massive restlessness. "There's a million things to get started at once."

I was numb again. The No was the last part of me to have escaped the numbness.

"So we stay until morning," I said. "Together."

He studied me. "You don't want to, do you?"

"No," I said.

He smiled. "I don't blame you. It got too rough." He sounded regretful, yet as though it were only a minor matter. Which, I supposed, to Reid Ulric it was.

"But why me?" I said.

"Don't ask Reid Ulric why," he said.

*"Not now and not ever. Reid Ulric doesn't
know why."* He gazed upon me solemnly. *"I
got the click. That's all I can tell you."* He
looked thoughtful. *"Actually, I think it was
Alice! all along. I can't feel, now, there was
ever any doubt."*

*"Then why did we have to go through
it?"*

*"Because Reid Ulric can do it only in
Reid Ulric's way."* He began turning his great
body. *"Come on. Let's have a drink."*

I followed numbly. I accepted the glass
of Jack Daniel's. I drank from it. My body
was so sore it would be painful to sit down. I
remained standing, moving gingerly to loosen
the muscles.

*"If you don't want to stay tonight, I
can tell the boat to come on back now,"*
Reid said.

"Thank you," I said.

"Anything Alice! wants, Alice! gets,"
he said. *"That's how it's going to be from
now on."* He was looking at me steadily. *"If
you desire to fuck Reid Ulric, we will fuck.
If you don't want to . . ."* He moved his shoulders to complete the declaration of my independence.

I thought of that great surrender under
the weight of his flesh. How much of it had
been real, how much false? How much of
Reid Ulric was real? I shuddered somewhere
deep inside.

*"I can't imagine wanting to fuck you
again."*

His voice was gentle. *"I can understand
why you'd feel that way."* He smiled. *"It isn't
all that important."*

I had hoped for a reaction of anger,
rejection . . . something.

"Call the boat," I said. *"Please."*

Without a murmur of protest, he went to the telephone. We sat drinking until the boat came. Reid, edging into enthusiasm, began to tell me his plans for Alice! By the time the boat arrived he was on his feet, leaning over me, exhorting Alice! to greatness; as though those indelibly terrible revelations had never occurred.

I sat silent. I was numb inside. For the rest of my life, I thought, Alice! will know only numbness.

Paul Riff displayed anxiety in every line of his body as he put out both hands to take mine in greeting.

"Everything go all right?" he said, his eyes searching my face.

"Everything went fine!" Reid Ulric's voice boomed from behind me. "Alice! will be the next great international star of stage and screen." He scowled ferociously. "But not television. The idiot box will never be graced by that lovely face."

I could not endure the thought of sitting, in the limousine, between Reid Ulric and Paul Riff all the way to my apartment.

"Reid," I said. "Get me a taxi."

A silence followed the words. Paul looked at Reid Ulric.

Casually Reid said, "Sure, Alice! There'll be a taxi." He motioned to an attendant, who hurried away toward the terminal. He turned to Paul. "The girl's had a tough weekend. Nobody will ever know how tough." He smiled at me. "But Alice! came out of it with colors flying."

I moved to stand separately until the taxi would be ready. Paul came hurrying after me when I was summoned. I closed the taxi door against him.

"You'd better stay with Ulric," I said. "He'll want to talk, I'm sure."

"Alice! Are you all right?"

I looked into his eyes. Numb inside. "I'm fine," I said. "I did what you wanted me to do, didn't I? I won."

As the taxi was passing the Waldorf, I realized that I couldn't go home to the empty apartment. I tapped the partition.

"Let me out here," I said. "Tell the doorman to please put the luggage in my apartment. Here's double fare for the trouble."

Grinning, he took the money, and I got out. I had never needed a drink in my life. I needed one now.

Seven years, I thought as I walked into the bar. Seven years.

Every man in the room turned his head to watch my entrance. I kept my eyes down until I found a small table in a corner. "Jack Daniel's on the rocks, water on the side," I said.

The whiskey was only one part of what Reid Ulric had done to me this weekend. And, I thought, so much more.

He changed Alice!

Picking up the glass, I drank deeply.

If Reid Ulric could change Alice! so profoundly in three short days, what would Alice! be like after seven years of Reid Ulric? I shuddered and drank again.

No way out. Numbness was the only salvation. I reached for the numbness, pulled it into my flesh, into my mind, like a blanket.

"You're Alice!, aren't you?" a deep voice said.

I looked up. A thick-bodied man, short of stature, with a bull neck and coarse hands. A coarse and powerful face. He had come, I

*realized without thinking, from a table where
he had been sitting in a group. The other
men were younger than he, smooth-faced
and well-dressed—and carefully not looking
in our direction.*

"Yes," I said.

*"I am Stavros Stephanos," he said.
"Will you consent to dine with me tonight?"*

*He'll see the bruises on my ass, I
thought irrelevantly.*

"I'd love to have dinner with you."

*Smiling broadly, he nodded. "One of
my people will make the arrangements. I
shall see you, then, at nine, in my suite upstairs."*

*I nodded and smiled and it was a good
numbness now, even as I wondered how I
would explain the whip marks on my naked
flesh.*

*Stavros Stephanos returned to his table.
He was replaced by one of the young men,
asking politely for my address and telephone
number.*

*When, after two more drinks, I arrived
somewhat unsteadily at the apartment, the
first flowers from Stavros, an enormous box
of steel-colored roses, were waiting.*

*Stavros Stephanos did not see the
bruises on my naked flesh. We dined tête-à-
tête in his Waldorf Towers suite, where he
talked quietly of himself, only obliquely of
me. Afterward we went to a nightclub where
there was no necessity to talk; and when his
limousine delivered me to my apartment, he
kissed the palm of my hand, smiled, and
begged permission to see me again.*

*The gallant man danced attendance on
me for a week. I had never been courted as
Stavros courted me. I found it charming to*

have fresh flowers delivered daily for my delight. However, I protested when small favors—a gold Tiffany key ring, a pair of antique earrings, a lovely sea horse brooch with ruby eyes—began to accompany the flowers.

Stavros declared it was his pleasure to give lovely things to such a lovely woman. Frankly, he added that I should not feel obligated in any way, for no ulterior motive lay behind these small gestures of appreciation.

Tenderly affectionate, after the first time he kissed not only my hand, but my lips, upon departure. Never, however, with the slightest suggestion of pressing his desire into my awareness.

When numb-Alice would have laid down for him at the asking.

Meanwhile, Paul Riff hovered anxiously. The negotiations were again proceeding at deliberate pace. Every day he assured me that soon now, maybe tomorrow, the contract would be ready for signature.

As far as Reid Ulric was concerned, Alice! was his already, body and soul. He came every day, arriving always unannounced, to discuss his increasingly complex plans. He promised me a script soon, he was assembling my retinue. I would travel accompanied by bodyguards, and my personal public relations man would insure crowds for the bodyguards to protect me from.

Numbly, from a cold distance, I studied the grotesque and massive figure of this ugly, powerful man. In me dwelled the stark memory of those three days in which he had shaped—or discovered—an Alice! I had not known could exist.

By contrast, the presence in my life of

*that other powerful man, Stavros Stephanos,
was intensely heartening. I knew about him
now; his empire of tankers and freighters to
match the other great ship-owning Greek
families, how he was now using the flow of
profits to stabilize the internal economy of
his business empire with wholly-owned banks
and office buildings and hotels.*

*"I have already the sea," Stavros would
say. "Now I shall acquire the earth." He
smiled. "Later, I will venture into the air—
one day, I shall operate a wholly-owned
commercial airline. But, for now, the land."*

*He was affectionate, attentive, every-
thing a suitor should be. Womankind lost so
much, I reflected more than once, when
chivalry, romance, went out of fashion.*

*I knew, of course, that sooner or later
the question of making love would arise;
Stavros, a man, yearned with all his passionate being to possess Alice!, a woman. But,
this courtship such a beautiful road to that
inevitable conclusion, I remained content to
await consummation. This royal progress to
the sheets satisfied something that, in all my
life, had remained profoundly unsatisfied.*

*At last, one night, when I arrived at
the Waldorf Tower suite for dinner—we most
often dined in private before going out—
Stavros greeted me with an intriguing new
intensity.*

*Taking both my hands in his blunt sea-
man's hands, he kissed me tenderly. "Tonight we shall be entirely private," he said.
"We shall talk."*

*Here it comes, I thought, knowing that
I wished it. I was astonishingly passionate to
experience this complicated man.*

I smiled. "That will be wonderful."

Gripping my hands, he led me to the tapestried sofa. He poured wine, watched me taste it appreciatively.

He put a hand on my arm. The touch was warm, passionate. "Alice! You do not like the life you lead. I can tell."

"I don't much like me." My voice was as serious, as direct, as his had been.

He smiled. "I think I know you by now. Perhaps better than anyone ever has. Beneath that great beauty, you are a simple and wonderful person."

A protest rose in me. "How can one truly know another person?"

He looked anxious. "I speak not only of a spiritual knowing. I hope it will not make you angry when I tell you that I have . . . spent much money in learning about Alice!"

I tightened inside. "What do you mean?"

"I commissioned a detective agency to . . . capture Alice! for me. Your beginnings in that small Midwestern town, your contemporaries in the high school there. Your first years in New York. Everything." He paused. "You understand, I did it only because I am a serious man," he added apologetically. "Most serious of all where I believe that I might . . . love."

So this, tonight, was not hello, but good-bye. A farewell, executed with the same grace and flair as the courtship.

"If you know all that, then you understand why I don't like myself," I said in a low voice.

"You must understand that the kind of money I dispose of, the power I have, attracts women like flies to a piece of dead meat." A scornful tinge to the words. "So it

is necessary to be careful." His voice hardened. "I will not be taken for a fool."

I touched his hand with mine. "Stavros, whatever you now think of me, be sure of this. I never took you for a fool."

"I know," he said quietly. "You are not the kind of woman to think men are fools . . . even when we are. You have a respect for us." He smiled slightly. "Perhaps a respect too deeply ingrained, for you have suffered much from it." He was watching me now. "Men have not treated Alice! well."

I looked at my hands. They were curled tightly in my lap. "I know," I said simply.

"I know also that you have arrived at a crisis point. The decision you make now will determine the Alice! you are, the Alice! you will become."

I was surprised. It was supposed to be a closely held secret. "You know about the contract, too?"

He nodded. "Yes." His voice hesitated. He drove it on. "I know about the weekend on the island in Michigan. In detail."

I began to tremble inside. No! It was not fair for Stavros to know such things, to use against me in this farewell.

He's not only getting rid of me, I thought. He is destroying me. As all men destroy me once they are through with me.

My lips felt frozen. "How could you possibly have found out about what went on up there?"

He looked almost regretful. "The little Terry, in Las Vegas, was so bitter about losing it took little money to persuade her to tell the story."

I was crushed. My only comfort had been the belief that no one, except those directly involved, could ever know what Alice!

had said and done—had become—on that island.

The wineglass was still nearly full. I asked, "Do you have any Jack Daniel's?"

"Of course," Stavros said. "If you wish it."

"I wish it," I said.

He brought the drink. I drank, thoughtfully and greedily. I cherished his courtesy. But just let it be over with, I thought; quickly, cleanly, then I can go on to the next thing. Whatever that next thing might be.

"Stavros," I said in a steady voice. "I can't tell you how much the opportunity to know you has meant to me." I smiled faintly. "Not least of all, the pleasure of being the—object—of your attentions." I rose. "I shouldn't say it, I suppose. But . . . I'm sorry it didn't work out."

He did not rise. "Sit down, please. I have not finished."

But I'm finished, I thought. Nevertheless, I sat down.

He smiled. "Alice!, it is now my deepest desire to show myself as a man worthy of the respect you have always shown, to your sorrow, for the male of the species. It is time for you to learn that not all men abuse beauty, when granted the gift of beauty in a woman."

I heard the well-rounded phrases without internal response. I knew, in spite of the formality of his utterance, the ultimate farewell it contained.

Why can't he just let me go? I thought rebelliously.

His tone became more formal still.

"I am aware of the crisis of decision facing you. I am acquainted with the man, Reid Ulric, who holds your fate in the palm

of his hand." He gazed at me earnestly. *"Ulric sometimes does good things. But he is not a good man."*

"I know," I said quietly.

Stavros Stephanos held my eyes for a long moment.

"I have determined to provide an alternative." His voice dropped. *"I wish to offer you . . . a Greek island."*

It thrilled through me. But I could not believe. Not yet.

He smiled slightly. *"Your experience of islands has not been good. Not even the island of New York, much less the island in Michigan. That is why it came to me, the right thing to do, exactly while I was waiting for you tonight."*

He was talking to allow time in which I could absorb the ramifications of his meaning.

Then, as behooves a serious man, he explained the ramifications.

"You will live there forever on your island. Your island, not mine. I shall come to you from time to time, as my schedule permits."

I had to know. *"Are you talking about . . . marriage?"*

A small pause.

"I have been married to the mothers of my sons," he said. *"I am now beyond the age for marrying."* His look was direct, unequivocal. *"Because I am a Greek, in a new marriage I should wish to make more sons. There are already heirs in plenty, each fighting the others for my favor."*

"Then you are asking me to become your mistress."

He smiled. *"Yes, my dear Alice! I wish to cherish you, protect you—and hold you for my own. I want to give you . . . sanctuary."*

Still inside, I watched his face. The idea of the island was enormous inside my soul.

"Stavros . . ."

He held up a hand. "Please do not answer quickly, Alice!, whether yes or no. You must understand the meaning of our bargain. If it is destined to be made."

"All right," I said. "I'm listening."

"First, I will deed to you the island in fee simple. I will assume all upkeep and maintenance. Upon my death, you will be assured of sufficient monies to maintain yourself in the accustomed style."

"That's fair enough."

"There is also a small unfairness," Stavros said. "You will remain faithful. I will not necessarily be faithful." He smiled again. "Probably, in fact, I will be, for I am a man of business, with many concerns to occupy my mind and my time. But . . . I do not promise."

"All right," I said quietly. "Just as long as, on my island, you are mine as truly as I am yours."

A tremor of passion revealed itself in his voice. "That goes without saying."

Stavros went on. "I cannot, of course, insist that you promise yourself to me for all time. Even if I should ask such a thing, you could not so commit yourself; you will inevitably become another Alice! once you possess your own island. But I must ask you, if you say yes, to promise that you will give it one year."

"I understand."

Stavros smiled. "Let us drink to your decision. Whatever it may be."

He picked up his glass. I picked up

mine. It was the wineglass I used, not the whiskey, for the toast to our future.

Stavros rose. "Now we shall dine," he said gaily. "Such serious talking makes for serious hunger." He picked up the telephone, said into it, "You may now serve, please."

I watched him. I was wondering what manner of man he might be. Though he knew—had accepted—everything about me, I knew almost nothing of him.

Except what I felt. And Alice! had learned long since not to trust her feelings as accurate perceptions of reality. Not where a male of the species was concerned.

But I had come to the decision not for the best of reasons; for the worst. Because, as Stavros had said in the beginning, I did not like my life. Because, as I had replied, I did not much like me.

After dinner, over much resin-tasting Greek wine, Stavros became as I had not seen him before. Putting on records, he insisted on demonstrating Greek dances. In his country, he informed me gravely, men danced out both their joys and their sorrows.

It was a marvelous exhibition, with leaps and spins and much slapping of the heels. In his enthusiastic dancing, he seemed suddenly a man much younger and happier than his years. When he collapsed with exaggerated exhaustion, we were both hysterical with laughter. With his arm around my waist, leaning against me, I kissed him impulsively.

Stavros sat up. "Well, Alice!" he said. "You know now."

A serious moment. I gazed upon him. This man had penetrated my spirit, my very soul, as no man, not even Reid Ulric, had

*ever penetrated my body. He possessed me
as I had yearned to be possessed.*

"Yes, Stavros," I said. "The answer is
yes. With all my heart."

Lifting my hand, he bowed his head,
took a deep breath as though inhaling the
scent of me into his soul. With fervent lips,
he kissed my palm.

"Before you go," he said. "Will you do
one crazy, small thing for Stavros?"

"Yes," I said.

"Allow me one glimpse of your body."
He grinned like a greedy boy. "I have, to be
sure, an appreciation. But now that I know
your body will be mine, I want very much to
view it entire."

I stood up. Slowly, feeling his eyes
watching every move, I took off my clothes.
Naked before him without the least instinct
toward concealment, I turned to walk the
length of the room. Then I returned, nearer,
nearer, under the weight of his seeing, until
I was close enough to be touched.

He did not touch. Simply, with glowing
eyes, he looked at my breasts, my belly, at
the honey-blond hair half-concealing my pubic mound.

He raised his eyes. "Such beauty warms
a man's heart," he breathed.

Playfully I said, "Why don't you take
off your clothes, too?"

He shook his head firmly. "I am ugly." He
paused. "Besides, if I were also naked, I would
be embarrassed by the lust that is in me."

I wanted him. Now. Being naked in the
sight of his eyes had made me lustful. I knew
an impatient desire to consummate our elegant bargain.

I spoke in a low voice: "I have said
yes."

*Again he shook his head. "When I take
you for the first time, it must be on your
Greek island, surrounded by my ocean."*

*"I see," I said. I could not hide the
disappointment in my voice.*

*It pleased him to know that I was dis-
appointed. He smiled. "Tomorrow you will
begin to make your arrangements," he said.
"As quickly as possible you must depart for
your new life. As soon as I can, I will come
to you."*

*More disappointment. "You can't go
with me?"*

*"I have much business to detain me in
New York." He smiled seriously, honestly,
passionately. "But that is not the true reason.
Before I come to you, you must have a time
alone on the island . . . a time in which to
become the Alice! that you will be. I have no
wish to make love to the Alice! this world of
men has made. Stavros Stephanos shall possess only the Alice! of the island."*

*Naked as I was, I put my arms around
him. He held me so tightly I could feel his
waiting hardness.*

But It could wait. And so could Alice.

Now, again, I was alone. My soul was nestled,
cushioned, inside the good body that God and the
vagaries of genetics had provided. As my body was
nurtured in the luxurious apartment, protected and se-
questered by the sheer unassailability of the millions
left to me by Stavros Stephanos.

All my life, I thought fatefully, I have lived on a
succession of islands. First the island of Daddy's love:
except that Daddy's love was only lust. Then all the
islands in between. And, last, the island of Alice!, as
provided by the Greek.

All my life long, there had been also the island

of my flesh, so desirable in the eyes of men. They had held me hostage in my body, both assaulting it and shielding it; They held me inviolate even as They violated me.

Alice should have remained innocent of men, I reflected sadly. Only abstinence, austerity, could have liberated me. But there had been, as I knew well, my own female hungers and appetites and needs and wishes.

Most of all, I thought, *the primordial instinct to please men.*

That was the stricture—the Holy Commandment —within my soul, planted first by Daddy, nurtured by the high school boys, Andy, and Paul Riff, even by Stavros. All the men. *Them.*

My life had been a continuous struggle to escape from the island of existence in which Alice served only the satisfaction of male pleasure and male possession. My vision of escape, however, had been limited to another island; never into the true untraveled continent of myself.

Now, I told myself, Alice is trapped on the most impregnable island of all. Unlike previously, I cannot visualize a way out.

I should have been selfish, I thought sadly. I should have been able to think only of myself. Indeed, in this return from long exile, I had sought a saving selfishness. But I had discovered only the ultimate loneliness.

I still went through the motions. Each time, with repetitive obsession, I had run through the thoughts all over again, I went out to find another man. An infinite variety of men, one each night and sometimes two; young, old, fat and lean, aggressive or impotent, with large or small or medium-sized cocks. After each man, I was left with the deep dissatisfaction.

Then I had to think the thoughts again. And again.

Nor was it only the men. Remembering those early discussions of the modern scene, with Prince Albert, I sought out many experiences.

I discovered that New York—America—was in a fever of self-discovery. I went to lectures on Women's Lib and spontaneous orgasm, demonstrations of yoga and Transcendental Meditation, I sat at the feet of gurus and group therapists.

My days were filled with mysticism and astrology and sacred chants and the laying-on of hands, as my nights were filled with the physical lust of men using my lustful body in all the ways a female body can be used.

Inevitably, I came out as empty as I went in. I found all these disciplines, both the real and the false, ultimately unsatisfactory. They were, it seemed to me, premised upon a yearning for instant illumination instantly achieved.

A group salvation, tribal rather than individual.

Perhaps, I thought, in the original context of Oriental thought, the more ancient disciplines had their value, their meaning. But, grafted, like a lotus to an oak tree, onto the western mind, they become faddish parlor games, touching not into the individual human soul. Only there, it seemed to me, could salvation possibly be found.

And so, time and again, I was forced back into the individual memory of individual experience.

Two weeks alone on the beautiful island Stavros had given me before he came to me for the first time.

The buildings were blindingly white under that Mediterranean sun which had lighted so much of mankind's history. There was, on the highest point of the island, the ruin of an ancient temple, so tumbled, now, one could scarcely trace the outline of architectural order which man, in his religious impulse, had ordained so long ago. Standing in these ruins, one experienced as a direct emotion the sacredness imbued into these stones by time and man.

And, walking the beach naked at sunrise, one felt the birth-of-being, in tune with the birth of a new day. A newness primordial and forever, the obverse coin of the old temple.

Returning from the long walk, my footprints were the only sign of a human presence; and, so often, the sea was tediously erasing them even as I followed my own spoor to the beginning of the morning's journey.

The perfect island. I knew from the first moment that Alice would remain here forever.

Perhaps I had known, before leaving New York, the island was the ultimate Alice-sanctuary, for I cut the ties that bound me with a ruthlessness I had not realized I could possess.

I was packing when Paul Riff arrived triumphant. "This afternoon at four o'clock we sign the contract."

I straightened to look at him.

His voice trembled with excitement. "It'll be a public ceremony, the press invited, everything. Your personal staff are on their way over to get you ready."

"I'm not signing, Paul," I said. "I'm going away."

He didn't believe me.

"Come, now, Alice!, a bit of stage fright is only to be expected. It's a big step we're taking. The biggest!"

"You didn't hear me, Paul. I said I'm not signing the contract with Reid Ulric."

He saw the bags then. "Now wait a

minute," he said rapidly. "Wait just a minute." His voice skated over the words as though they were thin ice. "Will you kindly tell me what's going on here?"

"I told you," I said. "I'm leaving."

His face stricken, he sank down on the bed. "But . . . what do you plan to do?"

"I am going to a place where I can live my own life," I said serenely. "I will not come back."

He stared, disbelieving. Then, desperately, he reached down into the very core of his soul.

"But what about me?"

"What about you?" I said inflexibly.

His voice rose. "After all I've done. All the planning. All the work. I've devoted every minute to the creation of Alice!" He stood up agitatedly. "You can't do it to me. I won't let you!"

"I don't know how you can stop me."

I had never seen Paul Riff angry. He was angry now.

"You can say this? After all I've done for you?"

"What have you done for me, Paul?" I asked quietly.

The question reduced him to gibbering rage. "What have I . . . You ungrateful bitch! I'm just another man to you, to be wrapped around your little finger. That's all you ever saw in Paul Riff. A man to be used and thrown aside. You didn't even have to fuck me, did you? Like you fucked every other man . . ."

He paused. His eyes were suddenly cold.

"I get it. You've made a deal with Ulric to get rid of me, haven't you?" His

*hand was on my arm now, gripping hard.
"Come on, Alice! Admit the truth for once
in your life."*

"No," I said.

*The single word stopped him cold.
Helplessly, his voice became a moan. "I lived
and breathed Alice!, I worked, I schemed, I
did things I never thought I'd have to do,
and all for Alice! Now you can stand there
as beautiful as ever and tell me such things."*

*"Yes, you did it all, didn't you?" I said
with sudden violence. "You sent me into the
competition for Reid Ulric. Without preparing me with the truth of what I'd have to
face."*

*He only stared. "But it was for your
own good."*

*Speaking the words so blankly, I knew
he had convinced himself of their truth.
Even, I thought, before he carefully did not
ask me to go.*

*Softly I said, "Would you have sent
Zella to Reid Ulric's island?"*

*He stared again. "That's entirely differ-
ent."*

"Yes," I said sadly. "I know."

*"So that's what's bothering you." With
a dramatic gesture, he took both of my hands
into his. "Alice!, I didn't like it any more
than you did. You don't know how I suffered, waiting for you to come home from
that weekend."*

*With a newly fervent hope, he squeezed
my hands. "That's all behind us. You won,
Alice! Now we can forget about it, go on together to greater things."*

I took away my hands. "No, Paul."

"But . . ."

I turned away. "There's no way to

*make you understand. No way I can tell
you how betrayed I felt when you showed
me how greedy you were for me to do Ulric's
bidding. So I'm not going to try."*

I stopped talking. Surprisingly, I felt
nothing; in this moment of the final break, I
simply saw Paul Riff whole, with neither anger nor compassion.

Because, I thought, I am free now.

"Paul, you will go to Reid Ulric, tell
him that I refuse him, and his contract."

Agitated again: "I won't do it."

"Then I will tell him," I said calmly.

I went to the phone, dialed the number. "This is Alice!" I said. "I must see Mr.
Ulric immediately."

"Alice!" Paul said in an agonized voice.

I put down the phone. I looked at Paul
Riff. I shook my head.

And I knew that the look in his eyes
would be pure hatred.

Reid Ulric sat in a massive chair,
hands braced on spread knees. A monster
presence.

"Why?"

"Because of what you made of me in
only three days," I said. "The thought of
seven years of Reid Ulric is unendurable."

His bullet head was lowered, his eyes
baleful. Not many, I knew, had dared thwart
him as I was now doing.

"I didn't do anything to you," he said.
"I only dug out what was there."

"That's the horrible part," I said.

His voice thrust from an oblique angle:
"You know when I realized you were the
winner?"

"No."

"When you put down the whip and told

me you didn't want to win badly enough to inflict such hurt on another human being. A hurt that you had already suffered yourself."

I didn't say anything. I was indifferent.

He stirred. "That's when I knew you were Reid Ulric's Great Woman. I knew then that you were capable of being moulded into my dream."

I was indifferent.

He held out one massive hand. "Alice!, you're throwing away a world of greatness."

"I don't want to be Reid Ulric's Great Woman in Reid Ulric's World," I said. "I want only to be me."

With all his magnetism, he was commanding me to surrender to his outstretched hand. I could feel palpable waves flowing from his being to mine. But it was not necessary to deny it. I simply walked away from him. As I had walked away from the whip. As I had walked away from Daddy.

At the door, I could stop, look back. "Choose Terry. Or Marlene. Or—the world is full of beautiful women. You can surely find one to take my place in your scheme of things."

He shook his head. "No. Once I chose Alice!, there could never be a substitute. The dream is dead the minute you walk through that door." There were tears on his cheeks. "I will have to find something else."

I gazed upon the great sadness in his ugly face. And I left.

I watched the gold-and-white seaplane come in, skimming the water as gracefully as a gull. The noise of the engines, intrusive in the island-silence, had drawn me to the window. I had just laid down for my afternoon

*nap; in those first days of the island, I had
slept long hours every night, and again in the
afternoon.*

*I watched the gardener put out in the
small motorboat. It coasted in, and Stavros
emerged. As soon as the boat was clear of
the plane, the plane's engines were started
again. I watched its long run, the swift lifting. After the motor noise had dwindled into the distance, I could hear the smaller noise
of the boat returning to the dock.*

*Stavros got out, walked toward the
house. He was wearing a black business suit,
tight on his sturdy body, a shirt of snowy
whiteness, a discreet tie. He was sweating in
the afternoon heat.*

*Until this moment I had not known that
the two weeks alone had also been a waiting
for Stavros.*

*Knowing it now, I did not go forth to
greet him. He would come to me here, where
he expected to find Alice!*

*Stavros entered. He did not speak. I did
not say anything, either, as he waited for his
eyes to adjust to the latticed dimness of the
room. My silence only responded to his silence.*

*I stood naked beneath a long white robe
of a coarse, soft, weave. I could feel the texture of the Oriental rug against my bare soles.*

*Stavros moved across the space separat-
ing us. He knelt to grasp the hem of the
white robe. He rose slowly, lifting the robe
gently, revealing inch by inch the lines of
my sungolden body.*

*I had not been waiting for only two
weeks. I had been waiting forever.*

*I stood naked. He gazed upon me fully.
Then he put his arms around me, lifted me,
laid me down on the bed.*

Passively, I watched him undress. He went about it quickly, neatly folding the clothes over the back of a chair. I was acutely aware of the enormous bulge of his penis in the white briefs. I had not yet seen his Thing. I had not yet felt It in me. He stooped to take off the last garment, stood naked before me.

The thickest cock I had ever seen, but very short. The flanged head, dark red, almost plum-colored, flared like the hood of a cobra. The flanges pulsed with the beat of his blood, slanting It toward my moistening cunt.

He got onto the bed, leaning heavily over me. The barrel of his chest and belly was enormous. He breathed deeply, evenly. In the black pupils of his eyes I could see a twin image of Alice!, tiny in her naked flesh.

"Alice!" he said.

"Stavros," I said.

He came into me strongly in one full thrust. I did not have to adjust to accommodate the movement. His Thing bulged into me, short though it was. I could feel the thick sliding of the flanged head cramming my pussy full, as it had not been filled by any man before.

We fucked in solemn silence, our senses concentrated into that joining of a man to a woman, a woman to a man. It was a consecration, not only of our bodies, but of ourselves. The wedding of our individual selves on Alice's island.

We fucked for a long time, the beat building slowly, almost imperceptibly, in intensity. But quickening there was until, without hesitation or adjustment, we came together.

His voluminous semen boiled out of my

*vagina, dampening the pubic hairs matted
between our bodies. Cementing us together.
He held me for a time. Then he rolled away,
and we slept.*

*I awakened to the caress of his hand on
my body. I rolled over, to meet his broad
smile.*

*"It was perfect," he said. "As I knew
it would be."*

"Yes," I said in contentment.

*His hand began lightly to stroke my
pubic hair. It moved up to my breast, slowly down again.*

*"And Alice! will be here for Stavros,"
he murmured, gladness in his tone. "You
promised a year."*

*"Forever," I said. "For as long as you
want me here."*

*His hand quickened. "A strange thing,"
he said, smiling. "You would think a beautiful lovemaking would be enough. But it
leads only to a greater desire."*

*I put my hand on the thick thatch of
black hair surrounding his Thing. "Yes," I
said. I circled my fingers delicately around
the shaft, moved it slowly upward, down
again. By the time it had reached the base,
he was ready.*

*I rose up over him, lying full-length so
I could put my mouth on his mouth after I
had absorbed his erection.*

*He watched my face as I fucked him,
aware of me wholly, taking in all of Alice!
at once. I fucked with sensuous movements,
savoring the slow thrust of my loins. Even
when he wanted to quicken, I refused it.*

*Suddenly he put his arms around me,
turning me under him. I lifted my legs, lock-*

ing them around his buttocks, and abandoned myself to his passion.

Lustful now, as we had not been lustful before. Both hands under my ass, his finger began to stroke my anus in rhythm with the beat. I thought he would come, when I wanted it to last forever. But let him flood me again with his semen. In my nostrils was the sea-scent of his first coming, it was smeared on our bodies, weighted the very atmosphere of the room, so let him add to it even though it was too quick.

He stopped dead still. I stirred impatiently. Then I, too, held still, for he was gazing tenderly upon me. He would not want to see in my eyes the impatience of unfulfillment.

With a quick backward thrust, he withdrew. Involuntarily, not wanting to let It go, I surged up after his retreating Thing. Both strong hands on my waist, he turned me over on my stomach.

I realized his desire. "No," I said gaspingly. "Please. It'll hurt."

The blunt cobra head pressed against my anus. Trembling because I must deny him, I sphinctered tightly against violation.

His body was heavy, pinning me down. His whisper came from over my shoulder.

"Are you telling me that, there, you are a virgin?"

"Yes, yes," I said desperately. "Please. "It's too big."

There was a lust in his voice as in his body.

"You are not lying, Alice!? Please do not lie about this thing."

"It's the truth," I gasped. "But it will hurt. I don't want to be hurt."

He lifted away his weight, allowing me to turn in his arms. I hid my face against his shoulder, ashamed that, on this first occasion of ourselves, I had to deny him anything. But I still trembled inside at the thought of such violation.

I expected anger. His voice came tenderly, in it the sound of laughter.

"Then you have never been loved by a Greek," he said. "Fuck a Greek, you get fucked in the ass. Didn't you know that?"

"No," I said.

His eyes were brilliant. "And you have brought me an unexpected gift. No man has been where this Greek cock shall now go."

Inexorably, his hands turned me again to my belly. I trembled, knowing there was no escape. Yet, with a cold shrinking, I realized it would be unendurable. Why had I thought this island to be any more, any less, than all the other islands?

Oh God!!! I screamed when It tore into me, a lance of sheer pain. Weeping in supine surrender, I broke into a cold sweat.

Stavros was not gentle. Perhaps he could not be other than ruthless to penetrate such instinctively sphinctered resistance. Ignoring my whimpering cries, he raped into me, taking that ultimate virginity of my flesh. It hurt more deeply, more vitally, than anything I had experienced. My flesh shuddered with each full thrust of that cobra-headed cock.

But then: a sea change. His hand under me now, stroking, and, incredibly, I felt my anus yielding, accepting his violation.

With one great thrust, he touched me into a wildness until now unrealized in the throes of sex. I cried out, not from pain this time, but with an unbridled passion. With the cry, I thrust strongly against him, want-ing It—having to have It—forever deep in me. With great dexterity and desire, I fucked in counterrhythm to his thrust, taking It all, glorying in It, laughing and crying and com-ing all at once.

Stavros rode me like a wild mare, teeth fastened into my shoulder as I bucked and tossed under him in a violence of orgasm I had never known. So totally into myself, I did not know when he began to come, for my senses swooned away, my head whirling red-and-black, my body shuddering down.

His arms turned me. Gazing into my face, with a great tenderness he said, "I love you, Alice!"

The simplicity of the words stirred me. "You have conquered me, Stavros," I whis-pered. "Conquered me forever."

"As you have conquered me," Stavros said. "I had not expected to love again."

I stretched my body languorously against his body. I put my arms around the great barrel of him and held him close. "It is wonderful to be loved," I said drowsily. "It is even more wonderful to love."

And so I loved Stavros Stephanos for fifteen years; as Stavros loved me. Yet, in the end, Stavros had betrayed Alice! Though he had promised, in the beginning, that the is-land would be mine forever, he had failed to secure it to me in his will. It had never been my island; only a borrowed Eden.

From the moment, the day after the funeral, when Stavros' eldest son had told me, with ill-concealed glee, that the island was no longer mine, I had pondered the mystery. There was only one possible answer.

Stavros was a great patriarch, a man of territory. His children—even when they disappointed him, as several had done—were close to his heart. When he had actually sat down to make his will, he could not bring himself to allow any land—even Alice!'s island—to pass out of family ownership. I was his mistress; but fifteen years of faithful love had not been enough to make me Family.

Thinking that the money could compensate me for his treachery, Stavros had left me those twenty-two millions of dollars. He had tried to assuage his soul-guilt with gold. But I would know forever that, money-making man though he was, the millions had not meant as much to him as the land.

He had, in spite of all love, withheld the essential Stavros. And, in withholding, betrayed our fifteen years of love.

I had not been to Lord Harry's for a long time. Nor had I intended to go there that night. But, returning home from a fucking, when I saw the sign I stopped the taxi and got out.

Because I was unsatisfied.

I had gone with a stranger, knowing, as I always knew now, that no matter how tender or strong or skillful or persistent he might be, no matter how many orgasms he wrung from my pliant flesh, I would rise up from his bed with a hunger still in my body, as in my soul. The good ones were no better than those who came prematurely, or could not come at all.

Yet, with increasing desperation, I sought the fulfillment that I could not find. Once, twice, sometimes three times a night; only to end at dawn in my own bed, curled tightly against the unsatisfaction of flesh and of spirit.

All right, I told myself as I crossed the sidewalk. Herb Gloss. If he hasn't already committed his creativity for tonight to another woman. So remarkably skillful, Herb's fucking was his truly creative activity. And I was fond of the silly man.

But, a small voice said inside my head, *you have tried Herb Gloss twice more, now, and found him lacking.*

Tony Saprito, then, I thought defiantly—though only last week, Tony, after waiting arrogantly one night in the lobby of my building for my return, had collapsed into impotence in his newly acquired awe of me-as-Alice!, who had given him a new chance.

A stranger, I interposed swiftly, someone entirely new. A miraculous stranger. Even though, lately, there had been a dearth of miraculous strangers.

Then . . . I saw him. The dear man, sitting alone at a table, knobby, ugly, his watchful detachment making around him a space of emptiness.

Only the slightest hesitation of a pause in the first moment of seeing. But, inside me, the pause was long enough to know.

I had liked Mark Judson.

Difficult, unbending, far too watchful, far too seeing, for one to be comfortable in his presence. Wary, uncompromising, a grudging giver of himself.

In spite of all, I had liked Mark. When he had left me, he had left behind an emptiness. Not love—though I recognized, in that flash of an instant between one step and the next, there had been the possibility of love. Not even friendship, though we had been friends. A simple liking for an incorrigibly male human being.

Not least of all, an unacknowledged lust to experience that impossibly awkward body.

There was a singing in my soul.

With Mark, I could give as well as receive. I *had* given, without knowing it; as I had received. That, I realized—so simply and wholly I had to wonder why it had taken a long life to learn it—was the ultimate selfishness. A generous selfishness the true Alice had never, until now, been able to encompass.

In giving, one calls forth a reciprocity far greater than passion . . . or even love.

I came back to the beginning: I liked the impossible man. When I had never *liked* a man, as a man, in my life. I had lusted for them, had tried to love them, been used by them. I had yielded myself to being used, because that had seemed all there was for Alice; all, I had felt deeply, there could be.

Not once in my halcyon life had I felt that simple, friendly *liking* I held for Mark Judson. No matter how familiar, how beloved, they were also strangers. *Them.*

Mark Judson—though indubitably, incorrigibly, a man—was not one of Them.

An instant's hesitation; then the halted step completed itself. To be followed by another, and another, until I stood beside his table.

Unaware of my presence, Mark brooded over the untouched drink. Whiskey, I saw. It looked rich enough to be Jack Daniel's.

"Buy a girl a drink?" I said.

Mark looked up, his face filled with *No, sorry.* With a shock, he recognized me.

I took the chair across the table. "What's your name, anyway?" I asked brightly.

With a faint smile, he said, "Nobody uses their real name in a place like this. Call me anything you like."

I tilted my head. "I think I'll call you Mark," I said. "Is it all right if I call you Mark?"

"Sure. Fine with me." He pondered for a moment. "Suppose I call you . . . Alice."

I smiled brightly. "That sounds like a good name to go with Mark. Alice-and-Mark. Mark-and-Alice. Can I have some of that Jack Daniel's?"

"You'll have to pay for it. I'm just about broke."

He leaned back, spreading both hands in a gesture of resigned explanation. "That's the way it is."

"I think a girl *ought* to buy her own drink," I said. "Don't you?"

"No," he said, beckoning to the waitress.

"I was going home to a very lonely bed when I decided to stop in for a nightcap," I said. "Glad I did, now. Even a stranger is better than an empty bed. Don't you think?"

He did not respond to that gambit. I kept on watching his face. "I hope I'm not being *too* bold. But I've decided, lately, a woman ought to ask for what she wants. Just like a man. Or don't you agree?"

He looked at me so equivocally, I thought he meant to shatter the make-believe pattern so quickly constructed between us.

Then he said, "Sure. If you can know what you want."

I nodded swiftly. "I know," I said. "I just found out. Somehow, it's like I've always known."

My drink came. I drank. Mark drank with me. We sat across the table from each other, the make-believe between us as fragile as a fairy web.

"I live just around the corner," I suggested. "Or don't you go home with women you don't know?"

"Are we strangers?" he said.

"Aren't we all strangers?" I said. "Everybody in the world? Mark-and-Alice most of all. We have whole continents of each other to explore. You *are* an explorer, aren't you?"

"I have been a seeker most of my life," he said gravely. "I've been trying to dump the habit, lately. But . . . I guess I haven't succeeded."

Opening my purse, I put money on the table. I stood up.

"Come with me, then, and seek some more." I held out my hand. "God knows what we'll find."

I had always known Mark Judson had a beautiful smile. I had not realized how much I had missed it since he had gone away.

We went together into the street. Without touching, we walked side by side toward the apartment building. At the alley, he hesitated.

"We don't have to go that way," I told him.

He turned. "Then you ought to get rid of that tacky wig you're wearing."

In a quick move, he snatched it from my head and flung it into the street. Roughly taking my arm, he led me on.

"I want to tell you something about this stranger you've picked up in a bar," he said as we walked. His voice was firm. "I'm dead broke, and finished in this town. I'm all packed, ready to leave tomorrow."

"But where would you go?"

He shrugged. "Maybe some little newspaper somewhere. I don't know. I just know that I'm finished with New York."

"But you . . . don't you love this town?" I said. "A person like you, I should think you would."

"Yes," he said. "I love the damned impossible place."

Like I love the damned impossible person, true-Alice told me. "Then why go away from that which you love?"

He stopped to look at me. "Alice Stranger, I'll tell you the secret of my life. I went to work for this woman, you see, a very lovely woman. The best job I ever had. But . . . I had to quit."

"Why did you have to quit?"

"Because she was not only beautiful, but a beautiful person. She had everything. Including so much money I couldn't even dream about that much money. She had *me,* though she wasn't interested in knowing that she had me. Considering the position I was in, I didn't dare show her the love and the lust that grew stronger in me every time I looked at her."

"You could have tried," I said quietly.

"No. The woman had to try. But . . . she was attracted to the experience of strangers. When, all the time, she was a stranger to herself, knowing nothing of her enormous capacity to love and to receive love."

"Maybe she didn't know she *liked* the man. Because she had never liked a man in her life." I could feel the softness in my voice. "She didn't trust love, and she didn't know about liking."

The make-believe was so fragile now, we were forced to remain silent until we reached home.

Inside my door, I turned to look at Mark. Only to meet a wary expression. In the midst of make-believe, uncertainty dwelled in us both.

"Mark," I said. "Take me, Mark."

The simple words swept away our fear of ultimately making ourselves so vulnerable to each other. He put his arms around me, held me close against his knobby, awkward body. His face bent down to take my kiss.

My arms were tight around his neck. "No more islands forever, Mark," I whispered. "Whole continents to explore. Especially the continents of ourselves."

We turned together, in a simultaneous movement, and went into the bedroom. We got into the bed and made love. He was clumsy and inept, with passion too uncontrolled.

I loved every minute of it. Because true-Alice knew that it was forever.

DON'T MISS
THESE CURRENT
Bantam Bestsellers

SAVE $2.00 ON YOUR NEXT BOOK ORDER!

BANTAM BOOKS

Shop-at-Home ——
Catalog

Now you can have a complete, up-to-date catalog of Bantam's inventory of over 1,600 titles—including hard-to-find books. And, you can save $2.00 on your next order by taking advantage of the money-saving coupon you'll find in this illustrated catalog. Choose from fiction and non-fiction titles, including mysteries, historical novels, westerns, cookbooks, romances, biographies, family living, health, and more. You'll find a description of most titles. Arranged by categoreis, the catalog makes it easy to find your favorite books and authors and to discover new ones.

So don't delay—send for this shop-at-home catalog and save money on your next book order.

Just send us your name and address and 50¢ to defray postage and handling costs.